Escape to Christmas Cottage

CJ MORROW

Tamarillas Press

Cover images and design: CJ Morrow
Design: © CJ Morrow
Copyright: © 2020 CJ Morrow

.

ISBN: 978-1-913807-04-7

For my family

Other books by CJ MORROW

Romantic Comedy:
It's Pamela Rigby Actually
Sooo Not Looking for a Man
We can Work it out
Little Mishaps and Big Surprises
Mermaid Hair and I Don't Care
Blame it on the Onesie
A Onesie is not just for Christmas

Psychological Thriller:
Never Leaves Me

Fantasy:
The Finder
The Illusionist
The Sister

One

'What are you doing for Christmas, Ruby?'

I swear the next person who asks me that is going to either get a punch in the face or I'll vomit on their shoes. Which would be worse? I am only standing at the water cooler, filling my glass and minding my own business.

'Oh, you know, just the usual, family stuff, quiet one.' I force out a bland little smile before feeling obliged to return the query. 'What about you?'

'Oh, first we're going to Paul's parents' place for brunch, then it's over to mine for Christmas dinner at six, with all our lot... blah, blah, blah.'

Suddenly, I realise she's stopped talking and I have to respond even though I haven't been listening to most of it because it's the same old stuff everyone says.

'Sounds fab,' I say, my voice rising at the end, trying to sound interested and positive. 'Have fun.' I turn and shuffle back to my desk and wonder how much longer this hell will continue.

It's our last day at work before Christmas. We're not working tomorrow, which is Christmas Eve, and everyone is hoping we'll be let off early today. Even me.

1

Not because I want to get home and start stuffing my turkey or trimming my tree or any of that crap, just because I want to get as far away from jolly, festive people as I possibly can.

'Suppose we'd better put some of this away,' someone says, starting to pick baubles off the tacky plastic tree wedged on top of the filing cabinet. I look away. Don't involve *me* in *that*, I didn't put it up and I'm not taking it down. I can still feel the daggers of disapproval flung my way when I wouldn't participate in this farce. 'Not even a bit of tinsel on your desk?' someone had questioned, before backing off when I'd barked, 'No, thanks.'

I hate Christmas. In case you hadn't guessed. I haven't always hated Christmas, but I do now.

The office door opens and I watch my friend, Zara, waddle towards me. The smile on her face lasts from the door to my desk.

'Hey,' I say, genuinely pleased to see her.

'I'm so glad it's my last day.' She flops down in the seat next to mine, rubbing her immense baby belly.

'You got lots of nice stuff.' We had her *leaving to have a baby* presentation an hour ago and I've never seen so much baby paraphernalia. 'Do you need a hand getting it home?' I hope she doesn't, I really do. I know that's selfish.

'No, my colleagues will stuff it in the car for me and Ben and the kids will get it out at home.' She smiles, then nudges me. 'I bet you just want to get off out of here, don't you?'

'Yes. I cannot lie.'

'Who knows, by the time you get back from your little jaunt, I might have had this baby.'

'When's it actually due?'

'4th Jan, but as it's number four, it could come any time.' She gives a little light laugh as though having a baby is like popping to the loo, but we both know that the last time was hell on earth for her and the baby. Personally, I think she's mad to do it again, but what do I know? She said that she didn't like families in uneven numbers, definitely didn't want three children because there's always a middle one, and she didn't want that. She'd been a middle one herself and she *definitely* didn't want that for her own children. Hence number four; I still think she's mad.

'Well, if you're sure you don't need any help...'

'No, you're fine. What are your plans? Car packed ready to go straight off?'

'Yes. Clothes and stuff. But I'm going to go food shopping before I get on the motorway. It's so cold outside that I don't think I need to worry about anything I buy spoiling, do you?'

'God, no. It's bloody freezing outside. Snow forecast, apparently. Not that I believe it. We'll just get drizzle like we always do. At least this year we won't be having thermostat wars all over Christmas like we usually do, Ben too hot, me too cold. I've got my own hot water bottle here.' She pats her baby bulge. 'I almost envy you.'

'What?'

'The peace and quiet. It'll be the usual bedlam in our house and inevitably tears before lunchtime on Christmas Day. Mine probably.' She rolls her eyes and stands up. 'Have a good break, Ruby. Recharge those batteries. Message me when you get back. They're letting me go now, cos *I'm* special.' She grins and as I look at her I see how tired she looks. She should have finished work weeks ago, in my opinion, but it's none of my business.

I stand up and give her a quick hug, mostly because she expects it. I swear her baby girl kicks me hard as I lean in. With three boys already, Zara was determined to try for a girl. I dread to think what would have happened if this one had been a boy too. Would she have tried for baby number five? Then a sixth if it wasn't a girl, to keep the numbers even?

'Message me if anything exciting happens.'

'I don't know if you'll even receive messages down there.'

'It's Devon, Zara, not deepest, darkest space.'

'I did tell you it was remote, though, didn't I? We couldn't even get a phone signal until we'd driven five miles away from the cottage.'

'Yes, but that was fifty years ago.'

'Shut up, you. Well, ten years, I suppose. In the days before we had children.' Zara's face takes on a wistful look and she smiles to herself, a secret little smile. 'I think we conceived our eldest there.'

Too much information for me. 'I was looking through the pictures Mrs Lane sent me again this morning,' I say, changing the subject. 'It looks like just what I need.'

Zara flops back down into the chair she's just vacated. 'Show me. Show me.'

I log into my personal email on my work computer and together we scroll through the pictures. I don't feel at all guilty for skiving, because it's exactly what everyone else is blatantly doing, except for the sly ones who pretend they are *super busy with so much to finish before the Christmas break.* No one's fooled.

I'm almost salivating as we scrutinise each photo, the picture-perfect stone cottage under a dark slate roof, there's even smoke coming out of the chimney. The inglenook fireplace, complete with wood burner, the two luxurious bedrooms and bathrooms. It's all just what I need, what I want. All to myself.

I've packed lots of DVDs so that I don't have to watch festive TV and once I get my shopping done, I'll be battening down the hatches and hiding away for the entire ten days I'm off work, unless I really feel the need for an exhilarating stroll on the beach which is supposed to be at the end of the garden. And in between all that I'll be knitting; I've quite got into knitting since I started it last year. It was Mum's idea to take up a hobby, but even she was surprised when I chose knitting – I'd never shown an interest in it before. I'm even getting quite good now; I've started a complicated Fair Isle sweater for myself. It will require all my concentration, which is good thing because it stops me thinking, and overthinking.

Yes, New Year will have been and gone by the time I get back. And thank God for that.

'Ahh, brings it all back,' Zara says, staring at my screen. 'Although they've done it up since we were there. It looks very boutique chic now. Which room are you sleeping in?'

'I don't know.' I hadn't even thought about it.

'Well, that one…' She points to one of the pictures. '…Is the largest and has the en-suite shower room, but that one…' Her nail trails over the screen to another picture. '… has the best view. I mean, *the* best view. I'd have that one if I were you. It's just behind the kitchen, if I remember correctly.'

'But it's not en-suite?'

'No, but the bathroom is just across the main living area and there was an enormous cast iron bath when we were there.'

'Like this?' I scroll through some more pictures. I'm already planning very long and luxurious baths.

'Yep, that's the one. Big enough for two.' Her face takes on that wistful look again. I don't even want to think about what Zara and her husband got up to in that bath.

'Well, I'm on my own so the whole place is en-suite to me.'

'That's true. Did you know it's called Christmas Cottage?' Zara searches my face looking for a reaction.

'No, I don't even have an address, just the postcode.'

'It's because it used to be part of a farm that grew Christmas trees, apparently. That's what Mrs Lane said, anyway.'

'Oh.' Christmas Cottage, who the hell calls a cottage that when it's usually only let out in the summer? Maybe they change the name to Summer Cottage during the warmer seasons. Mrs Lane, Zara's neighbour and owner of the cottage, hadn't told me that. I wonder if it was a deliberate omission, if Zara had briefed her? Mrs Lane has assured me that the postcode will take me straight to the door. I hope my old satnav is as convinced of this as she is.

'They probably did other stuff too. But they sold it off, she said, when her and her brother inherited. I'm almost envious of you,' she says, getting up again.

'Liar,' I say as she turns and smiles. She wouldn't trade the raucous fun she has with her family for a silent Christmas.

'Have you heard from your parents yet?'

'Yes. 2am, got a text. They've arrived safe and well and were going out for a late lunch with my brother and his family.'

'Regretting not going?'

'No. Definitely not.' My parents had begged me to come to Australia with them, begged me to spend Christmas with my brother and his family. But after last year, I knew I just couldn't inflict my miserable self on any of my family again. Even so, they've booked a much shorter holiday than they usually would. For me. I wish they hadn't. I'm okay. I'm going to be okay. 'Happy Christmas, Zara.'

'You too, well, you know what I mean.'

'I do, thank you. I'm really looking forward to being lazy. I'm not even going to blow dry my hair.' I grin as Zara holds her hand over her mouth in mock horror.

'You devil you.'

'I'm not going to wear a bra either.' I grin again.

'Oh my God. What bliss. It's usually the first thing I do when I get home from work, whip it off, but now, these great things are just too big for that. Pregnancy eh!'

I look at Zara's neat little boobs. They aren't as big as mine and I'm not pregnant. 'Look pretty good to me.' I nudge her.

'Saggy, darling, so saggy,' she whispers. 'I'm in over-the-shoulder-bolder-holders now.'

'Welcome to my world.'

She gives me a cheeky grin. 'Oh, have you got the key?'

'Already on my keyring,' I say, yanking open my desk drawer to check, more to reassure myself that Zara.

I watch her waddle back up the office and out of the door before I turn back to the photos on my screen. Yep, it really does look idyllic despite its name.

❄❄❄

We're let off early, one hour early, 4pm. It's already dark by the time I hit Sainsbury's along with a gazillion other people. The good thing is I'm not after the pigs in blankets or the festive party packs; I'm buying pasta and mince beef; the ingredients for a Victoria sponge, normal every week food. Though I do manage to buy two plastic tubs of chocolates, Roses and Quality Street, though I'll only eat the soft ones.

Cliff used to eat the hard ones, the toffees, the nuts, all the ones I didn't like. We were a good team – in chocolate eating world.

I grab a sandwich from Sainsbury's takeaway range and scoff it in the car. I line the Roses tin up on the passenger seat and take the lid off. If I get peckish en route I can just grab one or two. I take a quick swig of water and start the car.

Let the escape from Christmas begin.

The M4 isn't too bad, busy, but moving. Once I'm past Bristol – always a bit of a bottleneck – and settled on the M5, I start to feel relaxed. Yes, there is a lot of traffic. A lot. It seems that every man and his dog are heading to the South West. I wonder if they're trying to escape from Christmas, or, more likely, judging by the way the cars are stuffed so full that rear view mirrors must be obscured, they're just taking it with them.

The traffic slows and we're crawling along, but at least we are still moving. The predicted snow doesn't manifest but, just as Zara forecast, there's a fine and persistent drizzle that means the wipers are on permanently and because of the low cloud it's very dark, no moon to guide my way.

I reach over and grab an orange crème from the Roses tub, one of my favourites. Then I flick the radio on, not something I normally bother with; I don't have a hoard of CDs anywhere, or music on my phone to Bluetooth through, so it'll just be the radio. That's how boring and tedious this journey is becoming, that I, who never listens to the radio, *is* listening to the radio. There's a talk show on, people are ringing in with their Christmas hangover cures. I reach for another chocolate and this time I don't even attempt to sort out one of my favourite flavours. I'm living dangerously, taking pot luck – in chocolate world.

The journey along the M5 grinds on and on. Finally, the satnav tells me my junction is coming up in one mile, usually that would be short notice, but at this rate it may be another five minutes, or more.

I'm off the motorway. I'm on an A road, there's still a lot of traffic but now we're up to a heady thirty miles an hour. In a way I'm glad I'm still in a stream of traffic because with the rain and low cloud, visibility is poor and there are few street lights.

The radio is now playing Christmas songs.

'No thank you.' I reach over and change the channel. More Christmas songs. And again. It seems I cannot escape this crap. Then Chris Rhea's "Road to Hell" comes on, and I can't help smiling. It is so apt. I just hope the cottage is as lovely as it looks and isn't Hell.

I keep going at a painfully slow pace. The satnav estimated time of arrival keeps moving further and further back. Originally it had said eight-thirty, now's it's telling me ten-forty. I'm dying to go to the loo as well. I'm going to have to stop.

I pull over at a little service station and rush towards their toilets. When I've finished I head into the shop-cum-café and buy myself a strong coffee. It's getting late and I've still got at least another hour until I arrive. I'm so tired and irritable and just wishing I was there. I'm the only customer and even the guy serving looks like he wishes I was *there*, or at least, not keeping him open here.

I dash back through the freezing drizzle to the car where I fortify myself with another orange crème, wait for the satnav to do its stuff and put the radio back on. They're playing "Road to Hell", again. I hope it's not an omen.

The roads are minor now and the traffic sparse. I don't know if I prefer this or the heavy traffic on the motorway. I'm now wondering whether it would have been better to drive down during the day. Why didn't I wait until tomorrow?

On and on the journey goes. I have a headache from concentrating so hard to see, the drizzle has turned to driving rain; the wipers are working overtime and hypnotising me.

According to the satnav I should be arriving at my destination in the next five minutes. I find that hard to believe. I feel a sense of panic as I hope and pray that the satnav isn't going to send me down a one-way unmade lane to nowhere, or worse still, a sheer drop into an abyss.

Turn left, turn left, the satnav commands me. Do I follow its instructions or do I carry on? At least this road has a proper tarmac surface. I stop at the junction and attempt to peer down the road or lane or whatever it is, because it's too dark and dismal to tell, and wonder what the hell to do. Then I remember Mrs Lane's email telling me that the postcode *will* take me straight to the door. That, however, is assuming my satnav is good enough and up to date. I've had it a few years and I don't remember ever updating it. Can I trust it? But hasn't the cottage been here for years? It's not a new postcode.

I hover on the road, my foot pressed to the brake pedal so that my brake lights will alert anyone approaching that I have stopped. Not that anyone does pass, either behind me or coming towards me.

Be brave, I tell myself. If you get to the end of the lane and there's nothing there, you can sleep in the car and wait until daylight. If you fall into an abyss, you won't be worrying about sleeping anyway.

That's right, Ruby, look on the bright side.

I back up a little, then turn down the lane. I feel and hear the crunch of gravel and twigs beneath my tyres, as suspected, this isn't a proper road. I hate that it's not a proper road. Even with full beam on I can barely see ahead. Leafless trees flap their blackened limbs at me, waving frantically in a fierce wind I hadn't even realised had got up.

Should I stop the car and get out and walk ahead? Would that be better than driving? Or worse?

I stop the car, leave the engine running, the lights on and take deep breaths. I'm panicking. I'm being stupid. I wind down the window and stick my head out, immediately whipping it back in and closing the window. There is no way I'm walking anywhere in that; not only is the wind fierce, the rain is freezing too.

Pull yourself together, Ruby. Just go for it.

I put the car in first gear and edge forward slowly – it would probably be quicker to walk, but not if I get rain lashed.

Forward, forward until suddenly my lights hit a wall of white. And there it is, right in front of me, the cottage, just as picture perfect, even in this weather, as it was on the photographs. I steer towards the front door and park; I *think* I'm on gravel and not garden.

Once the car lights are off it is pitch black outside. I rummage around in my handbag for the head torch which Mrs Lane suggested I bring with me. She told me it would be dark, as the only external lights are solar and unlikely to charge well at this time of year. I pull the torch over my head and press the light to turn it on. I'm glad I kept my coat on after I stopped at the services, it was just too cold by then to take it off, even with the car heating on.

I wish my suitcase was in the front seat. I fight the wind to open my car door, finally manage to get out then go around to open the boot. The wind is howling around me, it's horrible. I grab my case and haul it out, but I don't bother with the shopping, it can wait until morning, the boot is as cold as a fridge so nothing will spoil.

I fumble the key into the front door and then fall inside the cottage, more fumbling until I find a light switch. Thank God for the head torch.

Then, there it is. A cosy sitting-dining-kitchen, bigger than it looked in the photographs, but just as pretty. There's even a low fire burning in the log burner. Mrs Lane had said she'd try to get the local lad to chop some wood and light the log burner for my arrival. I'm so glad she did.

I feel a sense of relief, the panic and stress of the last few hours lifting from my shoulders and floating away. I feel almost zen-like.

Just beyond the kitchen a door is open; my bedroom. I drag my case along towards it, step inside. The bed looks so inviting. I am so tired. I dump the case, head back to the kitchen and get myself a big glass of water then switch off the light in the living room, and use my head torch to navigate my way back to my bedroom.

I don't even bother finding my pjs, just rip off my clothes and climb into bed.

Sleep.

Two

I become aware of the sound of distant tapping as I wake the next morning. Thin daylight seeps through the gaps around the curtains that I hastily, and badly, drew last night.

I reach for my phone, the battery almost flat because I was too tired to find my charger before I leapt into bed, and check the time. It's after ten. Wow, how long have I slept? Probably the best sleep I've had in many, many months. That's what exhaustion does for you.

I snuggle back down under the duvet and take in the cosiness of the room. The duvet is thick and warm, the bed is super soft yet firm, the walls are painted a soft white, or at least that's the colour they look in the restricted light from the window. The furniture, just a wardrobe and chest of drawers are old and oak, and quaint. I shake my shoulders and slip further down the bed, enjoying the comfort, the security of my hideaway.

There's a heavy silence in the room, as though the outside world is a million miles away. Just what I wanted, what I needed. Except for that distant and insistent tapping. Is it a woodpecker? Or do they fly away for the winter? I have no idea.

Forcing myself out of bed, I notice a pile of thick towels on top of the chest of drawers and grab one, wrapping it around my shoulders. It's large and soft and will keep any chill off me. I go to the window to see this amazing view that Zara raved about.

She's right; in the distance a pale pink sky meets a navy sea, though it's not exactly what I would call at the end of the garden, which is long and wide and seemingly fenceless, almost an infinity lawn, it slides into the sea, the horizon.

In the corner a lone figure is chopping wood. The woodpecker; this must be the local boy that Mrs Lane mentioned. I wish he hadn't started quite so early. He's wearing a t-shirt and jeans, his discarded fleece just a heap on the grass. I watch him as he lifts the axe then brings it down quickly. That's quite a pile of chopped wood. Good, judging by how cold it was last night, I might get through all of that during my stay. Not, I have to admit to myself, that I'm particularly familiar with log burners, or even open fires. The house I live in has gas central heating *and* electric underfloor heating, all bases covered; and all computer controlled. So, I hope there's a manual for the log burner; there's sure to be if this is a rental cottage.

I rest my arms on the window sill, press myself against the warm radiator beneath it and marvel at the view. Even with the persistent chopping it is peaceful and serene. A reward after my stressful journey last night.

The local boy finishes his task, stacking the wood neatly under a wooden canopy, then looks around for his fleece. Seeing it, he grabs it and pulls it on over his head. Then he looks around for something else, his head of unruly hair ruffled by the breeze, not, thankfully, the gale force wind that greeted me last night. A giant dog comes running, quickly taking its place alongside its master and together they lope off across the garden, down to the right and out of sight.

I find my washbag and a book I haven't yet started, as well as another towel and wander out of my room. The bathroom door is conveniently marked with a ceramic sign showing a bath. Once inside, the great big bath tub from the photos entices me and I cannot help smiling. I've brought luxurious bath oils with me and as I pour some into the running water the smell is quite intoxicating.

An hour later, having rinsed off the restorative masks I've had on both my hair and face, and read three chapters of my book, a murder thriller – not sure how wise choosing that was given I'm all alone – I force myself out of the bath.

In the living room the logs in the burner are roaring away. I'm not sure that was still lit when I passed through an hour ago, and even I, with my limited knowledge of such things, know that log burners don't last all night unless topped up. Someone has been in here. Local boy, no doubt. I don't like the idea of that and decide that once I've retrieved my shopping from the car, I will be deadlocking all the doors. Happily, there's no sign of him now.

I stand in front of the log burner, my back to the warmth. It's so nice, I even lift the back of my towel to let the heat warm my bare skin. I feel as though I can do anything I like here, be myself, indulge my misery, allow myself to be happy, even run around naked – once I've deadlocked those doors. A ray of weak sunshine pushes its way through the windows and bathes my face, I close my eyes and enjoy the sensation.

I can hear the silence, the peace of this place. No memories – or at least not mine – running through the walls, no resentments, no accusations, just peace. I can be me. The me I used to be. Perhaps.

The snap of a door opening and my eyes ping open.

Standing in front of me is the local lad. Glistening chest wet from a shower, a towel around his waist, he's towelling his wet hair, his face obscured. Damn cheek.

A low growl.

Then I see it. The dog. The biggest dog I've ever seen. It sees me and moves in a blur, grabbing my towel in its beastly jaws. Yanking so hard that I cannot hold on. I'm knocked off my feet by the power of the dog's grasp, collapsing in a heap in front of the log burner. Attempting to cover myself with my hands – not an easy task given the size of my boobs – I'm yelping and howling as though I were a dog myself.

'What the f…' a male voice says, the local lad, the interloper. 'Kong, drop.'

The dog drops my towel, the lad, though actually, clearly, not a lad, but a big hairy man, retrieves my towel from the floor and, in one swift movement wraps it around me.

'I'm sorry about that,' he says.

'Sorry? Sorry?' I scrabble to get up, gripping my towel around me. 'What are you even doing in here? Who the hell are you?'

'I was wondering that myself. About you, obviously.' Is that the hint of a smirk on his face?

'Me? Me? I'm the idiot who rented this place for ten days, not some part-time woodchopper nipping in to use the facilities. I'll be reporting you to Mrs Lane.' I grip my towel tighter, pulling it up around my neck.

He's smiling now, definitely smiling. How bloody dare he?

'What are you bloody smiling at?' I'm incensed now.

'Sorry,' he says, but the smile remains. 'I've rented this place too.'

'No you haven't. You're the local la... man who chops wood. I saw you. Out there.' I point my finger rather awkwardly, in the general direction of the garden but have to keep my elbow clenched to my body because I don't want my towel to dislodge again.

'Y-e-s-s,' he says, drawing out the word. 'I was out there chopping wood, because I told the owner I was happy to chop it. But I'm *not* local and I *have* rented this place.'

'No.' I cannot believe it.

'Yes,' he says. 'There's obviously been a mix up. Somewhere.'

For a second or two I'm speechless. A mix up? How? Why?

He stands before me, still glistening, then starts to dab himself dry with his hair towel. His body is lean, but muscled. His body is not at all like Cliff's.

'Well, yes,' I snap. 'I suggest we both get dressed then come back and discuss this properly.'

'Okay,' he turns away.

'Yes, and you can put your giant dog outside too please.'

'Kong,' he calls and the dog trots alongside his master as the two disappear back into the bedroom next to the bathroom, the biggest one and with the en-suite too.

'Arrogant bastard,' I mutter. I do not want that dog menacing me inside my own holiday getaway, my Christmas escape.

In my room I ferret around for my phone charger and plug it in, while hunting clothes out of my suitcase and pulling them on. I feel so bloody angry. I check for a signal, there is none, it seems Zara was right.

I yank the towel off my hair and drag a wide-toothed comb through it. It had been my plan to have wild hair for the whole ten days, no blow drying, no tonging, just scooped up and out of the way if needs be, or hanging loose, whatever I like. Now I feel I have to dry it; I have to look presentable in front of this stranger.

No, I don't. Fuck him.

When I go back into the living room, he's waiting in the kitchen area. He's pulled two armchairs up to the wood burner, placing them on either side. He turns and smiles at me. I force myself to smile back.

'Coffee?' he says and I notice he already has two mugs out.

I could murder a coffee; now he's mentioned it, I'm desperate. But he's the enemy and I don't want to consort with him.

'Yes please,' I say, despite myself.

'Go and sit down, I'll bring it over. It's instant, I hope that's all right.'

'Yes, thank you.' My voice is meek and pathetic as I sidle over to one of the armchairs.

'So,' he says, offering me my mug, then sitting in *his* chair opposite me.

'I can't believe Mrs Lane would do this.' I'm not actually accusing him of lying, am I?

'I don't know who Mrs Lane is.'

'She's my friend Zara's neighbour. She's the owner. That's who let me have this place for Christmas and New Year, so I could escape all that.' I wince because I hadn't intended saying that last bit.

'Right. Well. I don't know a Mrs Lane. I rented the place from a friend of my dad's.'

'Who? What's his name?'

'Peter.'

'Peter what?'

'I don't know. He works with my dad, that's all I know.'

'Is he Mrs Lane's brother?'

He shakes his head. 'I don't know.' Then he smiles. Don't smile. 'I'm Noah, by the way. Noah Steele.' He holds out a hand.

I fumble my coffee cup into my left hand and hold out my right to shake his. 'I'm Ruby Sutton.'

'Pleased to meet you, Ruby Sutton.'

'Likewise,' I mumble. I'm not pleased to meet him. Not. At. All. The whole point of coming away was to not meet anyone. I sip my coffee and stare at the log burner, watching the wood sparks flare and fade behind the glass. The warmth from that thing is just so lovely. I'll have to master it once he's buggered off. 'When?' I ask, sounding snappish.

'When what?'

'When did you rent this place?'

He glances at me, his eyes cautious. 'Why do you need to know that?'

'Because I booked it months ago, that's why. So when?'

'More recently than that,' he says, his voice quiet.

Right then the sun shines on his face, he looks almost angelic. And sad.

'Is the sun shining on my car?' I jump up suddenly remembering my boot full of shopping. If anything is spoiled it's *his* fault for distracting me.

'I don't know,' he says, shaking his head. 'Where is your car?'

'Outside. Front door.' I rush off to find my keys. 'Shopping,' I call as I march back to the front door and yank it open.

Ten minutes later I've put his food onto the two top fridge shelves – he's a lot taller than me – and unpacked mine into the bottom two. The fridge is now fully stuffed.

'I think it'll be okay,' I say, not necessarily to him.

'Okay.' He's still sitting in his chair by the wood burner.

'Yes.' My tone is sharp, again.

'Does that mean you're staying?' he asks.

'Yes, it does. I was always staying. I booked first. It's you who is leaving.'

'I don't think so. I've paid good money to stay here.'

'You can get a refund.'

'No. I want to stay. You leave. You get a refund.'

Bloody cheek of the man. And, and, I think he's smirking again. I'm about to ask him how much he's paid then stop myself. What if he's paid more? Does that give him priority? Does it even matter? I booked first but he's not conceding that I should stay and he should go, so I doubt he'll give way if I've paid more. Anyway, I know I've paid a fraction of what this place would cost in the summer. He might win on the cost war. It's too risky to ask.

I grab myself a glass of water and go to sit back in my chair. It's obvious that he isn't going to give in easily.

He smiles as I sit down, as though we were in some pleasant social situation, not an embarrassing stand-off.

And I haven't forgotten that he's seen me naked. He glances at an expensive watch on his wrist.

'Did you have breakfast?'

'No,' I say, without adding that I feel very hungry because I haven't.

'It's nearly noon, I think I'll have lunch.' With that, he gets up and goes to the kitchen area. Right, so that's the end of the conversation, is it?

I get up and march into my room, grab my charging phone and check for a signal. Nothing. I pull my coat on and grab my bag.

'I'm just going to ring Mrs Lane,' I say as I head for the door. 'Get this mess sorted out.'

'Okay,' he says, totally unconcerned. 'You might have to walk a way up the lane to get a signal.' The cheek of him.

'Thanks.' I am not at all grateful.

I walk a little way and still no signal, and it's so bitterly cold that I don't think I can stand it. I go back and get in my car, start the engine and take far too long trying to turn the car around. I'm so grateful that I didn't attempt anything like this in the dark last night. Finally, I drive away, stopping frequently to check for a signal. Nothing. The trees that thrashed about and looked so menacing last night seem benign and calm today. The sun, which had been making appearances throughout the morning, is now hidden behind a thick layer of cloud. As I turn onto the main road, not that it's much of a main road, my phone suddenly pings several times. Hurray, I must have finally found a signal. I pull over and put my hazards on.

I read through the messages, a series of apologies from Mrs Lane, who, it seems, has just found out about the mix up. She's blaming her brother and offering me a full refund if I want it as she fully understands I want to be on my own. So Zara has definitely told her all the sorry details.

Or, she says, her brother is happy to refund Mr Steele. Who? Oh, him. Steele by name and steel, or steal, by nature. I laugh at my own joke.

Is there any point in ringing her now? I doubt it. But I do, and between profuse apologies, she just repeats what she's messaged.

Right, if he won't go, then I'll have to. I cannot bear to be in anyone's company, least of all a smirky stranger. But I won't be leaving without a fight.

I back the car up and turn back down the lane. As I approach the cottage, so cute and quaint, the white stone, the dark slate roof, even smoke coming out of the chimney and – I feel sick. Why should I give this up? Why should I?

As I get closer I realise there's a little car park to the left, that's where his great big black four-by-four is parked. Such an arrogant car. A bully car. Why am I not surprised he drives a car like that?

I drive over and park next to it; I'm almost disappointed to see that there's plenty of room because I would relish the opportunity to complain and make him move over, but there's no need. It will also be easy to back out of here too as there's a turning space behind us. Shame I didn't see this last night, though I wouldn't have wanted to trek my case even this short distance through the lashing rain.

'Mrs Lane's brother is happy to give you a full refund,' I say as I let myself back into the cottage. I keep my voice neutral; I know only too well how wise it is not to show emotion in a situation like this.

Noah Steele turns from the cooker and looks at me, then he smiles. I want to slap that smile off his face.

'No, I'm fine,' he says, before turning back to stir something that I have to admit smells absolutely delicious.

'Mrs Lane says she's discussed it with her brother and it's not a problem.'

'Cool,' he says. 'Are you hungry?'

I'm not sure how to answer this. Of course I'm hungry, absolutely bloody starving in fact. The last proper thing I had to eat was the sandwich from Sainsburys; you can't call orange crèmes food, can you?

'There's plenty,' he says, seeing my hesitation. 'I certainly won't eat it all.'

Eating with the enemy, is this a good idea?

'It's pasta Bolognese with a hint of pesto.' He doesn't have to work hard to make it enticing.

'Oh, did you use my mince beef?' He better not have done.

He shrugs, turns back to stir his pot. 'It was in the fridge,' he says without looking at me.

I bet it is mine. Did he have any? Did I move any minced beef to his designated shelves before I put my own in? I can't remember. Am I going to cause a scene over a bit of beef? Am I? I think I might.

Calm down.

'In that case, I'll have some.' I try my hardest to sound pleasant and casual while inside I'm seething.

'Cool. Do you want to set the table?' He nods over at the large oak table in the corner.

'Fine,' I say, hearing my own snappish tone. 'Happy to,' I add, with a smile. Then, when we've finished, we'll be having the conversation about you, Noah Steele, leaving, pronto.

After I've laid the table and sat down – I'm sitting diagonally opposite him, since I don't want to sit directly opposite, or next, to him – he brings our food over. He plonks two great big bowls down; mine is as large as his. I'll never get through that.

'Parmesan?' he asks, before darting back to the kitchen area.

That's definitely his and I am definitely having some. 'Yes, please.'

We sit and eat in that kind of strained silence where we each know we want to say something nasty to the other. But, oh, this tastes so good, and I am so bloody hungry.

He suddenly jumps up and dashes across the room. 'Nearly forgot,' he says, returning with a bottle of wine and two glasses. It's definitely not mine, it's red, I only bought white. He puts the glasses down, opens the bottle and pours one glass. 'Would you like one?' he asks, sounding as casual and friendly as if we were actually friends.

'Um, no. Thank you. Is it wise for you to drink when you'll be driving home soon?' Here we go, the perfect opener to our discussion.

'Not planning on driving anywhere,' he says, with no emotion in his voice.

'But Mrs Lane's brother, Peter, was it, says he'll give you a full refund.'

'Yeah, you said earlier. But I'm staying.' He takes a sip from his wine glass, before starting to eat again. 'There's still some left in the pot, if you fancy any more.'

'No, thank you. I'm quite full.' And so I should be, I've eaten the entire bowlful. 'About our dilemma,' I start. 'Obviously we can't both stay here, can we? And I booked first, didn't I?'

He shrugs before scraping his bowl clean. 'If you're sure you don't want any more, I think I will.' He gets up and heads for the kitchen area.

I swivel round in my seat and watch him fill up his plate with what's left in the pan. Then he saunters back to the table and sits down.

'I never had any breakfast and I'm starving,' he says as he sees me observing him.

Now *I* shrug. What do I care what he eats? Even if it is *my* mince beef.

'So, when do you think you'll be leaving?' I ask, pushing my luck.

'I'm not leaving. I've already said so.' He doesn't seem at all annoyed with my persistence, in fact, I think the bastard is enjoying it.

'Well, I think that's very unpleasant of you.' I stand up, grab my plate, march to the sink and place it, albeit noisily, on the draining board. 'And mean,' I add, before stomping into my room and slamming the door behind me. I'm worse than a teenager.

Ten minutes later I haul my bag out into the living room, dump it on the floor and stride to the fridge. I start removing my items and placing them on the worktop ready to pack when I find *my* mince beef. Oh.

'What are you doing?' Noah *Bloody* Steele asks from the comfort of his armchair beside the log burner where he is now sitting again, having, I notice, already cleared up the kitchen.

'Leaving, of course.'

'Have you checked the weather?' His eyes narrow.

'No, because I cannot get a phone signal. Remember?'

'I meant, have you looked outside.'

I stop taking my food from the fridge and stomp over to the front door and yank it open.

The savage wind makes the snow which is now falling thick and fast swirl into my face and inside the cottage porchway. I fight to close the door, only finding it easy when Noah Steele puts his weight behind it.

'That's set for the day,' he says. 'You can't drive in that. You won't be able to see, even with your wipers on full throttle.'

'I don't need your permission.' How petulant and irrational does that sound? 'I'll wait until tomorrow then.'

He slinks back to his armchair and, even though I can only see the back of his head, I know, just know, that he is smirking.

And now I'm going to have to put everything back in the fridge, too.

And drag my suitcase back into my room.

Three

After stuffing the fridge again, I scurry back to my room with my bag. How bloody undignified. For one or two mad moments I do consider braving the weather and leaving anyway, but the memory of my journey down, the road to Hell, is too recent, too strong. And, it appears it *was* an omen.

I pull out the clothes I'll need for tomorrow and my pyjamas. Then I flop down on the bed and stare at the ceiling. This really isn't how I expected my non-Christmas to be, stuck with a stranger, Noah Bloody Steele. Even his name irritates me.

Although he did make a mean pasta Bolognese and the addition of the pesto just made it perfect.

Cliff never cooked me a meal, ever.

I feel so full of food and so cosy that I could easily just fall asleep.

But I won't. I jump up off the bed. Why should I be confined to my room when he has the run of the place? No. Definitely not. I glance outside as I pull my knitting bag out from among my clothes. The sky and the sea appear blended together, the same shade of light grey. It's still snowing, in fact, it's probably getting heavier. I find this amount of snow in this part of the country hard to believe. What's going on?

Armed with my knitting I open my bedroom door. The chairs by the log burner are both empty. I peer around the room, there's no sign of Noah Steele. I head for the enormous sofa, imagining myself lying full length on it later. Putting my knitting bag down, I hunt around for the TV remote control.

I've just got comfortable, found an old episode of *Homes Under the Hammer* on one of the numerous channels – and you can't get any less Christmassy than that – and am in the middle of a tricky line of Fair Isle knitting when the rear door bursts open. The blast of cold air hits me like a slap. Then that giant dog comes bounding over and makes straight for my knitting. I freeze mid-stitch, hoping that by not moving, he won't attack my Fair Isle.

'No, Kong,' a calm, authoritative voice says.

Kong stops, then sits. He looks at me with expectation in his eyes, as though I'm going to give him a lovely treat. He's just lucky he didn't grab my knitting because I don't think I would have reacted very well. But you can't blame a dog for trying. The blame is definitely on the owner.

'Basket, Kong,' Noah Steele says, as he snaps his fingers. With a pleading look over his shoulder at me, Kong slopes off to a giant dog basket which has appeared in the corner.

'He shouldn't be in here,' I say, without even turning to look at Noah Steele.

'Don't worry, I'll move his basket into my bedroom tonight.' I can hear him shrugging off his coat, tugging off his boots.

'No, he shouldn't be in here, in this cottage. I'm sure it said no pets on the information Mrs Lane emailed me.'

'Peter said it would be fine.' His tone is so dismissive that I spin round and frown at him. He sees my reaction and I'm sure he smirks. Again. What's the matter with him? 'So, you really expect me to put him outside? In that?' He waves his arm towards the window where the snow is still swirling and the light is fading so fast it's almost dark.

'You've just been out walking, what's the difference?'

'We went to the end of the garden and back. He needed the walk after being cooped up in my bedroom most of the day, but even *he* didn't want to venture any further. It's bloody freezing out there. *You* didn't want to chance it in your car.' He stands with his legs apart and a defiant look on his face.

'Isn't there an outhouse or something? Or he could go in your car.'

'Really? You're serious? He'll freeze to death. You want dog murder on your conscience, do you?'

Sighing, I turn back to my knitting, to *Homes Under the Hammer*. 'Just keep him away from me then. And if you hadn't trained him to be such a perv, it wouldn't be so bad.'

'You what?' Now Noah Steele strides over to block my view of the TV.

'Don't pretend you don't know what I'm talking about. That trick with my towel.' I dodge my head around him so I can see the television.

'That wasn't a trick, he thought you were an intruder. He was protecting me.'

30

'Protecting you. Ha, that's a joke. It wasn't you left lying on the carpet stark naked while a stranger and his dog gawped on. *You're* the intruder.' If I didn't have my hands completely occupied with my knitting, I'd fold my arms to emphasise my point.

'I'm not an intruder,' he says, calmly. 'I've as much right to be here as you. Anyway, I needed...' His voice trails away. 'Would you like a coffee,' he says, after he's inhaled deeply. 'Or a glass of wine, maybe?'

'No thanks.' Don't try to tempt me or bribe me. I turn my attention back to my knitting which is starting to stress me out now, because I think I've lost my place and it's all his fault. Knitting was supposed to be my stress buster, my mind occupier, my escape. Irritating Noah Steele.

He flits around the room putting lamps on and drawing curtains. I have to admit, though not to him, it does make seeing my knitting easier, although if he hadn't been here I'd have done it myself. I don't need a man to switch on lights for me. Or for anything else.

He busies himself in the kitchen, which is fine, because although I can hear him, I have my back to him and cannot see him. He's ages and I don't know what he's doing, but soon I've managed to find my place in my complicated knitting and seen a renovated-house reveal on TV.

Finally, he comes and sits on the far end of the sofa. I don't know why he has to sit there, why can't he sit on one of the armchairs by the log burner, or at the table, or better still, in his room?

I turn to glare at him. He smiles at me. Then I notice the tray between us: a platter of sandwiches, two mugs of hot chocolate. I can smell it, taste it even.

'I'm hungry, I thought you might be. And everyone likes hot chocolate on a cold, snowy day, don't they?' He smiles again. He has a nice smile, but he's a bit too ready with it.

'What's in the sandwiches?' I ask, sulkily.

'Ham or ham and mustard, I didn't know whether you liked mustard.'

I am so tempted to tell him I'm a vegetarian.

'I'll have a ham one then, since you've made them.' I make it sound as though I'm doing him a favour.

'That side then.' He points to the sandwiches on my side of the platter, before handing me a plate.

'Bread's nice,' I concede, after several bites.

'I picked it up at a bakery on the way down yesterday. Needs to be eaten or it'll go off.'

I nod slowly and pick up another sandwich. See, I *am* doing him a favour.

Having put my knitting down to eat, I turn my attention back to *Homes Under the Hammer*, because I'm not, absolutely not, going to make small talk with this interloper, no matter how nice his sandwiches are. Or his hot chocolate, which is *so* nice.

'Cream,' he says. 'In case you were wondering what the secret ingredient is. That's what makes my hot chocolate so good.' He smirks again. 'I add a little at the end, as well as lots of milk.'

I shrug. No way am I admitting I was wondering exactly that.

After we've finished eating and devoured the glorious hot chocolate, he takes the tray away and clatters about in the kitchen clearing up. I don't offer to help him, instead going back to my knitting and losing myself in an episode of *Place in the Sun*. Once he's finished, he comes and sits back on the end of the sofa.

I glance up to see that he's reading a book. Then I remember my manners.

'Thanks for the sandwiches and the hot chocolate, very nice.' I offer the briefest of smiles then turn away.

'No problem.'

Out of the corner of my eye I see him turn the pages of his book and we sit in a silence only broken by the television. After a while he gets up and puts another log or two into the wood burner. Slyly I watch him, I'm vaguely intrigued by him, but it's not enough to outweigh my irritation. He comes back and takes his seat on the end of the sofa, but doesn't pick up his book.

'It's odd, isn't it, watching all that sun and sea in Spain when it's snowing and freezing here?'

'Yes, that's why I like it,' I say in a voice I hope conveys how much I'm into this programme, just in case he's got any ideas about turning it over.

'Not very Christmassy.'

'That's the idea,' I chirp, turning and giving him a quick, sharp look.

'You're escaping from Christmas, too.'

'Yes,' I say as curtly as I can and reach for the TV remote to turn up the volume. 'That and getting away from other people. All people.' I can't get any more pointed than that, can I?

'Me too,' he says. 'That's why it was a bit of shock to find you here this morning.'

'Yep. Ditto.' Now shut up.

'What's your story then?'

I turn and face him; he looks sad, very sad. But I no more want to hear his story than share my own. The whole point is not to dwell on it, not to churn it over, not to keep perpetuating it. To move on.

'Don't really want to talk about it,' I say and turn away.

'Yeah, I get that.'

'Good.' End of conversation as far as I'm concerned.

He gets up and paces to the kitchen, opens the fridge, looks in, closes it and comes back.

'I'm going to have a beer. Would you like something? Wine? Or beer?'

'Um, um…' Is it really so hard to make up my mind? He waits patiently while I dither, the hint of a smirk on his face. That smirk irritates me. 'No thanks, I won't bother.'

He slopes back off to the kitchen area and I attempt to get back into my knitting. Then he slinks off to his bedroom, returning a few minutes later, I'm guessing he's used his en-suite. Good, because I don't want him getting any ideas about using *my* bathroom, filling it with man-hair and man-stinks.

He brings two full glasses over, one beer, one wine, and puts them on the coffee table, the wine one in front of me.

'I guessed you did want one, or might do later. Just in case.' He beams at me and I find myself disarmed by his smile.

What can I say to that? How can I react without sounding like a miserable cow, a complete bitch? I can't wait for tomorrow to come so I can get the hell out of here, away from him and his forced jollity. Even if it does mean rattling around in that big, empty house full of memories, full of Cliff.

'Thanks,' I mutter, without looking at him.

'Don't worry, I didn't open one of yours, it's one of mine, the one I opened at lunchtime.' Another beguiling smile.

Just stop it.

'Thanks.' I attempt to concentrate on my knitting, but it's futile. I mark my place on the pattern, roll up the wool and push the needles through it to keep the knitting safe. I put the whole lot, pattern included, into my knitting bag and pick up the wine glass. Since it's obvious I'm not going to be left in peace to knit, I might just as well drink his wine. I put the glass to my lips.

❄ ❄ ❄

I'm glad I had those sandwiches earlier because otherwise this wine would have gone straight to my head. As it is, I am already aware, after just this one glass, albeit a large one, that I've been drinking. I suppose it's so long since I drank any great quantity of alcohol that I'm probably more sensitive to it.

'Another?' Noah Steele asks as he gets up from the sofa with both our empty glasses in his hand.

Oh, it's so tempting. It was nice wine, it just slid down, it's made me feel warm and soft inside.

'Maybe just half a glass,' I say and find myself smiling at him. I'm only being polite and pleasant. Stop smiling. Don't encourage him, he's bad enough.

He comes back with a full glass for me and another beer for himself.

I don't complain, but I do get up and get myself a glass of water. I need to dilute the effects of too much alcohol, especially as I'll need a clear head to drive home tomorrow.

A Place in the Sun comes to an end and then it's another show about people criticising each other's cooking. I can't stand this programme, so I reach for the remote, which I've tucked down beside me and start to flick through the channels. There's the inevitable slew of festive offerings, sickly, cheesy Christmas films, celebrity game shows where the set is decorated with tinsel, even though we all know it was probably filmed in July. Then I stumble across an old black and white movie.

'Oh,' Noah Steele says, leaning forward as though he's just been stabbed in the chest.

'You okay?' I feel a stab in my own chest, but I know it's panic. I hope he is all right, because I don't know what to do if he isn't. It's not as though I can ring for an ambulance from here. I'd have to go up the lane to get a signal, in the swirling snow, don't catastrophise...

'Yes, sorry. It's just that this was my mum's favourite film. We always watched it when I was a kid.'

'Oh. Okay. Why the groan, then?' Talk about a drama queen, or should that be king, or prince, maybe. Whatever.

'Nothing.' He shakes his head. 'It just reminded me of her, that's all.'

I smile and turn away, because I'm not going to ask him anything. I don't want to hear his story. I pick up the remote and prepare to find something else.

'Leave it on,' he says, his voice quiet. 'Please.' He sounds so pleading and borderline pathetic that I tuck the remote back down beside me. He may be calling the tune for now, but I'm in charge of the TV, I'm keeping the remote.

'Okay. For now,' I say.

'Thank you.' He picks up his beer and knocks it back. I glance over at my wine glass and see I've nearly finished it. How and when did than happen? I grab my glass of water and drink.

'More wine?' he asks, getting up to get more beer.

'No. Thank you. I need to keep a clear head for tomorrow's long drive home.' If I sound desperate enough will he agree to leave instead? I don't want to drive with a hangover, or worse, be delayed from driving because I'm still over the limit.

'Oh, that, right.' He smirks. 'You still plan on leaving then?'

'Yes. Of course. Since you won't. Will you?' I flutter my eyelashes at him. No, I really do. Shameful.

'No.' He shakes his head and goes back to the kitchen. When he comes back he has another beer and the wine bottle. 'Here, you might as well finish it.' He plonks the bottle down on the coffee table. Admittedly there is only an inch in the bottom, it would be churlish to waste it really, wouldn't it?

I empty the bottle and take a little sip, no need to be greedy. Then I lean into the back of the sofa and watch TV, *It's a Wonderful Life*. Clarence, the angel, is drying off his clothes after saving George's life. From memory, and it's a long time since I've seen this film, we're in for quite a sitting. Oh well, I've agreed he can watch it but if I find him wandering off or, worse still, dozing off, I'll be turning it over instantly. It's not that I don't like this film, I do, but it's a matter of principle. Noah Steele is not in charge. And this film is pure Christmas, and I don't want that.

I awake with a jolt. For a few moments I don't know where I am. The wood burner is still blazing away and that's what I'm blaming for my falling asleep, it's eating all the oxygen. I start to move then realise I've dribbled down my chin. How delightful.

'Ah, hello, sleeping beauty.'

'Um.' I jump up. I've fallen asleep, bad enough, but against him, Noah Steele. The enemy. The interloper. 'No need for sarcasm,' I snap.

'Don't worry, I dozed off too.'

'But you wanted to watch that film.' How dare he?

'I did. I saw it all. You didn't.' He grins.

I grab my knitting bag and march into the bathroom. When I come out I head straight for my bedroom.

'Night,' I mutter as I close the door behind me.

Four

Weak daylight wakes me. In my haste to go to bed last night I forgot to draw the curtains, but it doesn't matter, there's no one out there. Unless, unless, sneaky Noah Steele is sneaking around with his pervy sneak-dog.

I really don't want to get out of bed, it's so cosy. I have to admit that since I've been here I've had two of the best nights' sleep I've had since that hideous Christmas two years ago. No doubt last night's wine excess helped too.

The view from the window is both beautiful and shocking. It's not snowing. But it obviously has been, all night judging by the depth of the snow. All around us, everywhere I look, it's just a mass of white. Even the sea appears white as it blends into the pale sky. There is no hint of sun either which means the snow won't be melting soon.

Right on cue, just as I'm leaning against the lovely hot radiator and resting my arms on the window sill, Noah Steele and Kong appear. Together they lumber out of the cottage and out into the garden. Judging by how far it comes up their legs, that snow must be at least eight inches deep. Oh. My. God.

They plod along the garden, Kong staining the virgin snow with urine while Noah Steele hovers with a plastic bag ready to scoop up whatever else that monster dog does. Yuk, it doesn't bear thinking about.

I slink away from the window and melt back into my room; I do not want either of them noticing me.

Looks like it's going to be another long bath while I wait for the snow to melt enough for me to head home. I grab my book, which is definitely not suitable for being alone in a cottage with a stranger as the plot has now confirmed there's a killer on the loose. Oh well.

❄❄❄

When I finally come out of the bathroom – dressing gown firmly done up this time, I won't get caught again – the aroma of bacon hits me.

'Hey,' he says, turning from his frying pan. 'Cooked breakfast?'

'Um?' I really do fancy a cooked breakfast, especially after all that wine. But I don't want to accept any more meals from the enemy.

'It's *your* bacon,' he says, grinning. Cheeky bastard.

'Yes. Please. I'll just get dressed.' I can't really complain, can I? He's been feeding me his own food, and drink, these past two days. Even so, bloody cheek. He didn't even ask.

'Good timing,' he says, when I reappear wearing a cable knit jumper that I spent the whole of last summer knitting – my best effort to date, not including how successful I expect the Fair Isle to be, if I ever get the chance to finish it. I'm also, despite my best intentions, wearing a bra.

I slope off and sit at the table while he brings two plates piled high with our breakfast. One look and I know he's used all the bacon. All of it. I bought that to wrap around some chicken breasts not to fry up.

'Don't worry,' everything else is mine,' he says, seeing my face which is obviously betraying my thoughts.

'Thank you,' I mutter, taking in the fried potatoes, scrambled eggs, mushrooms and tomatoes. I have to admit it looks amazing, even if the portions are ridiculous.

'Don't worry if you can't eat it all.'

I stuff a forkful of potato into my mouth to prevent myself from telling Noah Steele to fuck right off and not tell me how much I can and cannot eat. Be nice, I tell myself, you'll soon be leaving.

'Anything you leave, Kong will finish,' he says. Kong, lying in his basket, leaps up at the mention of his name. Noah Steele clicks his fingers and Kong lies straight back down. See, that proves how well trained that dog is, proves he has trained it to be pervy.

I have to admit it's a great breakfast; it's accompanied by a pot of tea and a jug of orange juice. All his I know, because I didn't bring either of these items; coffee is my preferred drink. But I'm glad of the liquid and I don't leave much of the food for Kong.

'Cool sweater,' he says, as he takes our plates away. I suppose I should help clear up but I just sit there and let him get on with it. I never asked him to cook me breakfast.

'Thanks.'

'Perfect for this weather.' He scrapes what's left on our plates into Kong's bowl.

'Yeah.' Guilt gets the better of me. 'I'll wash up.'

'No need.' He turns and smiles.

Don't smile, it's too beguiling. Don't you dare try to win me over with your smile.

'Uh?'

'Dishwasher.' He waves at a cupboard door. 'It may be a cottagey kitchen but it has everything we need.' He smirks, then. Back to normal; smirk face.

I do at least bring our cups and glasses over from the table. Then Noah Steele and I dance around the dishwasher. It's all very cringe. I soon disappear back into my room to stuff all my things back into my bag and I'm glad to see that the sun has finally made an appearance and that means the snow should melt a bit.

I put on my coat, pull on my boots and take my suitcase out into the living room. There's no sign of him. I stop myself from performing a celebratory whoop and let myself out of the front door as quietly as possible. As I trudge along to my car, I'm glad my boot soles have good treads otherwise I'd be slipping all over the place. Once I get my bag into the boot I get in the car and start the engine. I'm not planning on driving straight off – I've left my handbag and my food inside – I just want to see how drivable this little road is.

I can't move the car at all.

I saunter back into the cottage. *He's* sitting in his armchair by the log burner with the TV remote in his hand. He turns the TV off when he sees me.

'I was wondering…' I start, trying to sound pleading but not helpless, and pleasant but not creepy. 'If you'd give me a hand getting my car out of the parking spot? I just need to back out and turn round, then I'm sure it'll be fine, once I'm driving forward.'

There's that bloody smirk again. I want to wipe it from his face, instead I just smile *my* most beguiling smile – or at least I think it is. Smiling is not my default, and certainly not of late.

'Yeah, 'course. Just get my coat.'

Once we're outside I see that he is armed with a shovel.

'Might have to dig,' he says, by way of an explanation, like I needed one.

'As long as it's not my grave,' I quip back. What? Where did that come from? That damn thriller I'm reading is creeping into my thoughts, my speech even. Why am I putting ideas into *his* head? Am I being stupid now?

He frowns and narrows his eyes but doesn't say anything. I think I might have insulted him. Oh well. Not to worry. I'll soon be gone and he and his giant dog can have the place all to themselves and my insults won't matter a jot.

'I tried to move it,' I tell him. 'But nothing happened.'

He bends over and shovels some of the snow out from under the front tyres, then moves back to do the same under the back tyres. Then he uses his boots to kick more snow out of the way.

'Try it now,' he says, without looking at me.

I get into the car, start the engine and move back a little. Yay! Then I hear the sound of snow crunching under the tyres and I grind to a halt. He's standing with the shovel resting across both hands and watching me. I wind the window down.

'Could you shovel a bit more out of the way? Please?'

He doesn't answer, just bends down and shovels again, then nods to me. I inch back then grind to another halt.

'A bit more?' I plead.

He obliges, again without speaking.

I inch back and stop.

We repeat the process three more times and I'm quite pleased that I'm now out of the parking space and on the lane. I have to turn now, which might be tricky.

'Could you...?'

'No,' he says, and it's only the second time he's spoken since I made the quip about him digging my grave. He hasn't smiled once since then, not even a smirk.

'Oh, but...'

'What do you want me to do? Dig out the whole lane? Then maybe dig out the road all the way to the motorway? Maybe they'll have cleared the motorway so I won't need to bother after that.' He stares straight at me, his eyes narrow, his face hard and mean. 'Put it back in the parking space and come to your senses, you won't be leaving today.' With that he steps around behind me and yanks open the boot, lifts out my case, slams the boot down and marches off.

Maybe that joke about digging my grave isn't so funny now.

I'm trapped here. With him and his dog.

I let myself back into the cottage, leave my snowy boots just inside the porch, next to his, hang my coat on the hook, and go into the living room. Thankfully, there's no sign of him, until I see movement outside. There he is, with Kong staining the snow again. Noah Steele has a ball and is throwing it for a slow, reluctant Kong to retrieve. Seeing that giant dog struggle through the snow I now realise how stupid my plan to drive home was. Yet he indulged me, dug my car out and didn't try to persuade me it wasn't sensible until I pushed him too far.

And I've evidently insulted him.

It was just a joke. It's not as though I really think he plans to kill me and bury me.

I grab my case, which he's dumped outside my bedroom door, and go inside. I flop on the bed and contemplate my Christmas escape holiday which isn't working out how I planned, at all. How long will I be stuck here? With him?

I look out of the window again when I finally get off the bed; he's still out there with Kong. He's making and flinging snowballs as far as he can and Kong, now sniffing around a snow-covered bush, makes no attempt to chase after them. I watch him, this stranger, this man who shouldn't be here, this Noah Steele who, to be fair, has shown me almost nothing but kindness since I've been here. In other circumstances, very different circumstances, perhaps a long time ago, I might have been vaguely attracted to him. He's tall, which I like, he's dark haired, and he has the most beguiling smile, even if smirking seems to be his default.

He's making a bigger snowball now; I can't imagine that travelling very far. Now he's rolling it on the ground, making it bigger and bigger. Suddenly I realise what he's doing.

And I want to join in.

By the time I get my coat and boots on and find my hat and gloves he's already made an impressive start. The snowman's body is already large and in position and he's rolling a head now. I stand behind him, conscious that he's unaware of me, and watch as he lifts the head onto the body.

'Does he need a nose?' I say, holding out a carrot I've taken from the fridge.

He turns. 'Oh. Hello. I didn't realise you were there.'

'No. I saw you from the window. It looked like fun. But I see you're almost finished now.' Now I feel stupid and embarrassed and wished I'd not bothered.

He smiles. There it is, no hint of a smirk, just a nice, genuine smile.

'No,' he says, taking the carrot and pushing it into the snowman's face. 'I need to build a snow dog too, otherwise Kong will sulk.'

I laugh, I can't help it. It's so stupid.

'You do his head,' he says. 'And I'll do his body.'

We beaver away, and Kong's likeness is rather more sophisticated than the snowman's. As we work the only conversation is about how we sculpt the snow to make the right shape. When we finish, we both stand back to admire our handywork.

'We should build you now,' Noah Steele says.

'Umm, yeah.' I suddenly get an image of me lying in front of the log burner naked. From the smirk on his face I think he does too. He had to go and spoil it. I'm just going to ignore that smirk, I was almost enjoying myself.

We fashion a second snowman, snowwoman, I suppose, alongside Kong. The one of me is roughly the

46

same height as the one of Kong sitting and a lot shorter than Noah Steele's snowman.

'We need another carrot,' I say as I turn to stomp back through the snow to get one.

'No, we can use this.' He yanks the carrot out of *his* snowman and snaps it in half, handing me the shorter portion for *my* nose.

'Thank you.' I sound shy, I feel shy. And silly. I push my nose into place.

'Let's get a picture, before they melt.' He pulls his phone out of his pocket and starts snapping away. 'Stand next to yours,' he says, waving to direct me into place before taking a few more photos. 'Kong,' he shouts.

Kong wanders over and sniffs our creations before Noah Steele positions Kong for his photo call.

'Let me get one of you,' I say, holding out my hand for his phone.

'Let's get one of all of us,' he says as I hand the phone back. 'Do you think we can manage a selfie with us all?'

We shuffle around while he holds the phone at arm's length and takes a few. I'm reminded of the selfie stick, still in its box, which Cliff bought me for that Christmas, two years ago. I didn't open it for weeks because we were going to do our presents when he came back.

It would have come in useful now.

We look at the photos together, laughing at them, at our smiling faces which are red with the cold. Then Kong starts to wander around our snow creations, cocking his leg and staining each one in turn, mine last. We laugh together again.

Now would be a good time, the little voice in my head says. I take a breath.

'I feel I owe you an apology,' I start, as Noah Steele frowns his puzzlement at me. 'For my quip about digging my grave.'

He grins. 'Oh, that. No probs.'

'Then why were you so…' How do I end that sentence without insult? He waits for me to finish. 'You know, a bit annoyed.'

'Oh that. Well, I could have told you that the snow was too deep for you to get out of here. But you're not the type to listen, are you? So I thought I'd let you see for yourself, then I realised that *I* would have to do a lot of digging before you'd concede defeat. Maybe the thought of it made me seem annoyed.' He doesn't follow this with a grin or smirk, just a look, a sad look.

'Oh. Right.' I'm not sure how to take that. 'So you don't like independent women then?' I manage a smile.

'Sure I do, but me digging wasn't you being independent, was it? *You* digging you out, that's independence.'

'Oh.' He does have a point, I suppose.

'Anyway, I'm getting cold and even Kong's had enough, I'm going in now.' He turns and strides towards the cottage leaving me there with my thoughts. After a few seconds I scamper along in his footsteps.

'Look, if I caused any offence, I'm sorry,' I try again.

He nods as he kicks his boots against the cottage wall to remove the excess snow.

'I did wonder what your hurry was.' He steps inside and holds the door open for me. 'I hoped I wasn't that repugnant,' he says as he marches off to hang up his coat.

'Well, no, but…' I say to his back.

48

He turns back and forces a smile, and I can see it's an effort, not like the smiles that seem to be his default face position, except when he smirks.

'Look, let's just try and have a happy Christmas, shall we, because we're both stuck here whether either of us likes it or not. Let's just be pleasant to each other. Yeah?'

'Okay,' I say. 'Um, Happy Christmas.'

'Yeah and you. Hot chocolate?' He strides over to fill the kettle for our hot chocolate and I, in a gesture of peace, retreat to my bedroom to retrieve the luxury chocolate biscuits I've been hiding. At least I haven't opened the box yet, unlike the Roses and Quality Street which are still in my car. I need to bring them in because even the orange crèmes will be rock hard in this cold.

Five

We fill ourselves with hot chocolate and chocolate biscuits. We review the photos again, especially the ones of the three of us with our snow statues. Noah Steele has done quite a good job of getting us all in, albeit without our feet.

'You'll have to send me a couple of those,' I say, without thinking it through.

'Sure, what's your number?'

'Oh, that won't work, no signal.' I come back quickly, rolling my eyes for emphasis. 'Bluetooth them to me.' I fiddle with my phone to enable the Bluetooth.

'Okay. He smiles and obliges. I don't know if he spotted my reluctance to share my phone number. I'm very careful about who I give my phone number to.

Two hours later while he is flicking through the TV channels and I am concentrating on my knitting without him interrupting my concentration, he breaks our amicable silence.

'That was an amazing Christmas lunch. I always wanted to do that when I was a kid, you know, chocolate lunch.'

I laugh. I know just what he means. 'Chocolate lunch mid-afternoon,' I say.

'Trouble is, I'm hungry for proper food now.' He gets up and goes to the kitchen, throws open the fridge door. I put my knitting down and follow him.

'I have some chicken pieces in there somewhere. And I'm sure between us we have plenty of veg, we could cook a decent meal from that.' Not, that the chicken will be wrapped in bacon, which was my original idea.

'Hey, yes. Sounds good,' he says. 'I'll put the oven on.'

Just over an hour later we're sitting down to roast chicken and roasted vegetables. We've thrown all the veg in together, even the broccoli I bought, and roasted the lot, and, even though I say so myself, it's really rather nice.

'That was a great idea, I'd never have thought of roasting veg.' He grins at me from across the table as he tucks into his food. I've dished out our portions so I've given him far more than me. I am hungry, but not that hungry and I wouldn't normally eat man-size portions.

'I do it all the time. I'm lazy, it's easy.' There is a modicum of truth there, I do do it, but only when I can be bothered, the rest of the time I live on beans on toast, or soup or cereal. That's the trouble with being the one left behind; you can't see the point of bothering just for one, but it had always been my intention to make a bit of an effort on this escape from Christmas, so at least I've achieved something – I've made a proper meal.

We clear everything away with a routine that seems practised, even though it isn't, obviously. I think we might have done a bit of team bonding while building the snowmen and cooking the meal.

This really isn't how I imagined my escape would be.

'Would you like a drink?' he asks after we finished loading the dishwasher.

Do I want wine? I don't think I do. 'Um, no. Not wine.'

'I have beer, it's low alcohol, or I could do you a St Clements.' He grins.

'Okay. St Clements.'

'This Christmas Day is nicer than I expected.' He leans back with his second beer while I sip away at my drink, I do like orange juice and lemonade – he even had the foresight to make ice cubes when he arrived.

'Or not as bad as feared,' I quip. And certainly not how I imagined it at all.

'No, suppose not.'

I've given up with the knitting and put it away. We've switched the TV off and we're listening to music from his phone via a speaker. I brought no music because I never thought beyond the radio in my car. His music is very calming. I do have those DVDs I packed, but as I've discovered, there's no player here so I won't be watching my non-Christmas films. Probably just as well, he'd probably talk all the way through them anyway.

'We're chilling,' I say, smiling to myself. Despite not having a drink I feel incredibly relaxed, almost happy. It feels as though we're two old friends slobbing about on either end of the sofa.

That's not right. I pull myself up and shake my shoulders.

'You okay?' He smiles at me, not a smirk, a sweet smile.

'Yes, just, you know, thinking about Christmases past.'

His face drops as though I've hit him with his shovel. Typical me; I've killed the mood.

'You okay?' I ask, and I'm genuinely concerned.

'Last Christmas I was happy,' he says. 'I had the best girlfriend in the world. Maybe if I'd asked her to marry me then, I might still be happy.'

I nod. I'm intrigued. Who wouldn't be? But I don't want him to tell me his story in case he expects me to reciprocate. I won't be doing that. We may be getting on because we have to but we're not friends, not really.

'I have mince pies.' I jump up off the sofa. 'Would you like one?'

'Yes, please. There's ice cream in the freezer too.'

If I keep eating at this rate, mostly to swallow down my emotions, and, apparently his, I'm going to be as fat as a house by the time I go back to work.

After another scoffing session and more drinks, I boot up and retrieve what's left of the Roses and the Quality Street from my car. And, hurray, he likes the nutty and chewy ones, not my favourite softies.

'My ex only liked the soft ones,' he says, softly.

'Same here. Well, no, Cliff only liked the hard ones, like you do.' Oooo, did that sound faintly flirty. 'It's so cold out there,' I say to divert him. 'I'm surprised these chocolates aren't frozen solid, though they are a bit hard.'

'Where's Cliff now?' He hasn't been diverted.

Oh no. Don't answer. Don't answer. But my stupid mouth betrays me. 'Dead.' I inhale quickly and turn away.

'Oh shit. I'm so sorry. I had no idea.'

'Course not. Why would you?'

'That's why you're here, escaping all the jollity.'

'Yep.' See, I did not want to discuss this. This is what happens when you let your guard down. Too much food, and choccy and I'm a right blabbermouth. And don't, please don't get me started on the wine again or I'll be blubbing as well as blabbing. I'm so glad I exercised a bit of restraint.

'I'm sorry,' he says. 'I can see you don't want to talk about it.'

'No.' I look down at my hands, I'm smoothing out a sweet wrapper on my lap, repeatedly running the palm of my hand over the orange cellophane.

He gets up and puts another log on the wood burner. I think he's being tactful, diplomatic, because I'm sure he last did that less than twenty minutes ago.

He sits back down and offers me a smile, sympathy, empathy, pity, I don't know but I don't want it. Right. Take action.

'What about you? What are you escaping from?' I didn't want to know earlier, because, you know, it's usually *you tell me yours, I'll tell you mine,* and I don't want that, but I have to divert his attention away from me. And, well, everyone likes talking about themselves. Don't they?

'Last Christmas I had a lovely girlfriend, I thought she was the one, she was the one. Now she isn't.' He stares off into the distance.

I nod. To be honest, that's enough for me. If he doesn't want to talk about it either, fair enough.

'She ran off with my best mate in February. They got engaged on her birthday, which was just before Christmas…' He turns to face me now. 'That was the day I booked this place. I just had to get as far away as possible.'

'Yes. I understand. What about your family.' Nosy. I'm just keeping his attention on him, not me.

'My mum died when I was a teenager, Dad remarried about fifteen years ago, he has a whole new family now. I love my brothers, but I just wanted to escape, be on my own, lick my wounds. They won't miss me.' He shrugs and smiles as if he's trying to convince himself as much as me. 'It's made everything very difficult, what's happened. There's a big group of us, we all go away skiing on Boxing Day, have done for the past five years, a fun filled week on the slopes. They're going, my ex and my ex-mate. I couldn't bear the thought. Told everyone I had a better offer.' He stands up. 'I'm going to open a bottle of wine; would you like to share?'

'Yes, please.' No, no, don't.

'How long were you together?' I ask, to keep the focus on him. He's poured us both a large glass of red and brought the bottle over too. I promise myself I'm only taking little sips.

'Three years and five months.'

'Did she tell you or did you find out?' I can't imagine how horrible either would be.

'No, my mate told me. Took me to the pub and bought me a pint and told me they'd *fallen in love*. So brave. While he was doing that, she was packing her bags and moving out of my house. That's the only good thing, it is *my* house. I own it. So no messy buying her out or selling it.'

'Some mate. That must have been horrible.'

'Yep. My best mate, from school. Met when we were eleven. Which means I've lost him as well as her. He kept saying he was sorry. He hoped we could still be friends. Fucker.'

'Have you seen her since?'

'Oh yes. We're in the same social circle. I see her, them, out all the time. I just couldn't face Christmas like that when everyone is out and about even more and drinking too much and things get said… Then the skiing.'

'Yes, I understand.'

'Do I sound pathetic?' he asks, knocking back his wine, emptying the glass and refilling it from the bottle.

I look at his face, gauge his mood.

'Oh yes,' I say. 'Definitely.'

'Yeah, that's what I thought.'

'Well.' I smile and shake my head. 'You're allowed.'

'I confronted her once, when I saw her out. I wanted to know why him, why not me. Why had she dumped me, except she never actually told me she'd dumped me. Do you know what she said, do you?'

'Obviously not.'

'She said I was too nice. I smiled too much. That's what she said.'

'You do smile a lot.' I've finished my glass of wine without realising and now my tongue is loosening up. And it's getting late and I should know better and just go to bed.

'Too much?'

'Can anyone smile too much?' It's a serious question. Can you smile too much? 'No, smiling is good.'

'Yeah. He's sulky, Liam, my ex-mate. Scowls a lot. She said he was sexy. Brooding. She liked it.'

'Oh.'

'Yeah, and I'm boring, according to her, Vic.'

'I'm sure you're not.' Am I? Yes, I am. He hasn't bored me at all, irritated the hell out of me, yes, but not bored. And, actually, he's not even irritating me now, more distracting me. From myself. 'Vic? That's her name.'

'Victoria, she prefers Vic.' He rolls his eyes a little and laughs. It's the first time he's laughed since he's been talking about her.

'Is she a car mechanic?'

'No. Err, why would she be?'

'Just, where I take my car for servicing, one of the guys is called Vic, mind he's fifty-plus and as grumpy as hell.'

'Right.' He squints at me as though I'm mad, which is fair enough. 'Would you like more wine or have you had enough?' Is that a judgement?

'I think I'd rather have hot chocolate.' I definitely don't need any more wine, that wine has gone straight to my head, but I don't usually drink red, so maybe that's why.

'Wow, twice in one day.'

'Well, it is Christmas Day.' Weird, I'd promised myself that I wouldn't be acknowledging Christmas Day at all, yet here I am sharing it with a stranger. And, I'm almost enjoying myself.

'Talking of which,' he says, jumping up. 'I have a present or two to open. Now's as good a time as any. They're in my room.'

He lopes off and returns with two beautifully wrapped presents.

'Wow, someone's good at wrapping.'

'Yolanda,' he says.

'Yolanda?'

'My dad's wife. She likes things to be just so.'

'Ah.'

'Would you like to open one?' He offers me a present.

'No. I have one of my own, my mum gave it to me.' Now it's my turn to retrieve my present from my room. She'd pressed it into my hands the day before they flew to Australia, said I could open it anytime I liked, but, until now, I haven't liked. If Noah Steele wasn't opening his now, I would probably have forgotten all about it.

When I return, he's waiting for me, his still wrapped presents balanced on his lap.

'I'll go first,' he says. He rips open the smaller of his two packages, and extracts a long, narrow box. 'Pen,' he says, before he opens the lid. He's right, it's a rather expensive one too.

'That's nice. Really nice.'

'Yeah, Yolanda likes nice things. Your turn.'

I open my present, probably less aggressively that he did his. It's a book. A self-help book. *How to move forward without constantly looking back.* Inside Mum has dedicated it to me, with love.

I lay the book on the sofa without comment. Using one finger Noah slowly rotates it so he can read the title. He doesn't comment either. I know my mum means well, but, really...

'My turn.' He rips into his second present, completely trashing the beautiful wrapping just like he did the first time. It too is a book, a journal. 'I think she wants me to write in this rather than moping around or continually going on about Vic.' He lays the journal on top of my self-help book.

'They mean well.' I know that's certainly true of my parents even if I don't know about Yolanda.

'Yeah.' He gets up. 'Hot chocolate now.'

After I've drunk my hot chocolate, I start to feel very drowsy. I've overdosed on chocolate in its various forms today and I just hope I'm not going to be a super spotty face tomorrow because chocolate does do that to me.

'I'm off to bed.' I don't add that I'm going now before I fall asleep dribbling on his shoulder again. 'Thank you for a surprising Christmas Day. It turned out better than I could have imagined.'

He smiles, again. 'You too,' he says. 'Sleep well.'

And I do.

Six

The snow is still here, and we've had a sharp frost overnight too. The snow glistens, sparkling in the weak sunshine. That, the sunshine, at least, is hopeful. Maybe the lane will defrost and I can leave.

Our snow sculptures look as though we've just built them, frozen in suspended animation, their carrot noses white with frost. That was fun, even Kong peeing on them was amusing. Noah was amusing.

'Morning,' he says as I pad out of my room in my dressing gown. He already has the log burner roaring away and the heating is on, so it's cosy inside. 'Did you sleep well?'

'Yes, I did. You?'

'Yeah. Though I had to get up earlier than I'd have liked to let Kong out. I hope he didn't wake you.'

'He didn't.' I manage a smile. It's all very nice exchanging early morning pleasantries with this stranger – just because he's told me his ex-girlfriend story doesn't make us besties – but I'm wetting myself. 'Bathroom,' I say as I move away.

He nods and shows off his smile again, the one Vic found so boring. 'Are you hungry?'

'I'm not. No. I'm going to have a long soak in the bath then decide what I'm going to do.' I mean when I'm going to leave, rather than what I'm going to eat.

He nods and a forced, polite smile flashes across his face before he turns away. Have I offended him? I hope not, but, on the other hand, I don't want him hanging on my every word, trying to please me, just because he's feeling sorry for himself. And me.

Is he needy? Is that why she dumped him? Needy and boring and too smiley?

In the bathroom I see the effects of too much chocolate and rich food on my skin. As predicted, I have a spot and it's right on the end of my nose. I look like bloody Rudolph. It's one of those blind ones too, nice and red and lumpy but no satisfying white head you can pop to hurry it away. Great. I thought teenage spots ended in your teens but they don't, here I am in my thirties and I still get them.

I was too tired to take my makeup off last night, and although I don't wear much, I now look like a panda. A dirty, spotty panda. Oh well, Noah Steele has seen me in *all* my glory, and I don't care.

An hour later and I'm looking far more presentable. I've read a sizeable chunk of my book in the bath – not the self-help book Mum gave me, which I left on the sofa – but the juicy murder thriller. Although, I am wondering about the sense of reading it, as it's set in a secluded cottage in the woods, when a handsome stranger comes a-knocking. It's fiction, I tell myself, get over it.

Oh, what the hell. Since Cliff died there have been many times when I wished I was dead too, so, I don't think I care. Except for my parents, they would care; they would be devastated.

There's no sign of Noah Steele when I go back into the living room. The fire is roaring and he's obviously tidied up, my book, and his journal and pen, are placed neatly on the coffee table. I wonder if he's written in it? I resist the temptation to check.

I wander around the room, it runs back to front and has windows at both ends, as well as a door to the porch, and rear French windows. Everything is double glazed, so it keeps the heat in. I look out over the back garden, it's still sparkly out there, but there's no sign of Noah and his hound. Maybe he's taken it for a long walk, faraway. I can hope.

I get myself a bowl of cereal, a cup of coffee and settle down at the table. It's peaceful, calm, quiet, warm.

The door from the porch suddenly bursts open and there he is. Noah Steel. With Kong. They usher a cold blast of air into the room. His face is red and blotchy from the cold and even Kong looks as though he's had enough.

'Hey,' he says. 'Nice bath?'

'Yes. Thank you.' Now be quiet.

He goes over to the freshly boiled kettle, makes himself a cup of instant coffee, mine, I notice, then sits himself opposite me at the table. We're facing each other now, staring straight into each other's eyes.

'You look different,' I say, without thinking. 'No stubble.'

'Yeah. Always shave on a Friday. Let it grow the rest of the week.' He grins. Without stubble he looks about fifteen, his skin is smooth and, now the red is fading, it's also pale. No spots, I notice.

'Why Friday?'

'Good for the weekend,' he says, with a light laugh.

'Right. Okay. I have to admit I didn't realise it was Friday. I've almost lost track.' It feels as though I've been here days and days.

'Yeah. Boxing Day too.'

We fall into a silence only punctuated by my crunching away on my cereal and the chink of the spoon as it hits the bowl.

'Nice walk?' I ask because I feel I should and I'm also wondering why he couldn't have been out longer.

'Haven't been walking yet. I've scraped your car and done a bit more digging.

'Oh.' Now take back all your nasty thoughts. 'Thank you.'

'You might want to try it first before you load it up. There hasn't been any more snow, but it hasn't thawed much either.'

'No.' I gobble down the remainder in my bowl and drink my coffee. I'm excited; maybe I can go home today.

Ten minutes later I'm heading out of the front door, wrapped up against the cold and surefooted in my good boots. He's cleared a lot of snow; in fact, I do wonder how long he took doing it. He's obviously as keen for me to leave as I am to go. No doubt opening up about his ex last night has proved, in the cold, sober light of day, to be too embarrassing for me to stay.

'Do you want to give it a go?' he says from behind me.

'Oh, sorry, you didn't need to come out.'

'Kong needs a good long walk today.' He shrugs his shoulders as if to say that he really hasn't come out for me at all. 'He's eaten too much and not been out enough.' Is he talking about himself too? Or me?

'Right.'

'Try while I'm here, then if I need to dig any more, I can.'

I get in my car and start the engine; he's scraped the ice off the windows too. He really *is* keen for me to leave.

I manage to back out, then turn, then move along the lane a little. This is a massive improvement on yesterday. He stands watching me, impassive, his face blank, the shovel, which I hadn't noticed before, in his hands. My joke about digging my grave comes back to me. I shudder.

Then I grind to a halt.

I'm stuck.

He dashes in front of me and rapidly shovels some more snow. I creep further forward. He shovels again.

I turn off the engine. He's round at my door in seconds.

'Everything okay? Car's not stalled, has it?'

'No. This is hopeless, isn't it? It's the same as yesterday. You can't dig me all the way out, can you? Like you said before, not all the way to the motorway.'

'The main road might be clear by now; they must have gritted it. Surely.' He sounds desperate.

I get out of my car, lock it up and glance up the lane. The snow looks deep, and because much of it is in shade, I doubt there's been much, if any thawing going on.

'I'm going to leave it here,' I tell him. 'Not much point it putting it back in the space, is there?'

He shakes his head. 'Hey, why don't we walk up the lane and have a look? It's less than half a mile. Then we can decide what to do.'

I'm about to say it's pointless, he can't possibly dig out half a mile of snow, even if the main road is clear, but he sets off at such a pace with Kong bounding along beside him that I have to almost run to catch up with him.

We march on, him slightly ahead, Kong bounding around and evidently enjoying himself. It's cold, but I think it might not be quite as cold as yesterday. Or maybe I'm getting used to it, or deluding myself. Or the effort of attempting to catch up with him and Kong is warming me up. Finally, and slightly out of breath I catch up with them. We've walked at least half way up the lane and this snow is far too deep for me to drive my car through.

'What do you think?' I puff.

'Let's see what the main road is like?'

On we march and at a pace too. Kong is still bounding around enjoying himself. That's one out of three then, because Noah Steele doesn't look particularly happy and definitely isn't smiling and I'm bordering on exhausted. We reach the main road. It is driveable, or at least the middle of it is; instead of two lanes, it's now a single lane.

'Could you manage that?' He turns to me and waits for my answer.

'Yes. Yes.' I'm saying this to convince myself, aren't I? 'But I don't know what happens when I meet a car coming the other way. There's nowhere to go, is there?'

He steps forward and peers both ways down the road, the visibility is good and the road straight so we can see a long way.

'Doesn't look like it.'

'You couldn't dig all along the lane anyway, could you?'

'No. Maybe I could try driving my car down here, sort of clear the way. Maybe.'

Oh yes, his big black four-by-four. I glance up and down the lane, then back up and down the main road.

'Do you think that would work?' I ask.

'Who knows.' He shrugs, again. 'We could try. If I get stuck you won't need to bother and if you get stuck you can just abandon your car until the snow thaws. Up to you.' He turns and starts to plod back down the lane, presumably to his car. For him to move his car at all I am going to have to move mine back into the parking space.

'You think this is stupid, don't you,' I say as we approach the cottage. It's twinkling in the weak sunshine, smoke billowing out of the chimney and its windows look like lazy eyes. It has a sly beauty in this weather and it makes me wonder how it looks in summer.

He shrugs and turns his mouth down. I swear that is far more irritating than the smiling.

'Do you really think your car will make it up that lane?'

'More chance than yours.'

'Okay, if it does will it clear away the snow enough for me to get up there?' Do not shrug again.

'I don't know. As I said, I'm willing to try if *you* want to.'

I stand for a moment or two considering my options, thinking it through, imagining our cars both stuck in the snow.

'I think it's pointless,' I say and watch the relief flood across his face.

Why didn't he just say so in the first place?

He puts the shovel back in his boot while I put my car back in the parking space. Before I turn the engine off, I put the radio on, I'm just in time catch the local weather forecast. There's no sign of a thaw and there's a possibility of more snow later today. People are being urged to only make necessary journeys. Aren't all journeys necessary? I know I never drive anywhere for the fun of driving. I don't find driving fun at all.

'I'm going to take Kong for a walk, maybe see if I can get down to the beach. The sea should be interesting in weather like this. Would you like to come, since you're stuck here anyway?' There's the smile again and I definitely prefer it to his shrugging.

'It's supposed to snow later.'

'We'll be back long before then.'

'Okay. Thanks.' I don't add that the reason I'm coming is to ensure that he does come straight back before it snows again because, for some unfathomable reason I don't want to be stuck here on my own. Which, given that that was my whole reason for coming here, is absolutely, bloody ridiculous. I also don't want to have to worry if he doesn't come back or be responsible for sending out a search party. How would I do that? I'm definitely overthinking this.

We weave round the back of the cottage, across the garden and swerve right. This is all new to me, I haven't been farther than the back garden so far.

'You've got good grip on your boots, haven't you?'

'Yes.' Don't treat me like a kid.

'Good, because when I walked down here the other day, before it snowed, I did have to pay attention, so it might be trickier now.'

'Now you tell me.' I laugh, but I'm also a little apprehensive.

'You'll be fine. And it is definitely worth it once we round this bend.'

He's right. It takes my breath away. The sea, which looked amazing from my bedroom window, looks magnificent now we're closer to it. It's glistening and dark and menacing and majestic.

'Wow,' I say. Then I lose my footing, nothing serious, just a slight misstep, but it means that I reach out and grab his arm for support. I feel a complete fool and such a cliché.

'You okay?'

'Yeah. Thanks. Sorry about that. Just slipped.'

'No problems.' He smiles and there's no sign of a smirk.

Unfortunately, as we find our way down to the beach, which is completely covered in snow except where the sea meets the shore, I grab onto him twice more. So pathetic.

Kong runs off, leaping and bouncing around; he's remarkably agile for such a great big dog. He hops in and out of the sea and wags his tail with pure delight.

'Is that a good idea? Him getting wet, I mean, with it being so cold.'

'He was already wet from the snow. I'll make sure to dry him off when we get back. Maybe let him sit in front of the log burner.' He gives me a sly look but I refuse to rise to his bait even if I do have an image of a steaming Kong stinking up the cottage.

Kong bounds down to the end of the beach then disappears. Noah Steele strides after him and I scamper alongside to keep up.

'There's a little cove down there, he found a dead seagull and tried to eat it.'

'Oh, is he going back for it?'

'Oh yes. But he won't find it because I buried it in the sand. Not that that will stop him hunting.'

We stride on across the beach, across virgin snow that shows no human footprints, just Kong's and those of birds, gulls probably. The snow crunches and compresses beneath out feet. There's no wind, it's eerily quiet, even the sea is almost silent apart from the occasional soft whoosh as it brushes the shoreline.

Kong is already digging when we round the corner and come across the cutest little cove.

'Kong. Stop,' shouts Noah Steele. The dog ceases mid-dig.

'I bet this is even lovelier in summer.' I can imagine secret trysts between lovers, picnics of wine with grapes and cheese. 'What?' I say, suddenly realising that Noah Steele is speaking while I'm indulging in a strange romantic daydream.

'I said I think this cove disappears at high tide. I bet it would be easy to get trapped here.'

That's my daydream ruined then, replaced by the horrors of drowning or climbing the sheer cliffs to escape the sea while the romantic picnic floats away on the tide.

He whistles for his dog who comes back with his tail between his legs and a sulky look on his giant face.

'There's a pub back there. I saw it the other day. Fancy seeing if it's open?'

'Why not. Yes.'

We retrace our steps and I pull my scarf up around my face. It's definitely getting colder; is this the sign of more snow?

We find the pub nestling in a small valley beyond the main beach and up a little. Smoke is coming from its chimney and there are cars in the car park.

I'm so cold now my hands and feet are starting to ache.

'Do you think they do hot chocolate?' I imagine the hot cup warming my hands.

'Only one way to find out.'

'What about Kong?'

'It's dog friendly,' he says with confidence.

'How do you know? Have you already been here?'

'No, it was in the folder.'

'What folder?'

'The one at the cottage, with all the info.'

I *knew* there must be one. 'I haven't seen it.'

'Sorry, I think it's in my room.' He grins. 'Bedtime reading. Sorry.'

'You can buy the first drink for that.' I push the door open before he can and march into the pub.

It's warm inside due to the enormous fire burning in the grate next to a Christmas tree whose needles have already started to drop all over the floor. Gawdy decorations hang from the rafters, tree lights are draped along the bar. People glance over at us, one or two smile before they continue their conversations, several pat Kong who, along with other dogs, is most welcome. We approach the bar and I ask if they do hot chocolate. They do. Noah Steele orders a half-pint of local beer.

We find a table in the corner by the fire and settle down. I take my coat, scarf, gloves off and nestle into my seat, an ancient settle that is padded out with cushions.

Noah Steele picks up the menu on the table.

'Busy, isn't it, for Boxing Day?'

'Yes. They're serving food until three. We could have something.' He studies the menu, then grabs one from another table and hands it to me. 'My treat,' he says when I don't greet his statement with enough gusto. 'To make up for you getting stuck here.'

'I can afford to pay my own way.' I narrow my eyes at him.

'Okay,' he says, his voice so mock meek that I could almost laugh, but I won't give him the satisfaction.

❄❄❄

'Freak weather we're having,' the waitress says as she puts our meals down in front of us. 'TV says there's more on the way. Roll on summer, I say. You're not local?'

'No, we're staying in the cottage above the beach,' he says.

'Ah, Christmas Cottage. Nice. Remember it when it was a bit more humble.' She laughs. 'How long for?'

'Until New Year,' Noah Steele answers for us both again.

'Just as well. You're probably stuck down that lane anyway.' She laughs again. 'Worse places to get stuck, eh?' She turns away, still laughing.

We fill ourselves with good food, and, now I'm suitably warmed up, I move onto the local cider. It's good too. And strong. The pub is busy, very busy and the clatter and chatter from so many people eating and talking means there are no awkward silences to fill and no need to constantly attempt conversation. No need to revisit our sorrowful pasts.

I'm relaxed and comfortable.

I see the waitress heading our way and assume she's going to swerve elsewhere any second because we haven't ordered any more food, but no, it's us she's after.

'You'll have to move now,' she says, smiling. 'The band's just arrived. You're sitting in their spot.'

'You didn't say earlier,' Noah Steele says, frowning.

'No, I didn't think you'd still be here when they came. Not a problem. I've got a nice spot for you in the corner, and you'll have a good view.'

The nice spot in the corner means we're squidged too close together for my liking, or his, I suspect. Our shoulders are touching, our thighs are touching. It's too, too intimate. We both squirm, attempting to move apart but there is just nowhere to go. We'll have to grin and bear it, or leave.

Sitting opposite us is an old couple who, judging by their pink faces and cheeky grins have had as much cider as I have.

'I'm Arthur, this is Joan. You up at the cottage then?' The old man comes straight to the point.

'Ruby Sutton and Noah Steele,' I say, before Noah Steele can answer. 'And yes, we are.'

'Honeymoon?' Joan asks, making a face that looks like ahh sounds.

'No. No.'

'Ahh, just having a break. That's nice.'

Both Noah Steele and I force smiles, I'm cringing inside and no doubt he is too. And I can feel the muscles in his thigh tighten as he attempts to move away from me again. Just grin and bear it, I tell myself. You've suffered worse.

I glance sideways at him to see how uncomfortable he looks but he's smiling away at Arthur and Joan, and the whole pub in general. That's when I notice the small piece of green on his front tooth. Spinach? Lettuce? I didn't pay much attention to what he had. Should I tell him? Maybe not. I reach down for my handbag, pull out my mirror and lip salve and apply some, while checking my own teeth for green debris.

'Would you like another drink?' he asks, his eyes crinkling as he smiles.

'I'll go,' I say. 'Since I'm on the end anyway.' I stand up and at the same time I push my little mirror into his hands and whisper, 'Teeth.' I'm really not that mean, am I?

'Thanks,' he says, pressing the mirror into my hands when I return with our drinks. He smiles, his teeth are spinach free and I feel all warm and glowing inside, it could be the cider or it could be that I enjoyed having the upper hand there, not that it makes up for the pervy-dog trick.

The band, two men, one with a violin the other with an accordion, together with a woman singer, set up quickly and start to play. They have no amps or mics or anything technical at all, just themselves, their voices and their instruments. They also have three pints of cider on the table, *our* table.

I don't know the songs, they're folky and sea shanty, but, like the rest of the pub we're soon tapping along with them, clapping, joining in with choruses when told to and, bloody hell, enjoying ourselves. I have another cider and Noah Steele another beer. I don't even notice his thighs anymore.

I don't know how long they play for; it seems a long time, but suddenly, they're packing up and leaving.

'Snowing,' Arthur says, leaning over the table and grinning at me.

'Oh,' I say, trying not to sound alarmed. I may have had quite a few ciders but I'm still aware that the walk back via the beach path will be treacherous. And dark. Why did we stay so long?

There's a mass exodus, even the bar staff are leaving. Noah Steele gets up and fetches our coats which we've left on the back of our original seats. He holds mine out for me to put my arms in; I wish he wouldn't but it would be churlish to snatch it from him.

We step outside, the car park is empty, the snow is floating down around us, and apart from one lamp post in the car park, everywhere is dark. It's eerily quiet with the snow damping down any sounds.

Kong who has spent most of the time we were in the pub either asleep, eating titbits from strangers' plates or being petted, saunters a few feet ahead of us and waits.

Noah Steele strides forward. I hesitate and shiver, though it's not even that cold, slighter warmer than earlier maybe.

'Okay?' he says.

'Not looking forward to trekking along the coast path.' What an understatement. 'In the dark,' I add, shivering again.

'Good job I can light the way then.' He pulls a beanie hat out of his pocket, puts it on his head and switches on a bright LED light in the front of it. I'd laugh if I wasn't so worried about our journey back. He looks hilarious. Just as hilarious as I must have looked with my head torch on. Shame I never brought it out with me, but why would I? I didn't know we would be out so late. Noah Steele stoops to put Kong's lead on. 'Can't have him running off in the dark. Ready?'

'No.' I'm saying no to Kong running off and no to me being ready. I'm frozen to the spot with fear. Trouble is, if I stand here long enough, I probably will be frozen, literally.

'Link my arm.' He crooks his elbow for me.

'How's that going to help when we have to walk in single file with a dark swirling sea beneath us?'

'Come on.' He shakes his elbow and, reluctantly, I link arms with him.

We set off, but not in the direction I was expecting. We're soon away from the one lamp post in the pub car park and I'm glad of his head torch hat, even if it does make him look like a Dalek. The snow is thick and crunchy beneath our feet and reflects the bright white light from his torch.

'Where are we going?'

'Home,' he says. 'Well, back to Christmas Cottage, anyway.'

'But this isn't the way.'

'It is. Look.' He lifts his head and illuminates the darkness in front of us. In the distance a white wall reflects his torch light.

'Is that the cottage?'

'Yes.' Now he lets himself laugh. 'The pub is just at the other end of our lane.'

'You might have said. I was dreading that walk along the coast path.'

'I thought I'd surprise you. I thought you'd be relieved.'

'Yeah. I'd have been more relieved if you'd told me earlier.' I let go of his arm and stomp ahead.

He moves his head and the way before me is plunged into darkness. If only I had my own head torch. He catches up with me.

'We need to be together if you want to benefit from my light.' He holds out his arm again.

I take it. Begrudgingly, I have to admit to myself that I feel a lot more surefooted hanging onto his arm.

I'm not telling him that though.

Seven

Once we're inside the cottage Noah Steele pokes the fire and puts several logs on. We both stand near it warming ourselves, even Kong ventures onto the rug once he's been towelled off.

'Sorry,' he says out of nowhere.

'About what?'

'Not telling you we were so near. Not letting on you wouldn't need to face the beach path again.'

'Ah. Yes.' I can't pretend I'm not a little annoyed about it.

'It was stupid. I thought it would be funny. Sorry. Misjudged that.'

'Is that the sort of joke you played on your ex-girlfriend?'

His face drops just as I realise what I've said, or rather, that I've said it aloud. That hadn't been my intention. I'm going to blame too many ciders. Maybe he's had too many beers and won't take offence.

'Now it's my turn to say sorry.' I focus on my hands as I warm them up.

'Let's call it quits.' He marches over to the kitchen and fills the kettle. 'Hot chocolate?'

'No, thank you. I'm a bit chocolated out. I'll make myself a tea.' It's his tea, oh well.

'Great idea. I'll make a pot. Need something hot to warm up with.'

I'm sitting on the sofa when he brings the tray over. 'Ooo, biscuits.'

'Yeah, I think they might be yours.'

'They are. But you're all right. You can eat them too,' I say as I reach for one. At least we never had any pudding in the pub.

'It was funny when you introduced us in the pub to that old couple,' he says, sitting down and dunking a biscuit.

'Why?'

'Well you gave them our full names. It just sounded funny. What do they care?'

'I didn't want them thinking we were together, that's all.'

'But they did anyway.'

'They did.' I roll my eyes and sip my tea.

'Anyway, going back to that, did you say your name was Sutton?'

'Ruby Sutton, yes.'

'And your husband was Cliff?'

'Yes.' My voice is almost a squeak. I know just where this is going and I'd rather it didn't. So far today I've managed to not think about Cliff for quite long stretches of the day. Hours, even.

'He's not *the* Cliff Sutton?'

'Yes. He is. Was. He's not *that* famous though.'

'He is, sorry, was, in my industry. The games industry, that is.'

'You make games?'

'Code, I code games. Which means I'm familiar with Sutton Software. I even went for an interview there, when I left uni, when I was trying to get into gaming software.'

'You didn't work there though?' Please say no.

'No. I didn't. His wife…' he sees my face and changes his words, 'Sorry, first wife, Susannah, was it? She interviewed me.'

'You didn't get the job then. That was a lucky escape. Susannah can be… difficult.'

'I did get the job. I turned it down. Often wondered if that was wise.' He gives a little shrug and a smile.

'Why did you turn it down?'

'Her. Susannah Sutton. I didn't like her and I knew I'd have a lot of dealings with her. It was about fifteen years ago, they weren't big like they are now, probably just on the cusp of hitting the big time. They were in some tatty little place on an industrial estate in Newbury.'

'They're still there, but it isn't little anymore and it certainly isn't tatty.'

'She was some piece of work.'

'She still is.' I clamp my mouth shut because I don't want to start slagging Susannah off, not here, not now. I don't want to rake up the past, I don't want her spoiling my escape, infiltrating my mind and my peace.

'Another cup,' he says, smiling.

'Why not?'

'So,' he says as he pours us both another cup from the pot, 'Do you live in Newbury?'

'No. No. We, I, live in a village near Swindon. It's not far from the M4 so Cliff could just zip up there quite easily.'

'Not Lyffingdon, is it?' He laughs as though he's just cracked a joke.

'Why do you ask that?'

'My dad and Yolanda live there. I know there are a lot of villages near the M4 but wouldn't it be funny if you lived in the same village?'

'No, I live in Great Lyffingdon, about a mile down the road.' I feel my heart sink. Is nothing private?

'Nooo.' His eyes widen in amused amazement. 'I was only joking. Okay it's not the exact same village as my dad lives, but it's so close. What are the chances?'

I shake my head. I'd prefer not to think about the chances. I'm beginning to feel as though I'm being stalked, though not by Noah Steele, but by fate. Oddly, a part of me wants him to ask about my domestic arrangements, a part of me wants to talk about it, but at the same time I don't.

'Did you live there when that murder happened?' He takes a completely different tack, though, sadly, a familiar one.

'Everyone asks that. No. The trial was just before we moved there.'

'My dad was obsessed with it. Says he'd met that magician and his assistant and you'd never think they were murderers. It was all very odd. The brother just disappeared too, didn't he? They didn't even find the body, it never washed up further down the coast or anything.'

'I don't know. As I said it was before we moved there and I only ever heard the odd thing.' I really am not interested in this and if that makes me shallow or uncaring, then maybe I am. I've been asked this so many times, but no one in the village discusses it. They're all too horrified. I certainly don't want to dwell on an old murder. Gives me a sudden shiver though, especially since I'm trapped here alone with a stranger and with no way of contacting anyone.

Noah Steele glances over at me and smiles softly. Maybe he can detect my mood from the look on my face. He finds the remote control, switches on the TV and flicks through the channels. He stumbles across a Bruce Willis film, *Die Hard*, glances over at me and raises his eyebrows in question. I shrug in response. I really don't care. The film is about half way through, but that's not an issue; I've seen it several times before so if I want to follow it, I can. Cliff loved it.

It's easy watching and although it's set at Christmas it isn't Christmassy, not unless you think Christmas is about robbing a vault and toting a gun and crawling around a half-deserted office block in a dirty vest. I slump down and watch it.

When the film ends, I say goodnight and go to bed, but I don't sleep, I keep thinking about Cliff, about Susannah, about Noah Bloody Steele.

The full extent of the overnight snowfall is evident the next morning. Our snow sculptures are still there, but now misshapen and expanded by another layer of snow. There's a frost this morning again, so everything twinkles in the hazy sunshine. I know, without even thinking about it much, that I am trapped here for another day. With *him*, though there's no sign of him or his dog outside yet.

I'm tired. I didn't get enough sleep last night, I just kept thinking and overthinking. Noah Steele's observations about Susannah have churned all my feelings up again. I was supposed to be escaping all that. I feel jumpy and irritated and sad and it's not just because I have a bit of a hangover.

I drink several glasses of water and take a few paracetamol; I'm regretting those ciders yesterday, however much I enjoyed them at the time. Then I get myself some breakfast, switch on the TV and sit on the sofa with my cereal – okay, I've used the last of the milk, but it was *my* milk anyway. I'm still wrapped in my dressing gown and am wearing thick pyjamas and fluffy socks. I don't care if he sees me, he's seen everything anyway after the pervy-dog-towel trick. I might not even bother getting dressed at all today – no bra, bonus! In fact, since I am stuck here with him, I should just carry on with my original plans, which were knitting, eating, chilling out and knitting.

That's what I'm going to do and he can just fit in or not. I settle down for a comfortable hour of *Homes Under the Hammer* with my knitting on my lap and the whole cottage to myself.

They're just getting to the final reveals on the renovations when *he* bursts in through the porch door.

'Hey,' he says. 'Morning.'

Kong leaps into the room and bounds over to his water bowl where he slurps so noisily that I have to turn the TV up to hear how much profit's been made after the renovation.

'Hi,' I say, making it obvious that I'm busy by alternately concentrating on my knitting or the TV.

He pours himself a big glass of orange juice and drinks it down with the fridge door open. Shut the fridge. So annoying. You brought enough cold in here when you came in, don't add to it. Then he puts the kettle on.

'Coffee?' he calls over.

'No thanks,' I answer, without even looking at him.

He puts instant in his cup then opens the fridge, again.

'Ah, no milk.'

I don't reply. I'm not going to apologise for using my own milk.

'No probs. I'll have black.'

He brings his coffee over and plonks himself on the end of the sofa.

'So what are you up to?'

I lift my knitting a few inches off my lap.

'Cool. Hey, *Homes Under the Hammer*. Love this. Have they had the reveals yet?' he asks just as the closing music starts to play.

'Yeah. Just.' And despite my best efforts I missed most of them because of him and his noisy, chilly interruptions.

'What do you want to do today?'

'I'm doing it,' I reply, at the same time flicking through the channels to find another episode of *Homes Under the Hammer*, it's usually on somewhere.

'Just chilling,' he says, laughing.

'Yeah.' Now go away, but if you must sit there, be silent.

'It's damn cold outside.' He waits for me to reply.

'Yeah.'

'Still, nice and warm in here. I stoked the fire up before I went out, I haven't let it go out at all since we've been here which is good, because the heating goes off at night, so the fire keeps the temperature just nice, overnight.'

'That reminds me,' I say, finally turning to look at him. 'Have you got that folder, about the cottage?'

'Oh, sure.' He jumps up and rushes off to his room, returning with a red, loose-leaf ring binder. He hands it to me, and I put it on the coffee table. I'll read it when *I'm* ready.

I continue my channel surfing but I can't find what I want so settle on something similar and American.

'US houses are like mansions compared to ours, aren't they?'

'Yeah.' Shut up.

'Though you probably live in a mansion.'

He's teasing me, I know it, I should just laugh it off but he's touched such a raw nerve. I feel my throat tighten, my cheeks tweak. Oh no.

I start to cry. Great big stupid loud howls. Oh, for God's sake. I'm so consumed with my self-pity that I drop my knitting.

'I'm sorry. I'm sorry,' I hear him say between my howls. 'I was just joking. I didn't mean anything by it, I'm so sorry.'

Still I howl.

He shuffles along the sofa and puts his arms around me and I let him and then I snot and slobber into his shoulder, then his chest. It seems to go on forever, the howling. Then I stop, pull myself together.

I'm such a bloody cliché.

I look around for a tissue, as if one will appear mid-air, by magic.

'Here,' he says, offering me his cuff. 'Use this. I'm going to have to change my shirt anyway.'

So I do, because he is.

Such a cliché.

'I'm so sorry,' he says again. 'I didn't mean...'

I hold my hand up to silence him. I do not want his sympathy; it'll start me off again.

'Cuse me,' I mumble, before escaping to the bathroom where I tidy myself up, wash my face, take deep breaths.

When I return he's changed his shirt. He offers me a small smile. I slump back down on my end of the sofa and he sits down on his. No more shoulder crying, no more snot. We both stare, without seeing, at the TV.

'You're right, I do live in a mansion,' I start, wondering why I feel the need to explain, and yet I do.

He doesn't reply, he doesn't need to, I know he's listening.

'We chose it together, chose everything that went into it together. It's amazing, even if I do say so myself.' I remember the day we came across it on the internet, we'd been actively searching for a proper house for a few months by then. We'd been married six months and living in Cliff's bachelor flat, but we were at the stage when we were taking steps to start our own family. Yes, Cliff already had his three boys with Susannah, but I wanted children and he wanted me to have them. Cliff always wanted me to have whatever would make me happy.

Maybe, if we'd know how hard that was going to be, we might not have been so eager.

'However, after he died I found out that the house I called home, the house I thought I co-owned with my husband, wasn't mine at all. It belonged to his sons, he left it to them. Oh, I can stay there as long as I like, my whole life if I want to, but I can never sell it, never move away, never remarry – not if I want to keep that house. Basically, I'm trapped.'

'Oh,' he says. Well, what other response can he give? Call Cliff a bastard? I've done that myself a thousand times. It wouldn't have been so bad if I had known, if he had discussed it with me. Instead he led me to believe that it was ours, and ours alone.

'You see, Noah Steele, I loved my husband, I would have fallen for him and loved him if he'd been penniless, because I adored him. I would have loved him if we'd lived in a cupboard or a shoebox.'

'At least you have a nice home,' Noah Steele says, sounding far too cheery. Is he trying to make me see the good side, the bright side?

'That's what I thought, initially. Except I can't afford to run it.'

'What do you mean?'

'I can't afford to run the house, pay the bills, pay the insurance, all the rest of it which includes a maintenance fee for the area, it's in a private gated community. All that costs money and I can't afford it.'

'But surely your husband…'

'Left me money,' I cut in. 'Yes, he did. Ten thousand a year. Which just about covers the costs of living there. Which is why I have to work. Which, of course is fine, why shouldn't I work? I'm not some rich, entitled lazy person. But ten thousand a year makes me sound like an Austen character, only in this day and age, ten thousand a year isn't a lot. And I only get that if I stay in the house.'

'Ah,' he says and I can see what he's thinking, I've thought it myself, that I'm ungrateful, that I do think I'm entitled. Maybe if Cliff had been honest with me, straight with me from the beginning it wouldn't have come as such a shock. But Cliff wasn't expecting to die, and that was the biggest and most dreadful shock of all.

'I know I sound ungrateful and greedy, Noah Steele, but I'm grieving and bitter too.'

He laughs, he tries not to but he can't help it.

'Glad you find it funny.'

'No, no, of course I don't. It's just that you keep calling me Noah Steele, my full name, like you did in the pub. That's what's funny.'

I suppose he's right; it is mildly amusing. I've called him Noah Steele in my head since the minute I learned his name; to his face I haven't called him anything until just now, but then he hasn't called me by my name either, full or otherwise.

'Ruby,' he says, as if reading my mind, 'I can see why you feel cheated. I can understand.'

'Can you? I'm sure Susannah had a hand in the arrangement, she still had a massive influence on him even though they'd been divorced five years or more. She certainly wouldn't want me having anything she thought her boys should have. Thank God we never managed to have children; I dread to think what would have happened then.'

'Can't you fight it?'

'I thought about it, I took advice, but it's legal and you've met Susannah, it's her I would have to fight.' I stand up. I've already said too much, far more than I wanted to. 'I'd better get dressed.' I head for the bathroom; it seems I'm not going to spend the day braless in my pyjamas, as previously planned.

❄❄❄

When I finally emerge from my bedroom, fully dressed in thermal leggings and my Aran sweater, there's no sign of him. I sidle over to the sofa, and switch the TV back on. Perhaps Noah Steele has taken the hint and gone out again, then I notice Kong. He's standing in the corner watching me, his eyes flitting between my knitting, which is on the coffee table, and my face.

'Hi,' Noah Steele says, striding out of his room. 'You okay?'

'Yes, thanks.' Shut up. Don't mention it. I'm already regretting telling you anything, cursing my big blabbermouth.

He goes into the porch and comes back holding his boots, sits down to pull them on and lace them up.

'Going out?' I ask, my voice maybe a little too jolly.

'Yes. There's a shop down the lane, past the pub and up the hill a bit. I'm going to see if I can get some milk.'

'Is it open?'

'Should be. Hopefully. Did you want anything?'

I'm starting to feel a little guilty for using all the milk, and, now I think about it, he definitely brought milk with him too, I remember seeing our two bottles side by side in the fridge door.

'I could go instead,' I say.

'I couldn't let you go on your own.' He's serious too.

'I don't think you could actually stop me.'

He smirks. 'I'd follow.'

'You do know how creepy that sounds, don't you?'

'Yes.' He smirks again. 'So, to save me being creepy, why don't we go together? I have to take Kong out again anyway.' He sees my face, which probably shows that I don't know what to do. If I'm honest with myself, I do fancy a walk in the fresh air. And now, this time of day, is probably the best time to go. What would I do if I was here on my own, as planned? Not have drunk so much hot chocolate probably, not have used *all* the milk by now.

'Okay,' I say.

Eight

'Is that Kong's poobag?' I ask as he swings an Asda bag for life while we make our way towards the pub. I'm being funny, I think, or maybe snide.

'Yeah,' he says, giving me a sideways glance.

'Really? Oh my God.' Kong is a big dog, but well, I hadn't realised how big.

He laughs. 'No. This is.' He pulls a small bag from his pocket. 'Not that I'm expecting to need it, he went this morning when we were out.'

'Thanks for that bit of information.'

'You asked.'

Now I feel stupid, my silly joke has backfired. We walk on in silence. To our left is the sea, not visible in the dark last night on our way back from the pub, now it glints and twinkles in the weak sunshine.

'Looks as though the snow is thawing a bit,' he says.

'Yeah.' Though not enough for me to escape just yet.

We pass the pub and start to head uphill where the lane is a lot clearer, obviously all the traffic to and from the pub has helped melt the snow.

'How do you know about this shop? Is it in the folder?'

'No. Well, it might be. I met another dog walker when I was out this morning, got chatting and he just mentioned it. Didn't realise we'd need it quite yet, if I'd realised I'd have gone there when I was out earlier.'

'Sorry about the milk, I finished it off.' Guilt makes me confess. I could at least have left enough for him to have a coffee.

'No probs. We've had so many hot chocolates and coffees and teas and cereal, no wonder we've gone through so much so quickly.'

'Let's get plenty,' I say without looking at him.

'Let's hope they've got some left.'

We carry on up the lane, it's quite steep in places but I can see that's it's been gritted which is just as well because I don't think we'd be climbing it so easily if not.

Finally I can see a building through the trees. And yes, there it is, a petrol station with a mini-supermarket attached to it.

'This meets a main road,' I state the obvious. 'Is that the same main road that the lane to our cottage comes from?'

'I don't know.' He pulls his phone out to have a look at the maps. 'Oh, I've got a signal here too. He starts scrolling through messages, I presume, before he finally looks at me and remembers why he got his phone out in the first place. 'Yes, it does. It's a big loop. Look.' He shows me his phone and, it is indeed, a big loop, like a horseshoe and we're on the bend down and the pub is on the bend up.

'So we could get out this way, then?' My mind is working overtime, planning my escape.

'It's only clear as far as the pub from this end,' he says, now he's stating the obvious, so obvious it hadn't occurred to me.

'Oh yeah.' I'm about to ask how feasible digging out the lane between the pub and the cottage is when I stop myself. I know I'm being ridiculous.

'Do you mind hanging on to Kong while I go inside?' He holds out Kong's lead.

'Oh, but, I…' I start. 'Yeah okay. I'll go in after you.'

I wait outside with a well-behaved Kong who looks at me with a doleful expression, tilting his head occasionally as if appraising me. I wonder if he remembers whipping the towel off me? While I wait I check my phone and see that I also have a signal. I flick through my messages, one from Zara sent on Christmas Eve and asking if everything is okay, so I quickly reply that it's great. No need for her to know all the details until I see her in person. She replies instantly.

Are you sure? I heard there was a strange man there? And you're snowed in!!! Of course, Mrs Lane has snitched on me.

Everything's fine, I reply. *Having a good time. Yes, snowed in, but not an issue.*

Worried because I hadn't heard from you.

Phone signal is rubbish, as you know. Lol. Don't worry. xx

I don't want Zara worrying about me and I don't want to continue this conversation with her because it's pointless. I'm stuck. So is he.

Noah Steele bursts out of the shop and Kong immediately stands up and wags his tail. 'I got four pints of milk,' he says, rubbing his dog's ears. 'Do you think that's enough?'

'I brought four with me? How many did you bring?'

'Two?'

'So that's six in how many days?' I can't even be bothered to work it out. I also feel less guilty about leaving him with no milk this morning; he brought less than me but has drunk just as much, probably more. 'I'll get another four.' I hand him his dog lead and head into the shop where I experience a weird feeling of suddenly arriving in civilisation. Which is patently silly because although we're snowed in, we're hardly in the middle of Antarctica, we're in North Devon.

The old chap behind the till greets me and we exchange pleasantries about the weather as I pay for my milk.

'Can it go in your bag?' I ask once I'm back outside again.

He switches his phone off, shoves it in his pocket and holds the bag open.

'The chap in the shop was telling me they've never had snow like this before, ever, in his entire sixty-eight years.'

'He said the same to me,' Noah Steele says, his voice quiet.

'Been checking your messages?' I'm making conversation, that's all, but if looks could kill I'd be dead via the hate rays coming out of Noah Steele's eyes.

'Yeah.' He turns around and marches back down the lane while I trot along to keep up with him.

'That main road looks pretty clear, doesn't it?' I say as we pass the pub where the snow is still deep and crisp and apart from our footprints, virgin.

'Yeah.'

'Do you think you could drive your big car through this? Sort of clear the way for me to get out. It's not as bad as it is on our end of the lane, is it?'

He doesn't reply. Doesn't even look at me, just quickens his pace and strides away.

'Charming.' I'm not going to run after him. Sod him.

❄❄❄

He's already taken his coat and boots off and is putting the milk in the fridge when I finally arrive at the cottage. I can feel something emanating from him, something that isn't smiley. That silly ex-girlfriend was wrong, he doesn't smile all the time. Kong looks like he's sulking in his basket too.

'Okay?' I ask, as I flop down on the sofa after taking off my own coat and boots. 'That walk did me a world of good. It was almost refreshing. What about you?' Why do I care? Why am I trying to jolly him along?

'No,' he says while filling the kettle. 'The answer to your question about me driving my car through the snow to clear the way for yours, is no. It's too deep. And steep.'

'Oh. Okay.'

'Sorry about that but you'll just have to stay stuck here with me until it thaws.' So that's what he's sulking about.

'Okay.' I'm even trying to make my disappointment sound jolly. Although, if I'm honest with myself, I'm almost relieved, because I don't know why I'm in such a hurry to go back to that big mausoleum of a house that hasn't felt like home since the day Cliff died.

'Sorry about that,' he says again as he stomps past me and into his room. Hang on, he was already in a mood before I asked him to clear the snow. He was grumpy the minute I came out of the shop.

He stays in his room for two hours. Two hours. He boiled the kettle but didn't even make himself a drink. I don't even want to think about what he's doing in that room. The good thing is I watch a crappy film on TV and really get stuck into my knitting without any interruptions.

Until, that is, Kong gets up and starts to pace about, nudging the back door with one of his giant paws. He keeps on doing it, then looks over at me. I suppose I could just let him out. But what if he runs off, disappears down that beach path and falls into the sea? No, I'm not having that on my conscience.

I creep over to Noah Steele's room and listen at the door. I can hear nothing until Kong starts to whine. Should I just let him out and hang the consequences? Or ignore him? I imagine how much pee Kong could produce and I don't want to think about the smell or how to clear it up. I give Noah Steele's door a tentative knock.

No response.

'Noah Steele,' I call, not too loudly. 'Noah Steele. Your dog needs you.' I knock again, louder this time. 'Noah Steele.'

His door flings open. 'Yes, Ruby Sutton,' he says, his face angry and grey.

'Your dog needs…' my voice fades away as he darts past me and heads for Kong. He yanks the outside door open, letting the cold in and Kong hurls himself outside.

'You could have let him out,' he says in a nasty voice.

'Yes, but I didn't know if he'd run away and might get lost…' I don't bother finishing the sentence because he looks so angry I'm almost afraid.

He stomps off to the porch, pulls on his coat and boots and follows Kong outside. I'm tempted to deadlock the door behind him so he can't get back in. Rude bastard.

❄❄❄

He's gone a long time, hours and it's dark. I've done a massive amount of knitting and I've made a lasagne. I'm just cooking some peas to go with it when he bursts in through the back door. Kong flops down into his basket.

'Shomething smelsh good,' Noah Steele slurs, a big grin spreading across his face.

'Would you like some?'

'Yesh pleash.'

I pull two plates out of the cupboard and dish up our food before taking it over to the table where he has slumped down onto a chair. He's dumped his coat and boots on the floor behind him. I'm tempted to make a fatuous remark about him going to the pub but don't, because, actually, it's none of my business what he does. I'm not his keeper. Nor he, mine.

'Thish ish good, you'll make someone a good wife shomeday.'

'How much have you had? I can't help myself, also, why should I? He's being tactless in the extreme.

'Enough. Just whiskies, didn't mix it. Enough to forget…'

'Good. Eat up.' I put on my jolly school teacher voice, as though I'm coaxing a three-year-old.

He whacks into this food with gusto and takes several gulps from the glass of water that I've brought over too.

'You're all right you, Ruby Shutton.'

'Thanks for that.' Now shut up and eat.

He winks at me before he continues eating. I hope the food sobers him up. He gets about half way through before putting his knife and fork down. 'Yeah, you're all right. You're girly enough to be girly without all that stupid girly stuff.' He winks again and this time one eye remains open while the other is closed for a full twenty seconds, maybe more. He looks as though he's been freeze framed.

'Eat up, Noah Steele.' Teacher voice again.

'And you're funny,' he says before picking up his cutlery again and tucking in once more. 'Not too serious, despite your circumstances.'

I don't think I'm funny; he must be very drunk if he does.

I let him finish his food and refill his water glass twice more and pray he sobers up. I hate drunks, incoherent ones especially. Like Noah Steele now is.

'Toilet,' he says, standing up and staggering towards his room. With a bit of luck he'll go to bed and I can continue my peaceful evening without him. I'm glad I cooked a decent meal; he needs something to soak up the drink but I didn't cook it for him, I cooked it for me.

He's gone ages and I assume he has, indeed, gone to bed. Then I start to worry, maybe he's fallen asleep on his back and choked on his vomit. Imagine the post mortem – he died after inhaling lasagne. My lasagne. I can't bear it. I have to check on him now. I have to.

Here we go again, me knocking on his door, calling his name, him ignoring me.

I press my ear to the door and hope that he is snoring. If he's snoring that means he's not dead.

Unless it's a death rattle. Doesn't that sound like snoring?

But I can't hear anything. I knock and call his name again.

Then I hear a noise that sounds like choking.

I'm going in.

He's sitting on the bed, leaning against the headboard – wow that's a big bed, no wonder he chose it – his eyes wide open. He's staring at his phone which he holds out in front of him, alternately pulling it nearer and further away.

'You okay?'

'Look at that. Jusht look at that.'

Urgh. He's still drunk.

'Go on. Look.' He throws the phone at me and I have to catch it otherwise it'll hit the door and probably break.

'Look. Look.'

So I do.

He's on Facebook and, as I scroll down his feed, I see endless photos of people having fun on a skiing trip.

'Here, here, give it here.'

I hand the phone back.

'See, that's them, Liam and Vic.' He stabs his finger at a couple smiling into the camera, they're twinkly-eyed and rosy-cheeked. She's a stunner, just as I expected her to be. Soft silver blonde hair waves around her face and over her shoulders, thick lips, luscious eyelashes. Him, Liam, he's okay. He's certainly not as attractive as Noah Steele. Nowhere near.

I slump down on the bed facing him, leaning against the giant wooden bed end. I'm stunned. I can't quite believe my own thoughts. Noah Steele is definitely good-looking. He has one day of stubble on his chin, his thick hair is messed up from being outside, and his lips are soft and inviting. He's at least a match for the cheating Vic and way better looking that his ex-friend, Liam.

'Come on, Noah,' I say. 'Stop tormenting yourself. Put the phone away.'

'Steele,' he says. 'You forgot to say Steele.'

I sigh, long and hard. 'Yeah. Well. I think you've just humanised yourself.'

'What?' His face contorts in confusion and I hope he doesn't ask me to explain, because I can't. It sounds like bullshit to *me*, and I'm not drunk. But I think I know what I mean.

'Is this why you've been in such a foul mood since we came back from the shop?' Of course, we'd found a mobile signal there. It all makes sense now.

'I bet your fucking Facebook isn't full of arseholes rubbing it in, how bloody happy and perfect they are.' He stares at me as if wanting me to prove him wrong. In his anger he's no longer slurring his words; maybe he's sobering up.

'I don't do Facebook anymore. Would you like some coffee? Come and have a coffee.' I move off the bed and stand, waiting for him. He looks at me as though I'm speaking a foreign language, so I hold my hand out for his.

He grabs it. His hand is warm, his skin surprisingly hard, not the hands of someone who sits at a computer all day. But then, he has been chopping wood here and stoking the fire too.

Still holding onto my hand, he gets up and follows me back into the living room. I deposit him on the sofa and make us both a coffee.

'Why don't you do Facebook anymore?'

I shake my head. I really don't want to think about why. I wish I'd never mentioned it. 'Just don't.'

'But you did?'

'Yeah.' I look down into my coffee cup and hope he takes the hint that I don't want to discuss it.

Of course, he doesn't. He's not sober enough to pick up on subtle hints. 'So why? And when?'

'I'd rather not talk about it.'

'Why not? I've shown you mine, now show me yours.' He grins, but it's not one of his – what I now realise is – nice grins, it's a stupid, nasty, drunken grin.

'You really want to hear this?'

'Yeah. Go on. You've seen my shit-storm of a life. Your turn. Have we eaten all those chocolate biscuits?' He attempts to stand up but I push him back down.

'I'll get them.' Who knows, they might help him sober up. Who am I kidding?

He eats three in a row without stopping. Good, I feel happier now that the focus is off me.

'What did you think of Vic?'

'Very attractive.' What does he want me to say?

'She is. She's bloody gorgeous. Stunning.'

'Yeah.' Okay, don't rub it in. She's certainly more girly than me. Apparently.

'Everyone used to say we made the perfect match, you know, in the looks department.'

I nod slowly. 'Yeah. I can see that.'

'What did you think of Liam?'

I shrug. 'He's not pug-ugly.'

'He's moody and mean. That's sexy. Did you know?'

He doesn't wait for me to reply, which is good, because I don't know how to reply to that.

'I'm not sexy,' he says. 'I'm boring because I smile too much.'

This again.

'Do you think I smile too much?' He presses on. Not this again. 'Do I? Tell me. I can take it. I know it's not sexy to smile. Liam told me that's what Vic thinks.'

His eyes search my face and I think he might start crying. I really don't want a drunken man crying on my shoulder. Most days it's all I can do to hold myself together; if he cries, I know I'll join in.

'I think you're sexy,' I say.

He grins.

Oh shit.

Nine

He blinks and then stares into my eyes, and the part of me that hoped he was too drunk to understand what I've just said, knows he's not.

'Really? I thought you hated me.'

'I never said that.'

'Not with words. But you've begged me to dig you out of this place every day since we've been here so you can get away from me.' He grins. 'Nah, you don't think I'm sexy. You hate me.'

'I don't hate you. I don't know you. I didn't want to be on my escape from Christmas hideaway with a bloody stranger, that's all. Surely, you felt the same?'

'No. Not really. When I saw you warming yourself by the fire, naked on that rug, I thought all my wishes had come true. Best Christmas present ever, I thought.' He smiles at me and I don't like how his smile affects me.

'You're very drunk. And your dog's a perv.'

He laughs. His eyes twinkle. I know it's the drink, but just looking at him makes me doubt myself again. He is so bloody attractive. And, if I'm being honest with myself, I've thought so all along.

'Anyway, why were you trying to escape Christmas and hide away? What are you hiding from?'

'Grief.' I almost spit it into his face. How bloody dare he? 'My husband died. Remember?'

'Two years ago.'

'Are you saying, are you suggesting, I should be over it by now?' Damn cheek.

'No. No. Course not. I'm not saying that, am I? No, you should be spending Christmas with your family, letting them help you, that's what I'm saying.'

'My parents have gone to Australia to visit my brother and his family.' I don't know why I'm explaining myself to him.

'You should have gone too. Why didn't you?'

'Because, because,' I spit, 'I spent last Christmas with my parents and I bloody ruined it for them with my crying and sulking and general self-pitying behaviour. They didn't go to Oz last year, like they do every Christmas because I wouldn't go with them, instead they stayed for me and we all had a bloody miserable time. That's why. Even this year they've only gone for a couple of weeks instead of a month or more. Because of me.' I do feel guilty about that, I begged them to go for longer but they wouldn't.

'Right. Okay. Right.' He nods as though wisdom has come to him. 'Bit like me, then, I suppose.'

'Not really.'

'Fucking feels like it to me. I've had my heart broken and Facebook is rubbing it in. And I couldn't even go on my usual skiing holiday with my mates. Looks like they're having a fucking amazing time too.' He folds his arms; there's that child again. The drunken one.

'Come off Facebook then.' I fold my arms now even though I'm neither a child, nor drunk.

'What would that achieve? It wouldn't stop it from happening, would it?'

'No, but you wouldn't see it, wouldn't have it rammed down your throat every day, would you?'

He starts to snigger as I realise what I've said.

'Well, you know what I mean; rubbing your nose in it. Sort of.'

He sniggers louder, he really is a child.

'Oh, there's no talking to you.' I pick up my knitting and try to concentrate on it. I've done quite a lot today but I'm not where I expected to be, Noah has completely wrecked my schedule.

'You haven't told me why you came off Facebook.' He sniggers. 'Did you think I'd forgotten about that?'

I roll my eyes at him in the most obvious and theatrical way I can.

'Well?'

'Well what?'

'Why did you come off Facebook? Come on, you can tell me. We're nearly best friends now, or housemates at least. Cottagemates, Christmas cottagemates, that sounds better, doesn't it?' He's grinning to himself. Idiot.

'Urgh. Shush. I'm busy.'

'What's with the knitting, anyway? Isn't that what old ladies do? My gran used to do that. Knit these godawful things that I had to wear to school.'

'You know that thing about you being too nice and smiley?'

'Yeah.'

'Well, that wasn't very nice, was it? Your gran probably worked very hard knitting for you.'

He looks at me as though I've slapped him around the face, which part of me wishes I could in the hope that it would sober him up.

'You're right. That wasn't very nice. Maybe I should drink more often, then I wouldn't be so nice and boring. I don't normally drink, you know. The odd pint, here and there, but I'm not a party drinker like Vic and Liam are. I've always been the designated driver in the group when we all go out. Maybe that's where I've been going wrong. Do you think I should drink more alcohol? More whisky? I could really get into whisky. Do you think that would make me more sexy?' He grins again.

'No. It wouldn't. You shouldn't. You're an irritating drunk. Anyway, I'm not sure what you're saying is true, you brought plenty of beers with you here and you're always knocking them back.'

'They're low alcohol.'

'You're still an irritating drunk,' I say. 'And you haven't been on low alcohol anything today, have you? You're very irritating.'

'That's because you're sober. You should have a few, catch up with me. I'll open a bottle of wine.' He makes at attempt to get up but I grab his arm and pull him back.

'Drink your coffee.'

He nods then picks up his cup. I wish I'd left him sulking in his bedroom.

'So, the knitting?'

'What?'

'Why do you do it?'

'Why not? It's a hobby. I enjoy it.' He's really annoying me now.

'Do you do it to take your mind off your troubles?'

103

I turn and glare at him. Of course, he's hit the nail right on the head but I'm not going to admit that to him, least of all drunken him. Mum had suggested it, spent hours teaching me, now she says I'm better than her. I don't think that's true, but it's nice to hear it nevertheless. And I do have to concentrate so it does take my attention away from thinking about my problems.

'Urgh,' I groan.

'Yolanda suggested I take up a hobby when Vic left. Yolanda said I should do woodworking, or something useful. She thinks I'd be good at that.'

'Yeah.'

'I didn't though. Maybe I should.'

'Well it's better than tormenting yourself slobbering over your ex on Facebook, isn't it?' I snap.

'So why did you leave Facebook again?' He leans over and pokes me in the ribs with his finger. I slap him away. 'Tetchy. Come on, Ruby, tell me all about it. I won't give up asking.'

'Fuck off,' I mutter.

'That's not very nice. You're not very nice, are you? I bet no one's ever accused you of being too smiley, have they? I bet your husband never said you were too smiley, did he?'

I gasp. How bloody dare he? I know he's drunk but that's no excuse for bringing up my husband; he didn't even know him.

'Don't talk about my husband. You've never met my husband.' I'm inhaling through my nose furiously to keep myself under control. I can feel the heat rising from my neck, moving up my face. If I looked in the mirror, I'm sure I'd be all blotchy.

'Your nostrils are flaring,' he says with a grin. 'Like a horse.'

'You're drunk and you're not at all nice. Maybe that's why she dumped you, you're just a horrible arse.' Oh my God, where did that come from?

Hang on, he deserved it.

He moves away from me, retreats further into his corner of the sofa, his end. He's blinking, too fast. I try to concentrate on my knitting while taking furtive glances at him and he's still blinking away.

'You're right,' he says after a while, his voice thick with drunken emotion. 'I am an arse, otherwise she wouldn't have left me, would she? Liam just sugar coated it, didn't he?'

I don't know the answer to that so I ignore him. He's not really talking to me anyway; he's now started rambling. Vic this, Liam that, woe is him. I can't cope with his self-pity; I've got enough of my own. His girlfriend just dumped him, she didn't die, he'll get over it, move on.

And I'm not very nice.

He's gone quiet. I glance over at him again. His eyes are closed, his mouth is open. He's asleep.

I flick the TV on, search for something mindless to watch and get back to my knitting. He starts to snore and I consider nudging him to stop it, but then I think about what he'll be like if I do, if he wakes up. I don't want to hear any more about perfect Vic, and Liam the traitor.

Am I too selfish? Probably.

The sound of the logs dropping in the fire makes me jump but it has no effect on Noah who continues to snore quietly from his end of the sofa. It looks as though the fire needs more logs. I put my knitting down and investigate. Fortunately, he's brought in a lot of logs and filled the basket next to the log burner. I hunt around for the tool to open the glass door and finally find it stored neatly behind the log basket.

After I've put a couple of logs on to burn I sit back down and feel quite proud of myself, see I am quite self-sufficient and, if I'd read that instruction folder like he has, I'm sure I could have kept that fire burning all the time too. Admittedly, I couldn't have chopped the logs but that wasn't strictly necessary as we're burning last year's seasoned logs, and Noah has just replenished the stock for next year. Apparently. Or that's what he told me when we last walked on the beach. So, not necessary at all.

He continues snoring and, now drooling, on his end of the sofa while I knit the evening away and watch TV. I'm just putting my knitting back in its bag when he wakes with a jerk. He blinks at me several times, smiles then gets up and heads for his room. All without a word. So I go to my room too.

❄❄❄

The sound of scraping awakes me in the morning. I leap out of bed worried about what's going on, open my bedroom door and find Noah on his hands and knees in front of the wood burner.

'Oh hi,' he says, sounding sheepish, he doesn't look at me.

'What's happened?'

'Nothing. We just let the fire go out. Not a big deal, the heating's on.' His voice is very quiet.

'Oh, that was me. I did put more logs on it but not just before we went to bed.'

'Probably time it had a clean out anyway.' He continues with his tidying and I head for the bathroom where I run myself a bath and decide to keep out of the way.

There's no sign of him when I pass back through the living room later but I can see Kong poking about in the garden and cocking his leg against each of our snow sculptures, although he revisits mine several times and my yellow stain is definitely darker than the others. It must still be very cold because they are still as intact as they were the day we made them and I can see Kong's breath as he exhales.

I come back out of my room after getting dressed to find Noah sitting at the table nursing a large coffee and a pint of water.

'Oh dear,' I say, perhaps rather ungenerously as I pass.

'Quite,' he answers, keeping his head down. 'Never again.'

'Have you had any breakfast?'

'No. Working up to it. Raking the log burner out has just about finished me off.'

'Oops,' I whisper and creep away to the kitchen. I don't think he's having a dig at me but after last night's nastiness, who can say? And I don't care anyway. Being trapped here with him reminds me of student days when a bunch of you happily agree to share a house only to find that some of you are arses and difficult to live with.

I yank the fridge open and study the contents. There's a new pack of bacon, he must have bought it yesterday. I also find some rolls in the bread bin. My own lips water at the prospect and everyone knows that the best cure for a hangover is greasy food.

'I'm doing myself a bacon bap; would you like one.'

His answer comes in the form of a groan.

'Honestly, it's the best cure.'

He groans again.

Not to be deterred and because I know best, I fry up a couple of rashers each and make him one anyway. I take our two plates over to the table and put his down in front of him. He looks up at me. His eyes are dark-ringed and bloodshot.

'Oh, dear. How much did you have?' I ask as I sit down and tuck into my bap. 'Whisky, wasn't it?' I'm almost enjoying his hangover, especially after his behaviour last night.

He groans again and takes a large gulp of water but doesn't answer me.

'Well, see how you go with that and if you can't manage it, I'll try to eat it as well as my own.' To be honest I probably could stuff it down, but I'd rather not.

'Okay,' he mumbles.

We eat in silence and I can tell he's struggling, but manfully, and eventually he finishes his bacon bap.

'Thanks for that,' he says, his voice quiet.

'Did it do the trick?' I take our plates over to the dishwasher.

'A bit, I think.'

'There, said it would. What you want now is gallons of water, or better still, full-fat coke.'

'Full-fat?'

'Yeah, you know, not diet. Did you bring any?'

'No.' He looks at me as though I'm stupid.

'Would you like me to walk to the shop and get you some?' I can't believe I'm making such a generous offer; it looks extremely cold out there.

'No, thank you.'

Instead I pour him another glass of water and put the kettle on to make us both a coffee. Then I take everything over to the table.

'Thank you. I don't deserve your kindness.'

I laugh. 'You don't, but you've got a hangover and that's punishment enough for drinking.'

'I have some vague memories of our conversations last night. I think I might have said some nasty things to you.' He looks up and catches my eye before I look away.

'It's fine.'

'No. I think I was rude and possibly hurtful. I'm sorry.'

'Maybe we both were.' I sip my coffee. 'And I wasn't even drunk,' I add, laughing. 'So I have no excuse.' I give another little laugh, light and soft, to let him know it's fine.

'Well, I just wanted you to know I'm sorry if I upset you.'

'Let's say we both are and leave it at that.' I don't want a replay of last night's conversation.

'Okay. Thank you. I might go for a walk along the beach, to clear my head. You're welcome to join us. Me and Kong.' At the mention of his name Kong leaps out of his basket.

He can see me thinking about it, remembering the slips and slides that meant I had to cling onto him. He offers me a smile, a nice one.

'Okay,' I say, hoping I won't regret it.

'Wrap up well, it's cold out there.'

✳✳✳

A couple of hours later and we're back. I'm frozen to the bone, my fingers and toes are numb yet I feel exhilarated, especially now we're back. We peel off our outer layers and while I rush to the loo Noah builds the fire back up.

We've not spoken about last night any more and I'm glad of that. I have no desire to rake over our insult tossing. We've chatted about Kong though, how Noah's dad bought him to replace the family pet when he died five years ago then realised he really didn't want a dog with so much energy and Yolanda had almost forced Kong onto Noah. Despite having pervy tendencies he's really quite a sweet natured dog, especially for something *so* big. It appears that Vic hates Kong and he doesn't really like her much either. He growls at her, a lot. I haven't heard him growl at all since the towel-tugging incident.

'How are you feeling now?' I ask as I open the fridge door. 'Headache gone?'

'Yes. Yes. Now I'm starving.'

'Ah, might be able to help with that, there's still half of last night's lasagne left. I can warm it up, and there's a bag of salad in the fridge that we really should eat before it goes off.' I pull the bag out and wave it about.

'Cool,' he says, moving towards the sink at the exact same time as I do. Our hands touch, it feels like an electric shock, a sharp tingle that makes me pull my hand away as though I've been bitten. He jerks his hand away too.

'Sorry,' we both say, neither of us looking at the other.

Ten

He's not drinking alcohol tonight. He hasn't said anything, but he came to the dinner table with a pint of water. I, on the other hand, have opened a bottle of white wine, my own. He visibly gagged when I offered him a glass. We're both tucking into yesterday's left-over lasagne.

'As soon as it thaws a bit, I'll leave so you can have a bit of peace,' he says suddenly.

'Oh. Right. Yes. Thanks.'

'I can't promise when that will be. How long were you planning on staying?'

'Until after New Year. Probably drive back home on New Year's Day.' Home, that place.

'Right, well, I'll go sooner. If I can. Hopefully it won't last much longer.'

I want to say no, to tell him he can stay and that he's not so bad after all, but after I've tried to make him dig me out and gone on and on about it, I don't feel I can. He's making a gesture, a generous one; I have to accept it.

'Thank you.'

'I'll do my best. Who knows, we might wake up in the morning and it could all be gone, just slush and puddles.'

I smile over at him. Despite us both coming back from our bracing walk along the beach with red cheeks and noses, he is now pale, incredibly pale. He yawns.

'Sorry,' he says. 'I'm not used to drinking like that.'

'I don't think many people are used to drinking like that.'

'No, well, you know…' He shrugs and grabs our empty plates, gets up and takes them over to the kitchen.

I want to say something nice, to tell him that I understand how he feels, even though I really don't, because my husband didn't *want* to leave me, not like Vic has left him. She did that of her own free will. At least Cliff isn't parading around with another woman now.

According to Susannah *I* was the other woman. I wasn't.

'I'm going to have some ice cream,' he says. 'What about you?'

'Yes, please.'

We sit and eat in silence. It's his ice cream and he's brought several flavours. Vanilla, strawberry and rum and raisin, he's given us a scoop of each. I've forgotten how much I like ice cream; we never had it, Cliff and I, because of the fat content. We tried the low-fat stuff but he hated the taste so we never bothered. Since his death I haven't thought much about food, least of all ice cream, so I'm surprised to realise how much I've missed it.

'You looked like you enjoyed that,' Noah says, smiling.

'I did. Haven't had much ice cream for years.'

'Oh? Why?'

'Cliff, he couldn't really have it, had to watch his fat intake.' I roll my eyes and smile. 'High cholesterol and type two diabetes. A heart attack waiting to happen.' I'm shocked to hear myself say that, I've never said it out loud before, just thought it.

'I'm sorry.' Noah takes our bowls away. 'Coffee?'

'Yes, please.' I take my wine bottle back to the fridge; I've only had one glass.

We plonk ourselves on the sofa with our coffees.

'He died in Susannah's arms on Christmas Day,' I say. Even though he hasn't asked I think he wanted to know and I know I wanted to tell him. He doesn't reply straightaway, just looks at me with kindness in his eyes. There's a silence now, only broken by Kong snoring in the corner.

'Do you want to talk about it?' he asks, eventually.

'You don't want to hear it.' I'm fairly sure he won't want all the detail because everyone else, my family, my few remaining friends, are sick of hearing about it.

He glances over at me and our eyes meet, then he looks away.

'I know it hurts when someone you love dies.' He's staring over at the log burner now and I feel annoyed. I want to snap at him, I want to remind him that Vic hasn't died so he doesn't know how much it hurts. Then I remember; he lost his mum when he was a teenager.

'Yeah.'

'Yolanda was my therapist,' he says before getting up to put another log on the fire. I watch him, watch the way he crouches down, opens the door, pokes the logs about before adding another. I can't say anything. I'm dumbfounded about the Yolanda revelation. He comes back, sits down. 'That's how my dad met her. Through me.' He gives a little laugh. 'I'd been a miserable boy then a naughty boy, well a teenager, sixteen by then and a difficult age anyway, after Mum died. It took a year before anyone really realised how much it was affecting me. The school called my dad in and it moved quickly after that, but only really because my dad's work health insurance paid for us to go private. And there was Yolanda, she specialised in bereavement counselling for children.'

'Did it help?' I ask when he falls silent.

'Yes. Oh yes. It did. I spent a year seeing her, every week at first, then two weeks apart, then a month.' He gives a little laughy snort. 'Of course Dad got to know her a bit too. Inevitable. They never did anything until I was discharged. Then they "bumped into each other" in a bar a few months later.' He makes air quotes with his fingers and winks at me.

'Wow. How did that make you feel?' I imagine resentment, anger.

'Surprisingly okay. I think Yolanda had done such a good job on me...' He winks again. 'Seriously, they kept it quiet for a long time. It was almost three years after Mum died before they told me they were together. I think if it hadn't been for the imminent arrival of my little brother they might have waited even longer. Technically I was an adult by the time they officially met.'

'Right.'

'Yeah, we're all good.' He smiles, his eyes light up. 'Mum wouldn't have wanted my dad to be lonely forever. He was still a young man really.'

'Yes.' I wonder if Noah's dad is like him, looks like him?

'So, what about you? Have you had any help?'

'Counselling, you mean?'

He nods.

I shake my head slowly. 'Never occurred to me.'

'I can recommend it.' He gets up again. 'Another coffee? Or hot chocolate?'

I plump for hot chocolate and idle the time away as he makes it by watching him. I have to spin around and sit sideways awkwardly on the sofa, but it's worth it. He's wearing a dark blue jumper and old, comfortable looking pale jeans. In clothes he looks lean, but I know there's a lot of muscle underneath. Not that I would mind if that wasn't the case. Cliff was hardly an Adonis. What matters, what really matters is what's beneath the exterior, the real person deep within. I think I like the Noah deep within, the one who isn't a nasty drunk or whinging about Vic and Liam.

I spin back to face the log burner just as he turns to bring our drinks over. I wouldn't want him thinking I'm watching him. I wouldn't want *me* thinking I'm watching him.

He plonks our drinks down on the coffee table.

'Okay?' he asks, with a smile.

I nod my reply slowly.

'Me too. Starting to feel a bit more normal now. Never again with the alcohol.' He flops down onto the sofa, then leans forward grabs my drink and hands it to me. Such a small thing... such an easy thing.

I inhale the chocolate aroma through my nose. It smells of winter, Christmas, cold, comfort. I feel compelled to carry on with my story.

'He went to her house on Christmas morning to see his sons. His boys. He'd wanted them to come over to ours for a few hours, wanted to pick them up, drop them back so they could have lunch with their mother, but Susannah wouldn't have it. So he went there. I can just imagine her fawning all over him, pretending they were still together, playing at one big happy family.'

I watch him as he picks up his own cup, takes a sip then looks to me to continue, as though I stopped to let him drink but that's not why.

'He'd spent a bomb on them, he always did.'

Noah glances at me.

'I know what you're thinking; he could afford it. Of course he could. He loved buying them things, spoiling them. They didn't appreciate it as much as they should, but I certainly didn't begrudge him spending on them. They were his sons. I knew he'd be just as generous to our child. The one I was carrying.'

Noah turns and looks at me, he blinks several times, then a little frown appears before he shakes it away.

'We'd had IVF. That was our fourth attempt and it was successful. It was early days, really early days, but it was real, it was there. Seven weeks. We'd seen the little squiggle on the expensive ultrasound Cliff arranged. No doubts. Very much there. So worth it after all we'd been through.' I'm listening to my voice as I speak, remembering those first few weeks of joy. 'Cliff had a vasectomy after the boys were born, *she* wasn't going through *that* again, never. Then he had a reversal. For me. Then we did IVF because it was still a struggle. IVF is hard, in case you're wondering.'

It had been hard, so hard, all those hormones, the ups and downs, the was I, wasn't I? Then we hit gold.

The joy of success. Cliff wanted a girl. I didn't care as long as it was healthy.

'He'd doled out all the presents, the boys had ripped the paper off them, left it on the floor, disappeared to their rooms to play with their new toys, well, games and PlayStation or whatever they were. He was preparing to leave then he just collapsed. Gripped his chest and fell among all the wrapping paper. She got down and held him, screamed for the boys to come down and call the ambulance. But it was all too late. I can still imagine him gasping for his life lying on a bed of Christmas wrapping paper. Hardly dignified, and he was such a dignified man. The paramedics brought him back, well, got his heart beating, but...'

Noah looks over at me, there's pity in his eyes, and empathy, I suppose. It feels strange telling this to someone who never met Cliff, didn't know anything real about him.

'He was young really, for that,' he says.

'Yes.'

'She blamed me. Said it was all my fault for putting him under so much pressure to be a father again. But that came later, much later. At the time she didn't tell me; she didn't ring me to say the ambulance was on its way. Nothing.'

I look down at my hot chocolate, cooling off now and the beginnings of a skin starting to form. I take a sip.

'He was late, so I rang him. The paramedic in the ambulance answered it. Told me. I raced up to the hospital, but she was already there, passing herself off as his next of kin. Bitch.'

He leans over and grips my knee. I could take it as a sign to shut up but I'm in full flow now and he hasn't heard it before, not like my family, and it feels good to say it all, put it out there. Again.

'I set the record straight and it was me they gave his belongings to. Not her. But she sat in the family room the whole time, probably waiting for her chance to tell me how he died in *her* arms, not mine. I don't know what she was playing at, I really don't. She got engaged on Christmas Eve to Adam, *her* younger lover. I wonder what he thought of her behaviour? I understand her being upset, but passing herself off as Cliff's wife, it wasn't right. I just slipped away; I couldn't face her then. Went back to my parents' empty house and lost the baby the next day. So I had nothing. Nothing of Cliff at all.'

'I'm so sorry.'

'That was one jolly Christmas. My parents were in Australia, so I waited until they came back to tell them. No point spoiling their Christmas too, was there? My mum was annoyed, but I... well...' I'm crying now, it was inevitable. He shunts along the sofa and sits closer to me then puts his arm around me. We seem to be making a habit of this.

'I didn't do anything about the funeral, not for a week.' I blow my nose on a tissue I've pulled out of my knitting bag which is on the floor at my feet. What an old granny I am. 'I assumed he was still in the hospital mortuary. But the funeral director informed me that he was there, with them, at their chapel of rest. She'd arranged it. Her. Hadn't told me. It was pure luck that I rang the same funeral place that she had used. Imagine if I'd rung another one and arranged everything and they couldn't find his body.'

He grips my shoulder and I look up at his face. He's crying, it's silent, but tears are running down his face.

'Sorry,' I say, pulling away as he wipes his face with the back of his hand. 'I've wrecked *your* Christmas now. It's what I do. Last year Mum and Dad wouldn't go to Oz without me and I wouldn't go, so we stayed home and all had a miserable time together. I wasn't letting that happen again.' I'm sure I've already said this, but I feel the need to emphasise the point.

'So you escaped to Christmas Cottage.'

'Yeah. Didn't know it was called that when I booked it. If I had I wouldn't have come. It was an omen, wasn't it?'

'Yeah.' He smiles. 'You've had a shit time, not just losing your husband but all that went with it. I'm so sorry.'

'Susannah always felt wronged, blamed me for everything. But it couldn't be farther from the truth. She had an affair years before I came on the scene. *She* broke up their marriage. They were already divorced before I even started working at Sutton Software.'

'Oh, what was your job? Are you in gaming?' His face lights up as though he's found a kindred spirit.

I give him a sideways glance. I just know what he's going to think when I tell him even though he'll probably be too nice to say anything.

'No. I was his PA. I replaced his PA who'd been with them since the beginning of the company, she retired. The agency sent me along and Cliff liked me.'

'Ah.'

'I know, it's such a cliché, isn't it? I wasn't looking for love, just a decent job. And Susannah didn't want him, didn't want him in her home, especially not in her bed, she just didn't want anyone else to have him either.'

He looks at me and he looks so sad, sadder than me even.

'And now I haven't got him either, so I think she's happy now. Though not as happy as she was to be the one whose arms he died in.' Do I sound bitter? Of course I do. I am.

'That's tough. For all of you. His kids too.'

'Yeah, it is.'

Noah glances at his watch. It looks expensive, all stainless steel and dials. Cliff liked an expensive watch.

'Nice watch,' I say.

'Yolanda chose it, for my twenty-first. From my dad obviously, but she's the one with good taste in presents.'

'Cool.'

He gets up and fiddles with the fire, puts more logs on. It's late. I'm tired, so he must be. I take our cups over to the dishwasher and load them in, switch it on.

As I turn around, he's behind me.

'Whoops, sorry.' He laughs. 'Just had this glass for the dishwasher, but never mind, missed it.'

He puts the glass on the sink drainer. He tidies up after himself, I've noticed that. Cliff never did. Susannah didn't either. They had a woman, Mrs Scrubit, they called her, not that that was her name, it was some sort of joke between them. She came in and cleaned up after them every day, did their washing and ironing, all their housework, cooked for them. Cliff wanted us to have a Mrs Scrubit too. I wouldn't. Couldn't. Once we got together Susannah wouldn't have me in the office. I wanted to get another job but Cliff didn't want that. After we married and moved to our grand house, I was a housewife, I cooked lovely low-fat meals. Would have been a mother. If he got a Mrs Scrubit, what would I do all day? Cliff and Susannah and their sons had become used to be waited on. I didn't want that for my children.

'Night then,' he says, turning at the same time as I do and we collide. 'Sorry.'

'No problem,' I mutter, but I'm looking up into his eyes. They're dark, the pupils dilated, his lips turn up at the sides, a half-smile.

Then suddenly, inexplicably we're kissing. He didn't initiate it; neither did I. It just happened. We shouldn't be doing this. It's silly. Wrong. But it feels so good. I reach up and put my arms around his neck. He puts his arms around my waist. It's wrong. It's right. I'm lost in this kiss. I think he is too.

Stop.

I pull away.

'Sorry,' he says and walks off to his room.

'Me too.'

Eleven

I yank my bedroom curtains open and lean against the hot radiator, my arms on the windowsill, I love doing this, it has almost become a ritual. The snow hasn't turned to slush and puddles. It's worse. Much worse. Another heavy fall by the look of it. Our snow sculptures are bigger than before, a thick layer of fresh snow expanding and blurring their outlines, blending them into one long up and down form.

The sea and the sky are the same colour, pinky-grey. Does that mean more snow is on the way? There is not a hint of sun in the sky, not even a sliver of blue sky.

He won't be going home today.

Damn it. I think. Or do I mean good?

I grab my book and peer out of my bedroom door. No sign of him or Kong, so I dart across to my bathroom. I'll have a soak and a read and keep out of his way. I'm still recovering from the shock of our kiss, the feel and taste of his lips, and I'm cringing because I enjoyed it. Enjoyed it far too much. It's a feeling that I've grown accustomed to not feeling.

I top up with hot water twice before I finally haul myself out of the bath. After I've cleared the condensation off the mirror, a big pink face gazes back at me, puffy and glowing. I wrap myself in towels and open the bathroom door. Kong's back and he jumps up from his basket and bounds over. Is he going to do the towel tug again? I'm pretty sure it's his party piece and he's been trained to do it. Pervert dog.

'Sit, Kong,' I say in my sternest voice.

Kong sits.

'Impressive,' Noah says, appearing from his room. How long has he been there, watching me, waiting? Was he going to let Kong disrobe me again? Was he going to watch my embarrassment again?

'Hi,' I say and march to my bedroom, closing the door behind me and leaning against it. Not because I think Noah will come barging in, but because a part of me wants him to.

❄❄❄

'You've seen the weather?' he asks when I reappear ten minutes later, fully dressed.

'Yes.'

'Sorry, I don't think I'll be able to leave today.'

'No.'

'Even Kong wouldn't go out in that first thing. He just peed by the door.'

'Lovely.'

'Sorry.'

I don't answer, just head over to the kitchen area and help myself to cereal. I check the dishwasher; he's already emptied it. I haven't done it at all since I've been here. More than once I accused Cliff of being lazy and undomesticated, I was annoyed that everything seemed to fall to me, as though I was a servant. He'd looked at me with genuine surprise, then suggested we get a cleaner, the previously mentioned Mrs Scrubit, who I declined. Maybe *I've* become lazy and less domesticated since I've been here, allowing Noah to do things I could, should. No, I've cooked for him. I haven't been completely lazy. Anyway, that was the whole purpose of coming here, to be lazy, to not do anything and *he's* spoilt it.

'Thanks for always emptying the dishwasher,' I call to Noah but without turning and looking at him. I can't look at him. Can't look him in the eye.

'No problem. Hardly taxing.' He appears next to me by the fridge; I need him to move because I want the milk.

''Cuse,' I say, still not looking directly at him, though I'm aware that he's wearing the soft jeans again, a loose t-shirt and nothing on his feet. 'Aren't your feet cold?' I glance down at them, big feet, like men always seem to have, but not ugly feet. Cliff had bunions.

'No, but I will put socks on soon.'

I take my cereal over to the table and within thirty seconds he follows me with his. Sits opposite me, so I have to keep my eyes on my bowl and take a sneaky look at his. It would appear that we both like a liberal slosh of milk on our cereal, no wonder we keep running out.

'It's stopped snowing,' he says. 'We have about four hours before it's due to start again.'

'Right. How do you know that?' I wonder if the weather app on *my* phone is working?

'Local TV news. I'm going to take Kong out later; might be the only chance we have. Would you like to come?'

'Yes,' I say, before I even have time to think about it. 'We're going to need more milk.'

'We should make a list.'

'Okay.' This is insane. We're playing house.

❄❄❄

Two hours later we head out of the garden with Kong in front of us. The air is still and it's biting cold. A thin sun is making a valiant attempt to break through the cloud but so far it really hasn't been successful. Our plan is to take the good lane across to the pub then head up to the garage mini-mart.

Kong has other ideas.

'Shit,' says Noah. 'Sorry, I'm going to have to go after him, the big bugger has decided he's going to the beach. You carry on and I'll catch you up. Meet outside the pub?'

'Umm…' I think quickly, imagining myself standing outside the pub for who knows how long, waiting and freezing. 'I'll come with you.'

'Okay. But be careful, it's probably worse than the other day, now we've had another snowfall.'

'Okay. Got my boots on.' Who am I trying to convince? Me.

It takes all of three minutes before I slip over onto my arse.

'Sorry,' he says as he yanks me up. Even through all the layers of clothing I'm wearing I can feel the fizz and spark of something between us where his hands pull me up. Judging from the way he stands me up and steps back, so can he. We carry on, I slip again but this time he catches me, then lets go immediately.

'Maybe I shouldn't have come to the beach,' I say by way of an apology.

'No. Why did you?' He asks his question calmly, there's no hint of accusation about it. But what would he be accusing me of?

'I just didn't want to stand up at the pub freezing my feet off.'

'You could have gone inside.' I can hear the smile in his voice.

'Yeah, never thought of that.' Why the hell didn't I think of that?

'Here,' he says, sticking his arm out. 'Link.'

I thread my arm through his and instantly feel safer; he's solid, he's stable. I feel foolish, I don't need a man to help me stand on my own two feet. Yet again.

Except I do. Apparently.

'Kong,' Noah bellows once we're on the beach. Noah unlinks our arms.

Kong comes bounding over from nowhere, a long stick in his mouth.

'Where the hell did he find that on this snow-covered beach?' Noah grabs the stick and hurls it for Kong, we watch him bound after it.

'It doesn't feel quite so cold down here.'

'Sheltered, I suppose. I'll give him five minutes to run off his energy then we're going back up.'

I stand and stamp my feet while Noah throws the stick several times for Kong. I could be sitting in a warm pub, my hands cupped around a hot drink. Stupid me.

'Let's go,' Noah says, sounding annoyed.

'Okay. You all right?'

'I'm fine. Kong,' he bellows again, yet I can't help feeling it isn't just Kong he's annoyed with. Where is super nice, smiley Noah?

We scrabble our way back up to the lane in single file out of necessity and when I slip, nowhere near falling over, he automatically takes my hand in his. We're both wearing gloves so there's no skin to skin contact and yet it feels so intimate.

Once in the lane he lets go of my hand and walks a little away from me. I've obviously done something to offend him.

'Did you want to go in the pub and get warmed up?' He forces the sides of his mouth to curl into a smile, it looks like an effort.

'Yes. Good idea.' Will he leave me to it, or join me? Do I care?

'A whisky, is it?' the barman asks Noah, with a smirk.

'No, just two coffees. Are you doing food today?'

The barman nods to the menu on the wall. 'Just those today. Take a seat and I'll send Beth over.'

'We might as well eat in here. Save us bothering later. And I'm hungry. Are you?'

I am. 'Yeah, okay.'

Beth brings our coffees over and takes our order; we both choose steak and kidney pie and chips. Then we sit in silence, but it's okay because we busy ourselves with our drinks, so it's not awkward at all. Except it is. Of course it is. Is it the kiss? Have I said something offensive?

Is it his phone? Has he got a signal now? Has he looked on Facebook again? I don't recall him looking at his phone; in my mind I playback the last forty minutes or so, trying to remember.

'You asked why I came off Facebook,' I say, because thinking about Facebook has brought it to the fore. I'm going to tell him; he might learn something from it.

'I did.'

'It was because of her, Susannah. After Cliff died she posted pictures from the funeral, the coffin on its plinth, the two flower arrangements on top, mine and hers. Hers bigger, she pointed that out in her post too. There were pictures of the wake, people standing around drinking and eating, people I didn't know, but she tagged them all. Then after that there were the daily pictures, ancient photos of when they first met, their wedding, their sons. It went on and on.'

'Why didn't you just unfollow her?' He doesn't sound sympathetic.

'I didn't follow her. I've never followed her. Why would I? She tagged me on every post. Every damn time. Then there were complete strangers offering their condolences, "so sorry for your loss." There was no escaping her.'

'How long were they married?'

'You're going to side with her now.' I'm annoyed. I shouldn't have said anything.

'No. No. I'm not. I can understand her grieving if they were together a long time, he was the father of her sons. And no doubt those boys were suffering.'

'Yes. Of course they were.' What can I say? He knows exactly how those boys must have been feeling, probably still feel. 'But none of it was my fault. I didn't do anything. I let them, her, have the funeral she wanted. She insisted that Cliff had always wanted his ashes buried in a woodland. I even went along to the woodland interment weeks after the funeral because that was what she said Cliff would want. We had another little ceremony then, just close family and friends. What a joke. Just thirty or more people I didn't know. I never even knew if what she said Cliff wanted was true; we'd never discussed funerals. Why would we?'

'It must have been hell for you, losing your husband, then your baby.' He leans over and grips my hand, then quickly lets go as though I've stung him. Skin on skin contact, it feels like a sting.

'Anyway, that's why I came off Facebook. So I didn't have to see any more of their supposed perfect life before me. I've never gone back. I've never regretted it.' I pause and watch his face for a reaction but he's just staring into the distance.

'You said you wanted to know,' I add, my excuse for telling him, which I'm already beginning to regret.

As I say the words, throw out the challenge, our food arrives, and Beth goes off to find us cutlery and condiments. When she returns we eat without talking and Noah orders us a soft drink each. Full-fat coke for him, tonic water for me.

'You think I should come off Facebook then?' he says once we've finished.

'Yes. I did say. No need to torment yourself. Have you looked today?'

'No. No signal. Oh, might be one here.' I wait for him to reach into his pocket for his phone, but he doesn't.

He gets up and disappears, clicking his fingers as Kong rises. Kong slumps back down.

'We'd better get off to the shop before it gets dark and starts snowing again,' he says when he comes back. I assume he's been to the toilet; I'm wondering if I should go before we leave. He shrugs on his coat and picks up mine.

'We'd better pay the bill,' I say, letting him help me get my coat on.

'Done.'

'Oh. What do I owe you?'

'Nothing. Don't worry.'

I wish he hadn't done that; I don't want to be in his debt.

'I'll get what we need at the shop then, make us even.'

'Okay.' He puts Kong's lead on and we all head for the door.

Outside it's even colder and I pull my hat out of my pocket and pull it down over my ears. He does the same, but he doesn't need to switch on the headlamp. At least it's not snowing. Not yet.

We set off at a pace and it doesn't take long to reach the shop.

'I'll go inside,' I say, striding towards the door. He can stay outside with his own dog.

I pull out the list we made before we left: milk, eggs, bread. The staples, the basics. I get a wire basket from the stack by the door and hunt around for the things we need. I buy a newspaper. Just before I go to the till I spy cake decorations. I've brought flour and sugar with me, my plan to make a cake, which I haven't done so far. Mostly because of him.

I peruse the cake decorations, gawdy Father Christmases that look as though they've been here years. Then I spot buttercream; I could make cupcakes. I check the sell by date then lob a tub into the basket, adding some cake cases too.

It feels even colder when I go back outside, probably the contrast from inside the heated mini-mart.

'I'll carry that,' he says, reaching for the carrier bag. I don't argue.

'Been checking your phone?'

'No. Might do later. It'll have downloaded here. Probably. And yours.'

'Yes, though you can't reply back at the cottage.'

'I've got no one to reply to,' he says. 'Come on, I can feel snow in the air. Let's just get on with it.' He strides on and I attempt to keep up with him just as a large snowflake settles on my face. 'Come on.'

It seems it's not just Vic and Liam who have upset him.

It's me.

Twelve

It's a relief to be back inside the cottage, ripping off our coats, kicking off our boots. Noah towels Kong down then goes straight to the log burner and adds another log. I pull my hat off and lay it on a radiator.

'Shit, look at it. We were lucky there,' he says, standing up and staring out of the window. The snow is falling thick and heavy and the light is fading fast.

'We were,' I agree and at the same time I feel as though he's blaming me that the last few minutes were so hard going. I don't know why. *I* didn't hold him up. *I* didn't suggest going for lunch. *I* didn't run off to the beach.

I dash off to my bathroom while he unpacks the shopping.

When I come back he's on the sofa reading my newspaper.

'I've left your blue stuff out,' he says without looking at me.

'What blue stuff?'

He doesn't answer but when I go to the kitchen area I can see the tub of buttercream icing on the worktop; he's right, it is blue. I hadn't noticed that. He's balanced the pack of cake cases on top of the tub. The cases which I thought were cupcake cases are actually muffin cases. Twice the size. Oh well.

'Do you need anything in the kitchen?'

'No,' he says, thoroughly engrossed in my newspaper.

I hunt around in the cupboards until I find what I need, turn on the oven and make my cakes; it doesn't take long before the whole cottage is filled with the aroma of baking.

'Smells good,' he says from the sofa, the first time he's spoken since I started baking because he's read the print off my newspaper.

'Thanks.' I hover around the kitchen, not knowing how long the cakes will take in this oven; I don't want them to burn. Finally, I pull them out and leave them to cool. They are enormous and so will I be if I keep eating at the rate I have since I've been here. I'm blaming him for that.

When I turn around, Noah has gone, probably to his bedroom to check Facebook and make himself miserable. Lovely.

I tidy up after myself, load the dishwasher and put it on, then I draw the curtains, it's pitch black outside now and it's barely five pm. I sit down and read my newspaper for five minutes, then check the cakes; they're cool enough to ice. Once I've finished, I arrange them on a large plate and put them on the dining table. The blue of the icing is positively vibrating. I'd have preferred white. But they look enticing, a dozen bright blue, giant cupcakes.

I head off into my bedroom to check my phone, though, happily, no Facebook for me. Sometimes I'm tempted to log back in and sneak a look at Susannah's page, then I remind myself how miserable it made me feel. I also know that what she posts is a lie, yes they were happy in the past but she ruined it. Her. Not Cliff. She broke his heart. He told me that, and he never thought he'd find love again, until he met me. I had nothing whatsoever to do with their marriage ending no matter how Susannah likes to spin it in her head. Anyway, she has Adam now, not that they've married yet. I wonder what he thinks of her behaviour.

I have an email from Mum with some pictures of them all on the beach on Christmas Day, squinting in the sunshine. How odd that seems, especially when it's so cold here. Talk about one extreme to the other. I'll have to wait until I go to the shop again before I can reply.

I slink back into the living room to find the TV on and Noah sitting on the sofa eating.

'Hey,' he says. 'Your radioactive cakes are good. I've had a couple; hope you don't mind.'

'Radioactive. Cheeky sod.' I laugh. 'No, they need to be eaten. That's why I laid them out.' I'll have to put what's left in an airtight box at the end of the evening otherwise they'll be stale.

I help myself to one of my cakes. His description of the icing is spot on. So bright.

I plonk myself on the sofa, peel back the cake case and bite into the cake.

'Crumbs.' I attempt to catch them with my hand.

'I'll get you a plate.' He leaps up and dashes to the kitchen. I notice that *he* had the foresight to get a plate first.

'They do taste good, even though I say so myself. Even the *radioactive* icing is nice. All that sugar, I'm going to get a sugar rush.'

He laughs. I'm pleased to see that he's in a better mood than earlier, very pleased in fact because I expected him to be even more morose after he'd tormented himself on Facebook.

'I've taken your advice,' he says, glancing over at me.

'Yeah?'

'Yeah. I'm off Facebook for the foreseeable…' Is he reading my mind, or did I say it out loud? I don't think so.

'Cool. Good decision.'

'I did have a look first though.' He grins at me like a naughty kid.

'Was that wise?'

'Oh yes. Liam has badly sprained his ankle so they're coming home sooner. He's on crutches. Result.' He does that thing men do, punches the air as though he's just scored a goal. I suppose this explains why he's cheered up.

'Result? Do you have a voodoo doll of him, or something?'

He eyes me suspiciously. 'No. Course not. Just wishful thinking. Couldn't happen to a nicer bloke.'

I can understand that; how many times had I wished that it had been Susannah who had died on Christmas Day and not Cliff. A wicked thought, I know, and I don't wish it now. Not very often anyway.

'I think I'll have another toxic cake,' he says leaping up from the sofa.

'Toxic?' I could be insulted but I find it amusing.

'Short for intoxicating, obviously.'

He comes back to the sofa with two on his plate.

'More like addictive, I would say. Mind all that sugar.'

'They are addictive. You're a good cook.'

'Baker,' I correct.

'Okay, baker,' he says with a laugh.

I return to my newspaper and he flicks through the TV channels. Eventually, he goes and makes a pot of tea and brings it to the coffee table together with mugs. Then he fetches the plate of cakes over too. I give him a look and raise my eyebrows.

'Well, they'll go nice with the tea and we wouldn't want them getting stale.'

'They won't get stale, they're radioactive, remember. Their half-life is probably ten years.'

He laughs, pours our tea and hands me my mug.

'Bloody hell, look at that,' he says, pointing to the TV where images of snow swirling dramatically flash before our eyes. 'Sorry, Ruby, but I don't think I'll be going home tomorrow either.'

'No, I don't think you will.' I pointedly turn the page on my newspaper and he sits down with his tea and two more cakes. And *I'm* worrying about *my* sugar intake.

This is easy, too easy. Comfortable. I'm half reading and half watching some cheesy film he's put on. It's warm and cosy in here and even when Kong pads over and rests his head in the space between us, I'm still comfortable. I even reach over and give him a pat.

'He likes you,' Noah says.

'Does he? Did he tell you that?'

'Well, yes, sort of. He doesn't bark or growl at you.'

'Does he growl? I haven't heard him, have I? Oh yes, when he yanked my towel away leaving me exposed on the carpet. But not since, I think. He's a well-trained pervert though.'

'No, he's not, are you, boy?'

'Says you.'

'He growls at Vic all the time. Even as she's filling his bowl with food, he growls at her. I'm beginning to think he's a good judge of character.'

I don't know what to say to that, so don't respond. I'm not going to join him in slagging off his ex-girlfriend because I've never met her and anyway, he might get back with her at some point. If that's what he wants. That thought suddenly makes me sad. He shouldn't settle for someone who could do that to him, dump him for his best mate.

We both return to what we were doing and Kong puts a paw on the sofa.

Time passes and it's so pleasant, we even have a second cup of tea and I get my knitting out and manage a couple of complicated rows uninterrupted, then he breaks our peace.

'I think I'm getting over Vic now. I feel a lot better about the whole situation.'

'Good.'

'Yeah, I'm a lot happier altogether, about everything.'

'Certainly happier than you were this afternoon.'

He looks at me but I don't meet his gaze. Why did I have to say anything?

'What do you mean?'

'You were, how shall I put it? Decidedly grumpy.'

'When?'

'A bit on the beach. Off the beach. In the pub. Once we walked to the shop, after the shop, especially after the shop. You stomped around like a moody teenager.'

'I stomped because I was cold and because I wanted us to get back and not get caught in the snowstorm again like we did the other day.' The sides of his mouth curl just a little, a tiny smile forming. Maybe.

'Okay. Whatever you say.' Let it drop now. Wish I'd never mentioned it.

He gets up, takes the teapot away, unloads the dishwasher, restacks it. And I watch. I like watching him.

'Just so you know,' he calls over, his back to me as he's wiping down the kitchen worktops. 'I *was* in a mood. But not with Vic. Or about her even.'

I wait for the punchline. He stops wiping and walks back to me, stands in front of me. He waits until eventually I force myself to look up from my knitting, which is irritating because I'm in the middle of a row.

'I was in a mood with you, if you must know.'

'Me? What have I done?' Immediately I've said it, I wish I hadn't because I don't want him listing my misdemeanours, supposed or real.

'You. *And* me.' He pauses and I shake my head. What's he talking about? 'You and me and… last night.'

'Ah. We never did anything last night, except…' I stop. I'm not saying *kiss* out loud.

'No, because we stopped. Or, rather, you stopped. You pulled away. Thank God. Or who knows what it would have led to?'

I shrug. I can't pretend I haven't wondered that too. I've wondered it rather too much. I spent a lot of time before I fell asleep last night pondering on it.

'We can't even say we were drunk, can we? Because we weren't.' He looks pointedly at me.

'No. Okay. But why did that put you in a mood? You seemed fine in the morning. Neither of us mentioned it, I thought we were just going to pretend it never happened.'

'If that's what you want.'

138

I shrug again. 'I never said that.' I'm aware that we're sort of flirting and arguing at the same time. It's weird. Gone is the comfort and ease of earlier, now the air is charged. Even Kong has noticed it and slunk off back to his basket in the corner.

'Kissing you last night made me realise that Vic's not all that.'

'Not all that?' He's seen too many American films, girly ones at that, I wonder if she made him watch them. 'You mean she's not as fantastic as you thought?' The idea of being compared to Vic is as flattering as it is laughable.

'Yes. That's it, exactly.'

'You are joking. I think you're forgetting I've seen the pictures of Vic on your Facebook feed.' I laugh. Hilarious.

'Beauty isn't all about the outside, the skin, is it? I think you know that.'

'Are you talking about my husband?' How bloody dare he?

He has the sense to look sheepish. 'Not specifically, no.' He now looks earnest, genuine. 'I meant we're all more than we appear on the outside. We're all so much deeper than the latest clothes, the glossy hair, aren't we?'

'I'll have you know that my husband was very good looking in his youth. Apparently. I've seen the pictures.' The bloody cheek of him.

'I'm sure he was. But I wasn't even thinking about him.'

'He was also very kind, and funny and clever, that goes without saying...'

'I don't think I can win with you. Come on Kong. Out you go before bed.'

I stay on the sofa while Kong reluctantly gets up and is forced outside for one last expulsion, he's not out there long and I can feel the cold blast that follows the opening and closing of doors. Noah comes back and stokes the fire, then banks it up with enough logs to last the night. I just watch him, feeling increasingly annoyed. Finally, I stand up.

'It was a backhanded compliment anyway,' I say to his back as he closes the log burner door.

'What was?' He turns and frowns at me as though the conversation we had just minutes ago has never taken place.

'What you said?'

'Which part?'

'The bit about kissing me making you realise that Vic's not so great after all.'

'Oh that. Well, sorry if I said the wrong thing. I can't really do right for doing wrong, can I?' Here we go again, Mr Moody.

He stands up and walks towards his bedroom and just at the same time I head towards mine and we almost collide. Fortunately, we're both agile enough to miss.

'Sorry,' he mumbles into his chest.

'No probs.'

I move to my left and he moves to his right and this time we do collide. But there are no apologies, no pulling back or running away, no words at all. Just lips on lips and hands in hair and on necks… and I never make it to my own bedroom.

Thirteen

I am alone in his bed.

I have no idea what time it is. Weak light is creeping in around the edges of the curtains, so I know it's probably after eight. Or it could be nine.

The bed is enormous, it makes sense that he chose it. I imagine what would have happened if he'd taken the other room and I'd crawled into bed with him that first night. The bed in my room is a king-size, this one is probably six feet wide. It's very comfortable and I spread out like a starfish because he's not here. Maybe he's in the bathroom. I listen for the sounds of water running, a tap, or maybe the shower. But there's nothing. I slither out of bed and pick up my clothes from the chair, I pull on the long sweater I was wearing yesterday. It will do for now.

I try the handle of his en-suite bathroom as I pass, it gives, he's not in there, so I nip in and use his loo. The bathroom is full of manly things, a shaver, aftershave, deodorant as well as two toothbrushes, one of which is electric. They're all lined up neatly on the worktop by the sink. I'd quite forgotten what this looks like, how it makes me feel. I didn't realise I missed this. After Cliff died it took me over a year to force myself to get rid of his things, many I just boxed up and sent to his sons, but some just went in the bin or to charity. So sad.

As I approach the bedroom door I can hear music, pop music.

Once I open the door, I see why I hear music.

He's dancing to a radio channel which he's put on the TV, since there's no radio here.

I have to rub my eyes because I cannot believe what I am seeing. He is dancing with his dog. Kong's front paws are on Noah's shoulders and they are dancing together. It's comical. And grotesque. I stand and watch for a minute or more before he spots me.

He pushes Kong's paws down, grabs the remote and turns the TV off.

'Morning,' he says.

'What was that about?'

'Kong wanted to dance?'

'Really? Does he want to do that often?'

'Err, no. Only when he's on a sugar high.' Noah grins at me.

'A what?' Then it dawns on me. I was so distracted last night that I left the cakes out.

'How many has he had?'

'Not sure. But there was still one left.'

'One left? Oh dear. My fault, I meant to put them in a sealed box, there's a drawer full of Tupperware next to the fridge.'

'I finished off the last one,' Noah says, another grin, this time sheepish, on his face. 'Sorry. Couldn't resist.'

'Don't worry, I wouldn't have fancied it after Kong had slobbered all over the plate.'

'It had no drool on it, I checked.'

I start counting on my fingers; I think there were six left last night. 'Kong has had five,' I say. 'And bear in mind they were double size because I bought the wrong cake cases.'

'He didn't mind. Neither did I?'

'Will it make him ill? Will he be sick?'

'Probably not. He's good, he'll go outside if he feels sick. He's going to need a long walk to use up the energy though. Anyway, never mind about Kong, how are you this morning? All good?'

'I'm good.' I smile; it's hard not to; Noah is wearing just his boxers and a t-shirt. He has well-muscled legs. They go nicely with his well-muscled body.

He moves towards me and wraps his arms around me, plants a quick kiss on my lips.

'You taste sweet,' I mutter, without thinking.

'Yeah, it's radioactive cupcake and dog slobber.'

'Urgh, no. Yuk. Go away.' I wipe my mouth with the back of my hand and dash into my bathroom while he laughs.

I'd forgotten how disgusting men can be. And funny.

❄❄❄

'Are you skipping breakfast after your cake fest?' I ask once I'm dressed.

'It's almost lunch time, so yes, I'm skipping breakfast.'

He's right, it's eleven-thirty. I don't know where the morning has gone. I do, however, know where the night went and why we slept so late. It's so, so long since I felt like that; completely lost in the moment, and enjoying every second of it. Over and over again. That Vic must be a fool to give him up.

'I might have a sandwich or something,' I tell him. 'Do you want one?'

'Yeah, what have we got?' He strides over to the fridge and together we choose our sandwich fillings. In the end he makes the sandwiches and I let him, content to sit and watch, although I do pour us a drink each and take it over to the table.

After lunch I check the weather outside. It is not snowing, and there is a glimmer of sun in the sky and one tiny little wedge of blue sky in the distance which is clearly visible if I press my face to the glass.

'It's improving,' I call.

'Yes. I know. The forecast is more positive too. Warming up nicely over the next day or so.'

'Great. That's great news,' I say, smiling brightly at him.

'Yeah. I could probably leave tomorrow.'

'What's tomorrow? I've lost track of the days.'

'New Year's Eve.'

'Really, already?'

'Yeah. Would you like me to leave tomorrow?' He looks downright miserable at the prospect.

'No. You're all right. Why don't you stay.'

'Thank you,' he says, not meeting my gaze.

'Don't make me regret it though. I mean, I hope you didn't sleep with me just so you could stay here longer.'

He looks at me in horror, then starts to laugh. 'Rumbled,' he says. 'Fancy a walk?'

❄❄❄

We make our way down to the beach and I hardly stumble at all. This is probably due to Noah holding my hand tightly. It feels like we're lovers. I love it. I feel

144

safe and secure and well… loved. I know it's an illusion, I know it's very temporary. Very. It's not love at all, it's lust, but I'm enjoying it while it lasts. For the first time since Cliff died I feel alive. Noah *is* nice, he's also smart and funny and hot, and I'm not normally bothered by that, but running my hands over his body last night… I shudder at the memory.

'You okay?' He looks at me with concern in his eyes.

'Yeah, I'm fine. Just shivered for a second.'

He puts his arm around my shoulder and pulls me in tight. 'Do you want my scarf?'

'No thanks, I'm fine now. Really.'

That stupid Vic is a bloody fool for letting him go. I hope she's regretting it. I hope she doesn't want him back because he's far too good for her.

'You know,' he says, smirking at me. 'I haven't missed Facebook at all. You were right to tell me to come off it.'

'Cool. But it's only been a day or something, hasn't it? Hardly a test. But I never missed it. Although I am sometimes tempted to log back in and snoop around.' I grin and so does he.

'Not saying I won't ever do that. But probably not while I'm here. With you. Much better things to do.' We giggle like kids, our heads together, our bodies entwined. He leans down and kisses me and I shudder again. I do, quite literally, go weak at the knees. Who knew lust could be so intoxicating? Even more intoxicating than radioactive cakes.

After that we round up Kong and scuttle back to Christmas Cottage as fast as we can. There's nothing like a bit of raunchy sex before dinner…

❄❄❄

I've been thinking,' he starts, as we're sitting at the dining table in our dressing gowns like an old married couple. We've had a cobbled together meal which involved mince beef, onions, garlic, potatoes and a frying pan. I'm not sure how that will play out later, but at least we'll both smell of it. And taste of it.

'Did it hurt?'

'What?'

'Your thinking?'

He laughs, which is kind of him, because that joke is ancient, juvenile and not really funny at all.

'Seriously, I've been thinking about your housing dilemma.'

I feel sudden alarm. I look up from my plate where I've been drawing circles with my fork in the residue of my meal, and stare at him. I hope he's not going to suggest something silly, something insane like I could go and live with him. He wouldn't, would he?

'Do you have a plan for moving out, moving on?'

'I do. But it's long term.' I get up and pick up our plates, take them over to the kitchen, busy myself clearing up. I don't want to discuss this with him. I don't want real life creeping back in and spoiling the fun, the distraction.

'The reason I ask,' he says, getting up and following me.

Please don't say something stupid, please don't offer me a home.

'Is that my dad is a financial advisor. He's really good at it too. He could help you look at ways to minimise your outgoings while saving for your escape and could help you get a mortgage of your own.'

I blink my response at him several times as though I'm speaking in Morse code, via eyelashes.

'Are you okay?' he asks.

'Yes, yes. Have you been reading my mind?' I follow this with a little laugh, trying to make light of it, but I'm still sure I don't want to discuss this with him. I know when I was down I blurted out my situation, but do I want him, or worse, his father involved?

He smiles and fills the kettle, then tells me to sit down while he makes us coffee. When he brings it over to the sofa he sits next to me, not at his own end. This is the first time we've sat on the sofa since last night, since this afternoon, since everything changed, and it feels strange.

'Well, the offer's there. I'm sure he'd be able to help you. He'd show you how to save some money for a deposit, where to put it to grow best, stuff like that. It's how I had my own place at twenty-four when all my mates were either living at home with their parents or flat sharing.'

'I do actually know how to save for a deposit,' I tell him, perhaps a bit too snappily. 'I've done it before.'

'Sorry, I didn't mean…' I feel his body stiffen and he moves slightly away from me.

I feel mean now. He was only trying to help.

'No, I'm sorry,' I say. 'I realise you're being nice.'

He rolls his eyes when I say nice. This is getting more awkward.

'Nice,' he mutters into his chest.

'Kind, then, kind. Look, the facts are that once I found out where I stood, once I got over the horror and betrayal of it, even though I know Cliff didn't mean to leave me penniless and alone, I took steps.'

'Cool. Cool,' he says, sounding cold, rather than cool.

'Yeah. Once I realised that the only way I was going to live on my own terms was to cut my losses and leave that house, I got a job and started saving like fury. After all I'm not a Jane Austen woman.'

'A what?'

'Ten thousand a year. Although it was usually the men who had the income, not the women. Unless they're Lady Catherine de Bourgh.'

He shakes his head again, evidently not knowing what I'm talking about. He looks totally bemused and bewildered.

'You know, "It is a truth universally acknowledged, that a single man in possession of a good fortune, must be in want of a wife". The good fortune in question was five thousand a year for Mr Bingley and ten thousand for Mr Darcy.'

Noah looks at me as though I am insane. Maybe I am.

'You've never seen Pride and Prejudice? I mean, I understand if you haven't read the book, but you've never seen the film? Or the TV series? My mum had the DVDs; we used to watch the series at least once a year while Dad hid in his shed or garage or garden or somewhere, though even he had seen it at least once.'

'No. Never. I've heard of it but don't know what it's about.'

'It's what made Colin Firth the heartthrob he is. The wet shirt part.'

'No. Sorry.'

'You've not seen Bridget Jones's Diary, because that's sort of based on Pride and Prejudice? It's why Colin Firth played the part of Mr Darcy, why the character's called Mr Darcy. Jane Austen basically invented chick lit and the chick flicks that have followed. Obviously, they didn't have film or TV in her day…' Oh shut up.

Noah stares at me blankly then shakes his head again. I can understand him never watching girly films when it was just him and his dad but what about Vic?

'Vic never…?' I ask, wondering if bringing her up is a good idea.

'No. She isn't really into stuff like that. She's sporty. And a party girl. She's high maintenance with the hair and stuff, but I suppose you'd call her a man's woman rather than a woman's woman.'

'Right.' Whatever the hell that means.

I don't like Vic at all.

'Well, just saying, if you ever come across either on TV you should watch and educate yourself.' I feel silly now for going on about it but at least it's distracted him from offering me financial advice from his dad.

'Okay,' he says and the smirk is back and half of me wants to slap it away and the other half wants me to kiss it away.

I choose kissing.

And everything that goes with it.

Fourteen

'Morning.' His smile greets me as I open my eyes. We're in bed, his bed and the dawn is just breaking.

'You haven't been watching me sleep, have you?'

He grins his response.

'Because if you have that's both creepy and a cliché.'

'That's me,' he says, with a smirk. 'Creepy and a cliché. Fancy a cuppa?'

'If you insist.'

'I do.' He leans over and kisses me on the nose. Not, I notice on the mouth, maybe my garlic breath is worse than his.

I take his absence as the opportunity to slink into his bathroom where I left my toothbrush last night, and hurriedly remint my mouth. I'm safely back in bed and propped up on pillows ready for my tea when he returns with a tray.

'And toast too. Lovely. You're spoiling me.'

'You're worth it.'

'Okay, enough of the cheese.'

'Ah, no cheese, we've eaten it all.'

'Shut up.' I laugh, because I can't help it and for once in a long time I'm actually happy, especially if I don't think too much about real life and the inevitable let down that will follow this little fantasy.

'It's New Year's Eve.'

'Yes, already. How quickly that has come around.'

'Are you still planning on going home tomorrow?' His stares into my eyes over his mug of tea.

'Yes, that's all I booked for.'

'Yes, but I booked until Sunday. When do you have to go back to work?'

'Monday.'

'Why don't you stay. We're having fun.' He grins. Boyish and sheepish and so bloody sexy, all at once.

'With you?' I say before taking a big bite of buttery toast. The hot butter dribbles down my chin and I cuff it with the back of my hand. How elegant. He dashes off to the bathroom and returns with a wodge of toilet paper for me to wipe my hands and face.

'Thank you,' I mumble into my toast.

'You're welcome.' He climbs into bed beside me and starts to eat his own toast. 'Seriously, why don't you stay? The weather's not so bitterly cold now, we can go for long walks on the beach, lunches in the pub, trips to the garage mini-mart... and still find time for ourselves.' Exactly what we've been doing so far and I am not complaining.

'Eat your toast and drink your tea,' I say, but I'm definitely considering it. Why not? What's waiting for me at home? A splendid, empty prison.

'Give it some thought. Promise me you will.' He looks so sad; I think he's joking.

'Okay.'

'You'll stay?' His eyes light up.

'No. I'll give it some thought.'

I hear him sigh before he takes a gulp of tea.

'Is madam going to lounge around in the bath for hours this morning?' he asks with a grin when we've finished our tea and toast.

'Maybe.'

'When you're done do you fancy a walk to the beach?'

'I suppose so.'

'Don't sound so enthusiastic.' He looks crestfallen; serves him right for bossing me about. I almost like it. I'd forgotten what it feels like to be part of someone else's plans.

'I might just have a shower today.' I climb out of bed and skip off to my own bathroom.

After my shower I go into my bedroom to dress, pulling on warm clothes and staring out of the window to see just how cold it is. The snow statuettes have noticeably shrunk, they're more like the size they were when we built them.

❄❄❄

Down on the beach the snow has melted a little, there are patches where the sand is visible and Kong really enjoys himself digging for something, though we're not sure what and he never finds it. Maybe it's the seagull he found days ago; the one Noah buried.

Noah holds my hand or grips me around the waist, I like it. I'd forgotten what this feels like; Cliff was never one to be overly demonstrative but he would hold my hand if he thought no one was looking.

'This has melted so much I'm wondering if we could get the cars out, or at least mine,' he says as he skims a stone across the sea. We watch Kong lollop in after it then quickly come back out, it must still be freezing in there.

'Oh?'

'The town is only about five miles away and it's supposed to be lovely, all little niche shops and artisan bakers, that sort of thing. Though it might be a bit cheesy and cliché for you.' He grins at me.

'Oh, I don't know, I seem to be quite partial to cheesy clichés.'

'We could get something for our New Year's Eve dinner tonight.'

'And wine,' I add, attempting to skim a stone myself and actually making my stone go much further than his.

'That was good.'

'For a girl?' I say, with a smirk.

'I never said that.'

'Make sure you never do.'

He laughs. I laugh and Kong comes bounding over so fast that he knocks into me and I go flying. Fortunately, my only injury is a wet backside. Noah helps me up and brushes the snow and sand from my coat. It feels strangely intimate, even more so than lying naked in his bed.

'Okay?'

'I'm fine.'

He leans down and kisses me on the lips. My knees almost buckle. Wow, this feels so good, so good. Remember these moments, savour every second.

❄❄❄

No digging is required to move his car; the snow has melted enough to turn to slush as soon as the wheels roll over it. He's backing his car out and executing the perfect three-point turn while I stand in the lane holding Kong's lead.

Finally, he pulls up alongside me and jumps out.

'Worth a go,' he says, as he opens the rear doors and ushers Kong inside while I climb into the passenger seat. 'We can always turn back, or attempt to if we don't get to the bottom of the lane.' He half laughs and I imagine getting stuck further up the lane and am grateful it's his car and not mine.

But we don't. His car glides effortlessly over the snow and soon we're on the main road heading for this little town he mentioned. The sun even makes an appearance, although it's thin and pale and hidden behind wispy clouds half of the time.

There's a small car park behind a Co-op, and he parks his car while I check how long we can stay there and how much it costs. There is no limit and it's free.

'We can go in there on the way back for anything we can't get elsewhere,' I suggest as we pass it, although Kong is straining at the leash to head in the direction of the Co-op. Noah pulls him sharply to heel and then he calms down.

'He's not really used to towns. I don't take him shopping at home,' Noah says by way of an explanation for his behaviour.

'I'm surprised you brought him here.'

'Seemed mean not to. Hope I don't regret it.'

We carry on into the high street, which is just as he described; gorgeous little shops showing off their Christmas decorations, lights shining in windows, baubles dangling from signs.

'Lovely,' I say.

'Told you. Knew you'd like it.' He puts his arm around my waist and pulls me to him. Then he lets go, because the melting snow is slippery and Kong is pulling on his lead.

'I might have to put him back in the car.'

'Will he be okay?'

'Yes. It's not like it's hot and he'll overheat, or too cold even, now. You could go in that shop there and I'll catch up with you in a few minutes.' He points to a shop full of candles and glass bowls and handmade pottery, gemstones and essential oils. Perfect, just the kind of place I like to spend time in.

'Okay,' I say, scuttling into the shop where the aroma attacks my senses in the best way possible. I stand just inside the door and inhale.

I choose a couple of scented candles, a rather lovely glass jar for my bathroom – I'll fill it with cotton wool balls – and some drawer liners which smell of heaven, although it says sweet pea on the label.

I'm alone in the shop and I take my items to the till, but there's no one there either, so I ring the bell on the counter. There's a display of massage oils next to the till and I hurriedly add one to my shopping.

'Just coming,' a male voice calls.

Then he appears. A man in his fifties, shortish, with a rounded belly, tight, curly grey hair and kind eyes.

I gasp and almost drop my shopping.

'Are you all right?' he asks.

'Sorry. Just. Well… I'm fine, thank you.' I push my items towards him and watch as he rings them up. I can hardly tell him that he reminds me so much of my dead husband that it took my breath away. As I watch him I feel as though I'm seeing a ghost.

'Would you like a bag?'

'Yes, please.' I notice the way he loads my shopping into a flowery paper carrier. His actions are delicate and quick, not at all like Cliff. I smile at him and remind myself he's a stranger.

'Everything okay, Sweets,' a male voice calls from the same direction as Cliff's ghost had called earlier. With that a second man appears, he's tall and dark and wearing a pink apron. 'Oh, sorry, didn't realise we had a customer. Just cooking up a storm in that kitchen.' He shakes his head and winks at me, then at Cliff's ghost.

The shop door opens and Noah slides in. Both men turn and appraise him, letting their eyes linger too long.

'Got everything you want?' Noah asks as I wave my card over the card reader.

'Yeah.'

'Have a lovely evening,' Cliff's ghost says as we turn to leave.

'You too, mate,' Noah says, holding the door open for me.

Once we're outside I hurry away from the shop then stop and take a few deep breaths.

'Are you all right? You look as white as a ghost.'

'I'm fine. Really. I'm fine.'

'Really?'

Do I tell him? I hesitate before deciding that I will, because I've lain in his bed enough, and while we hardly know each other, there's no need to be secretive about this.

'That guy who served me, he looked just like Cliff, for a moment.' It sounds stupid now I say it out loud. I expect Noah to smirk, to laugh even.

'Yeah? That must be weird. A gay Cliff.'

I laugh. I shouldn't. It's not really funny and I don't think he meant it as a joke, but I laugh and suddenly I feel better.

'How did you know he was gay? Not my Cliff, obviously. You were hardly in the shop before you were out.'

Noah gives me a quick sideways look and then the smirk appears. He shakes his head and links arms with me. 'Come on, now Kong's out of the way, let's get some serious shopping done before these shops shut because I suspect they won't be open late because...' He leans in and whispers in my ear, 'It's New Year's Eve.'

'You don't say.' I nudge him with my elbow, which makes him slip on slush and fall over onto his backside.

I'm mortified. I move to help him up but he's quick, and soon back on two feet.

'Remind me never to cross you,' he says.

'I'm so sorry. Oh my God, I'm so sorry. Are you okay? Are you hurt?'

'Only my pride,' he says. 'Anyway, I think I've got a few more trips to go before I catch up with you.' He grins and I feel a bit better. 'And you can use that massage oil on me later, that'll cure any bruises you've created.'

I feel myself blush. 'How did you know about that?'

'I was admiring you through the window, because I'm creepy and a cliché, remember.'

I'm tempted to give him another nudge, but dread what damage I could do, so I smile and so does he.

In the butchers we buy steak – he says he's a good cook which is good because I am definitely not good at steak; in the bakers we buy crusty bread and jam doughnuts, in the Co-op we buy vegetables and milk as well as wine and low alcohol beer.

Kong gets excited when we get back in the car but soon settles down for the drive back. The sun is already starting to set as we approach Christmas Cottage, it looks idyllic, smoke rising out of its chimney, the sun's reflection glowing orange in the windows.

I take in the sight of it, the hum of Noah's car, his presence next to me, even Kong's gentle breathing behind me. I want to remember this; I want to hold onto this sweet memory.

I want to enjoy it while it lasts. Because, of course, it cannot last.

Fifteen

'That was so good. You really *are* a good cook.' It's the best steak I've ever had, including ones I've eaten in expensive restaurants.

'No need to be so shocked,' he says with a laugh.

But I am shocked; Cliff never cooked anything. If he wanted to surprise me with a meal at home as a treat, he rang up one of his chef friends who sent something over, they didn't actually come to our house to cook it, but sometimes it felt like it. Not that I'm complaining, I had a good life with Cliff. I loved him so much and I miss him.

'Do you want a doughnut now?'

I shake my head. 'I couldn't.'

'Nah, me neither. Let's just slob out on the sofa for a while and watch a bit of shit New Year's Eve TV.'

'You sit down,' I tell him. 'I'll clear up your mess.' My comment is meant to be a joke but the joke is almost on me as there's hardly any mess, he's cleared as he's gone. There's just our plates and cutlery to add to the dishwasher. I'm soon joining him on the sofa where he's poured me another glass of wine and opened a can of low alcohol beer for himself. He's right about not being a big drinker because he's only had a very small glass of wine with dinner, now the beer. This is my third large glass. I need to watch myself or I will be drunk and indiscreet and he will be sober and remember everything. I definitely need to watch myself because we need to have *the* conversation.

We watch a few hours of dreadful TV, so bad it's almost good. Despite my best intentions I drink more and am feeling a little lightheaded.

'What did you and your husband usually do on New Year's Eve?'

'Well, we only had three together, I think, or maybe four.' I struggle to remember, how bad is that? 'The first year we moved into our house we hosted a party, a sort of joint New Year and housewarming party. It was fabulous.' It was fabulous, it looked amazing. Cliff had brought in party planners to decorate the house; the food was catered and there were waiters serving drinks. In the morning the cleaners came in and cleared everything up while we were still in bed. Mum and Dad would have come but it was bang smack in the middle of their holiday in Australia which meant they couldn't, so I hardly knew anyone, just one of my old girlfriends and her fiancée. 'We had people in to do the stuff, you know, food, a bar, clean up afterwards.' I give a little shrug.

'Wow, how the other half live.' He says this without a hint of malice or jealousy.

'Yeah. Another time we went to Cliff's friends for dinner. That was very classy and quite sedate. I liked it.' Except, again, I hardly knew anyone and they were all a lot older than me. I'm not telling Noah this, there's no need to. It really isn't of interest to anyone but me. 'Another time we went to a party at someone else's place, now that was palatial, swimming pool like something from a luxury spa, not like ours…' My voice fades away, not just at the memory, but at the look on Noah's face. 'What?'

'You with a pool in your house.'

'Yeah, well, as I said, it's not my house.'

'No. Sorry. Course not. Must be nice though.'

'It is.' I'd be a liar if I said it wasn't. 'Anyway, theirs made ours look like a paddling pool. But we didn't stay for very long that evening because *she* turned up, with her new boyfriend who was younger than me. Cliff was pissed off, which annoyed me. Why did he care who she was with; he was with me. *I* was his wife. It's all so complicated when you're with someone with so much history and baggage.' I've said too much, far too much. I was so in love with Cliff but sometimes I examine our relationship from a distance and see that it wasn't perfect. But then, is any relationship perfect? I doubt it.

'I don't suppose the young boyfriend lasted long,' Noah says, trying to cheer me up, I suppose.

'Oh yes. He did. They got engaged the following Christmas Eve, you know, the day before Cliff died in her arms. I don't know what he thought about all that, they're finally getting married later this year.'

'Ah.'

'Yeah. Well, like I said, it's all very complicated.' I take a gulp of wine. 'What do you usually do?'

'Usually still over with the skiing crew. We have a lot of après ski and party the night away. I usually wake up feeling fine when everyone else is nursing banging hangovers, so I do most of the clearing up. No servants for the likes of me.'

He grins, I roll my eyes and then we laugh.

'They weren't servants, they were, caterers, waiters, cleaners.'

'And the difference is?'

'Dunno,' I say, taking another swig of wine. I have to slow down the drinking. 'Anyway, not an issue now because I can't afford such extravagances.'

'That sounds tough.'

'Ahh, poor me.'

'I didn't mean it like that. I can see that it must be genuinely tough when you've been happy having these expectations with the man you love and then it…' He stops. 'Sorry.'

'It's okay. I know what you mean. Truth is I *was* getting used to it. Not having to worry about money is very liberating. Extremely liberating, but it lulls you into a false sense of comfort. Now it's all I do, worry about money.'

'Surely you can do something about your situation. Does she, his ex-wife want you living there?'

'She doesn't care one way or the other. The boys are too young to live in it, or sell it, so I'm just the caretaker in her eyes. Even if it was back under her control I doubt she'd sell it because there's no better earner than property, is there? Nothing grows in value like bricks and mortar, that's what Cliff always said, especially long term.'

'That's…tough. No chance then that she would pay you to leave.'

'No. Not that I've broached that subject, but no. I wouldn't take it anyway. I never earned the money, Cliff did. My share, my investment in it is tiny.'

'Your investment?'

'Yeah, I sold my little flat and put the equity into our lovely new house. Cliff said I didn't need to, told me to keep the money and spend it on myself, but I didn't want to do that. He actually told me not to sell my flat, to rent it out and have the rental income as a bit of pocket money. But I wanted to pay my way as much as I could. How stupid was I? I can't tell you how many times I've kicked myself for not taking his advice.'

'I'm sure my dad could help you. The offer is still there.'

'Thanks. Really. I have my plan, I'm saving for a deposit so I can start again, just me on my own and not entangled with Cliff's family at all. It's just taking time.'

'Well, as I said...' He reaches into his back pocket, pulls out his wallet, then extracts his dad's business card and hands it to me. I push it into my knitting bag, smiling my thanks as I do so.

'The irony is if I hadn't lost the baby, I'd be on fifty thousand a year. And it would increase every year. That's how it worked in Cliff's will. So you see he had provided for me, really well. He just hadn't expected to die like that. Who does?' I shrug and take another sip of my wine. I've been very indiscreet. '*He* never expected to die. *I* never expected to lose our baby. We had our whole future mapped out before us, then....' I fling my hands up because I can't say any more without crying. I inhale through my nose to stop the tears then grab my wine glass.

Noah doesn't say anything else. He can't without sounding judgemental, although there's not much he could say that I haven't thought. Much as I loved Cliff, after his death there were days when I resented him and his financial arrangements. I should have seen it coming really. I shouldn't have been so naïve. He had told me enough times that he would always look after his family and his business. I just thought *I* was his family.

'It's not all about the money,' I finally add.

'No.'

'It's not about the money at all, really. It's just the situation. The everything. I loved him so much and I miss him so much.' Don't cry. Don't start snivelling into his shirt again.

But I do, of course I do.

We fall asleep slouched on the sofa and wake up just as the countdown to the New Year starts on TV.

'Happy New Year,' he says and kisses me.

'You too,' I mutter back. I'm still half asleep and feeling thirsty.

'Coffee and doughnuts?' he asks, disentangling himself from me and getting up.

'Water for me, but definitely a doughnut.'

He adds more logs to the burner and brings our drinks over, together with the bag of doughnuts.

Here we sit, after midnight, before a roaring fire, scoffing doughnuts and watching the New Year fireworks live from London. I would never had done this with Cliff because of the fat and the calories. Despite the constant diet watching Cliff still had a paunch. He said it was his age. It never bothered me. I fell in love with his personality, his sense of humour, his kindness.

That worked out well.

I glance over at Noah who is now on his second doughnut. There's not an ounce of fat on him. How is that? Or will it catch up with him in middle age?

'Do you work out?' I say, without thinking.

'What, gym and stuff, you mean?'

'Yes.' I wonder if he drinks all that whey powder muscle builder stuff too. I once had a boyfriend who was into that, and he went to the gym before and after work. Our relationship didn't last long, mainly because he didn't really have time for me.

'Nah. Can't be arsed with all that. I ski. Well, used to. Cycle to work most days, and when I can't I walk. That does me.'

'How far to work?'

'Three miles, something like that. Easier that driving and I don't have to bother about the parking. And I walk Kong a few miles every day, more at the weekend.'

'And you chop wood,' I add.

'I do. Not just here. I do my own and my dad's.' He looks into the doughnut bag where the last one is waiting, strictly speaking it should be mine.

'You have it,' I say, not quite gagging at the prospect of another one, no matter how nice it is.

So he does.

'You think I'm a greedy fat pig now, don't you?' He says this as he bites into the doughnut, his third.

'Hardly fat.'

'We'll have to go for an extra-long walk on the beach tomorrow. Kong will enjoy it.' At hearing this Kong leaps up. 'I'd better let him out,' Noah says, jumping up.

I'm already in his bed when he comes back in with Kong.

'It's so bloody cold out there,' he says. 'I hope it doesn't freeze again. I'm glad you've decided to stay and not go home tomorrow.' He stands in front of me and pulls off his jumper and t-shirt.

I watch his muscles flex, he has abs, but they're not at all like gym-built ones.

'I think I might need to take up wood chopping,' I muse.

'Why?' He frowns at me as he kicks off his jeans.

'Tone me up like you.' I wish I hadn't started this conversation now; I've drawn attention to my body which definitely isn't sporty like Vic's.

'There's nothing wrong with you. You're lovely as you are. That's what's so attractive about you, you're not into all that body obsession stuff, worrying about your roots, your clothes, not like…' He tails off; he was about to compare me to Vic. I can't blame him; haven't I just done that very thing, comparing him to Cliff?

'Thanks,' I manage to mutter at his backhanded compliment.

'Anyway, I thought you preferred knitting.'

'I do, and I'm well off my schedule.'

'Is that my fault?'

'Definitely.'

He disappears into the bathroom and I cosy down under his duvet.

'I used your toothpaste,' he says as he climbs into bed beside me.

'As long as you didn't use my toothbrush…'

'Would I do that?'

'I don't know. I hardly know you.' I grin at him. But it's true, we hardly know each other. He could be like the serial killer in the book I'm reading, winning me over then chopping me up.

'Well, I wouldn't. Take it from me.' With that he wraps his arms around me and snuggles into my back, and soon, his breathing is gentle and soothing and I feel myself dozing, but not before I remember that we still haven't had *the* conversation.

166

Over a very late breakfast the next morning I attempt to bring up the subject. The subject I know must be discussed but am dreading.

'I've been thinking…'

'Yeah.' He throws a piece of bacon in his dog's direction and Kong moves like lightening to catch it before it hits the floor.

'Wow,' I can't help saying.

'Impressive for such a big dog.'

'Yes. It is.'

'You were saying…' he looks at me and smiles.

'Yeah, um…' Now I've brought it up I'm wondering if it's even worth discussing.

'Spit it out.' He winks at me. I wonder what he thinks I'm going to say.

'Yeah. Right. Um. Well, where to start.'

'At the beginning?'

'Yeah.' No, I'm not going to say it. 'Just thinking that I don't want to eat as much as I did yesterday, or drink that much either, cos I can feel the waistband on my leggings cutting in.' Not true at all, but he doesn't know that.

'Right. Well, that's up to you, but you should have said before I cooked you a mega breakfast.' He laughs. 'Is that it?'

'Yes.' No. But now's not the time.

'Okay, let's go for a walk and loosen your waistband for you a bit.' He grins, almost leers.

'Don't be so disgusting.' But I laugh, I can't help it.

Sixteen

After a long and very bracing walk along the beach we head back to the cottage. Thankfully it didn't freeze again overnight and the snow has thawed a little more since yesterday, but it is bitterly cold because of a sharp wind coming in from the sea.

As we enter the rear garden Kong makes a beeline for our snow sculptures and promptly pees on mine.

'Hey,' I call over to him, but he bounds away. 'Look at that, Noah.' I point to the base of the snowperson that's supposed to be me. 'He's only peed on mine. Look how stained it is but yours and his are clean.'

'Clean as the driven snow,' he mocks.

'Ha ha.'

'They've lasted well, but they are starting to collapse now.'

'Well, mine's had some help.' I'm joking of course, it's not like it matters.

'It's because he likes you.'

'He pees on me cos he likes me?'

'Yeah.' Noah kisses me and it's not just the cold that makes me shiver. 'Let's go inside and get warmed up.'

It's easy being with him. Lying together on the sofa, lying in his arms, lying in his bed. Easy and comfortable because I have no expectations. I just hope he doesn't. We have a few more days to enjoy ourselves before we have to go back to reality. I've decided I'm not going to have the conversation about there being no future for us, no expectation on my part and no disappointment either, just yet. Why spoil the fun? For now I'm going to enjoy this little fantasy in our own little snow world in Christmas Cottage. Even the name suggests it is a fairy tale. A nice one.

We're on the sofa now, I'm knitting and he's reading my bath book.

'I'm surprised you brought this to read,' he says,' Considering you were going to be on your own.'

'Yeah. I just grabbed it from the bookshelves at home; it was one of Cliff's. He liked thrillers.'

'Have you finished it?'

'Not quite. I was whipping through it but then I started getting distracted.' I grin at him.

'Yeah. I've read the last chapter. I wouldn't bother if I was you.'

'You cheat. You're not supposed to do that.'

He gets up. 'I'm going to make myself some pasta. I assume you don't want any since your outburst this morning about eating too much.'

'It wasn't an outburst, I just said I didn't want to overeat today.' I wish I'd never said it because I am feeling hungry now, the cold always makes me hungry.

He shrugs and pads off to the kitchen area where he starts clattering pans around and I attempt to concentrate on my knitting. Fair Isle is not something you can do when someone is talking to you.

It takes him about ten minutes before he lays the table with cutlery and mats and a jug of water. My mouth waters. I wish I'd swallowed my pride and just agreed to have some. I'll have to wait at least an hour now until I can make myself something to eat or I'll just look weird.

'It's ready,' he calls over.

I nod and smile and make a show of concentrating on counting stitches, but I watch him out of the corner of my eye. He's taking two bowls over to the table.

'Are you going to join me?'

I turn and look over. He's smiling. Grinning. Smirking.

'I know you don't want it, but I made you some anyway.'

I can't get over to that table fast enough. So fast that even Kong jumps up in alarm before realising it's only me and settling back down. He's made my new favourite; Bolognese pasta with pesto. My favourite and he doesn't even know it.

❄❄❄

And so the next few days are filled with walking on the beach, cooking for each other, going to the garage mini-mart for milk and a newspaper when we need to, one trip to the pub and one trip back into town to see a quirky romcom in the local tiny cinema. He even tells me he enjoys it and when I nod and tell him he doesn't have to say that, he assures me it's true.

'I'm just an old romantic at heart,' he says, pulling me closer as we head for the car park behind the Co-op. 'Just because I haven't seen a film like that before doesn't mean I didn't enjoy it.'

I can't decide whether he's joking or not. Cliff hated romcoms, or anything that wasn't action packed with multiple kills, he said it was because of the games industry but I think it was probably the other way around. He was in the games industry because he liked action packed killing films.

'You've gone quiet.'

'Yeah, just thinking. Don't feel you have to agree with my taste in films.'

'I don't. I genuinely enjoyed it. And she went for the nice guy over the bastard. Made me feel a lot better.' He laughs, but behind the laugh there's a tone of sadness.

'I think it's mostly the case in real life too. What woman in her right mind wants a bastard?' Whoops, I think that might have been tactless, but it's too late now.

'Yeah,' he says, opening the car door for me.

He's the perfect company, the perfect distraction from all my woes. There are times when I completely forget why I'm here, completely forget about Cliff, about Susannah. I'm carefree. There are times when I think he is too, and that he almost forgets about Vic.

It's our last evening together, the perfect Saturday night, we've eaten early in the pub, we've walked Kong until he refuses to stay out any longer. We're back in the cottage drinking a toast to ourselves and our lovely time, bemoaning the fact that it must all end tomorrow. According to the information folder we have to vacate by 10am, although as Noah pointed out, it's not very likely that we have to stick to that too strictly because it's not as though anyone will be rushing in to clean for the next holiday makers.

'To us,' he says, raising his glass to mine.

'To fun,' I say, perhaps a bit too pointedly.

A thin smile drifts across his face before he takes a sip of wine.

'To not being on Facebook.' He clinks glasses with me again.

'I'll drink to that.'

We both sit with our own thoughts. Perhaps now would be a good time to have the conversation. How shall I start it? What can I say? Should I leave it until tomorrow morning? I'll be sleeping in his bed tonight, lying in his arms, expecting something to remember all this by. If I say something now will I jeopardise that? Spoil it?

'How do you feel about me, us?' he says, pre-empting me.

'Um, what do you mean?'

'Us, you and me.'

'Well, it's been fun. It's really cheered me up. You've cheered me up.'

'Same here. Like I said before, when I saw you naked on the rug in front of the log burner, I thought all of my Christmases had come at once, and I was right.'

'Yeah, you and your pervy dog.' I roll my eyes in the most theatrical and exaggerated way.

'Where do we go from here?'

'Well,' I say, doing my best to misinterpret his question. 'There's a lovely big bed in that room there.' I point to his bedroom. 'And I, for one, am looking forward to some serious *last night in Christmas Cottage action.*'

He nods slowly. 'Yeah, me too.'

Hours later, after several bouts of serious action, when we're lying awake in each other's arms, I start the conversation, the one *I* must have.

'You've been the best thing that's happened to me in a long time.'

'You too.' He kisses me on the forehead and cuddles me tightly.

'And,' I start, before giving him a quick kiss on the lips. 'I don't want you to feel pressured or worry that you're stuck with me. I mean, I think if you had the chance you'd like to get back with Vic. And it sounds as though, from what you said she said about Liam, that you might have a chance.'

I hope he doesn't get back with Vic because I don't think she's good enough for him.

'Yeah,' he says, with a faraway sound to his voice.

'Come on, admit it, if she was waiting for you at home and begged you to take her back, you would.' I want him to say no, I want him to say never, so why am I pushing him so much?

'Yes, probably,' he says, his voice scratchy with sleep.

'You know you would.' Why am I pushing him?

'Yes.'

'And I think you should.' No, I don't. 'If that's what you want. You should build your future with Vic, if you want to, and not feel even the slightest bit guilty about me.' Guilty, that's not the right word.

'Right.'

'What I mean is, don't give me a second thought. Let's be perfectly honest here, we're each other's rebound fling, aren't we? You're the first man I've been with, had any desire to be with, since my husband died and, despite my initial reservations, I couldn't have chosen better.' I follow this with a quick kiss. 'It must be the same for you.'

'I guess,' he says. 'It has been very enjoyable and you're a great girl, sorry, woman. And I'd like to see how things are between Vic and Liam, see if she wants me now.'

'Good. We're in agreement.'

'Yeah.'

Then I hear the soft, regular breathing that lets me know he's asleep, so I snuggle down and go to sleep myself but not before feeling slightly, if only momentarily, second best to Vic.

❄❄❄

I'm the first to wake up in the morning. I watch him as he sleeps, so now I'm the creepy cliché. He's nice. He's smiley and helpful. And kind. Cliff was kind but he wasn't always nice, he said it was because he had to play the hardnosed business man and sometimes he forgot to turn it off. Maybe Noah isn't quite so nice at work, though I can't imagine it.

He's also very attractive. He's got thick, slightly unkempt hair, and it's dark too. I like that. He's only shaved a few times since we've been here so I've seen his face smooth and stubbly and every stage in between, and I like them all. He's tall and looks lean, but without clothes he's really quite muscular. I like that.

And he can cook. And, and, which is possibly more important, he can clear up after himself too.

I'm finding him far too attractive. It's a good job we've had the no strings attached conversation. I don't need a full-on relationship at the moment, I have enough to focus on. I think the same goes for him too.

Oh, but it would be so easy to slip into something serious.

Then get my heart broken.

'Are you watching me sleep?' He grins.

'Yeah. Creepy and a cliché, I know. But the precedent has already been set.'

He laughs. 'Our last few hours together,' he says, leaning over and kissing me. 'What shall we do?'

An hour later when we've given each other something to remember our time together by, we climb out of his bed, wrap ourselves up and cook up everything in the fridge.

Then we shower and dress and take Kong for a long, long walk on the beach.

'Imagine how amazing this place must be in the summer, or even the spring,' he says, shading his eyes against today's strong sun which is rapidly melting the remnants of snow.

'Imagine how much is must cost.' I laugh, but I could kick myself for saying it. He must think I'm obsessed with money, especially after hearing me bleat on so much about my situation.

He throws a stick for Kong.

'Apparently,' he starts, 'This beach is a bit off the beaten track and it doesn't get crowded even in the height of summer.'

'Like a little secret cove.' A fleeting image of the two of us lying on towels, a beach umbrella poked in the sand between us, a champagne and strawberries picnic, passes across my mind.

'Kong would love the sea. Hopefully it would be a bit warmer in the summer.'

'Would you go in?' I imagine him striding out in swimwear. I try not to imagine that.

'To be honest, probably only paddle, or maybe go in wearing a wetsuit. I don't delude myself about the temperature of the UK seas. This is not the Mediterranean, it's the Atlantic.'

'Yes,' I agree, remembering many holidays as a child where I'd braved our seas, my teeth chattering, my fingers and toes almost blue from the cold even when the sun was shining. Cliff always insisted on holidaying abroad. He co-owned a villa with Susannah in Portugal. We had to play awkward negotiating games so we could go when it wouldn't clash with her. If we wanted the boys to come — not that I particularly wanted them to come because, well-schooled by Susannah, they hated me — we had to go in the school holidays. The villa was stunning, a white stucco building surrounded by a lush green garden, its infinity pool overlooked the sea. I can't go now of course, not without Cliff. I suppose Susannah takes her fiancé there now, with the boys. No doubt the boys love him because Susannah will have taught them to.

'Do you think you'd come here in the summer?' Noah's face is serious in question.

I shrug. Would I? I don't know.

'It's nearly noon, we should get back and pack up. We've probably taken the piss enough already.' I divert the conversation and never give him an answer.

❄❄❄

It doesn't take long to pack everything up at the cottage. I just stuff my clothes into my case. We divide what's left in the fridge between us, but there isn't much. We wipe down the fridge shelves, leave everything neat and tidy. We stop at stripping the beds because I know Mrs Lane pays someone to clean and wouldn't want to interfere with their regime.

'I'll bring my car up to the front door and load it up,' he says. 'Then I'll bring yours up too.'

176

I stand at the window, see him back his car out of the space and drive it to the cottage entrance. He's already put all his bags outside on the path and he loads them into the back. Kong joins me at the window, watching his master, then he leans his head against my leg as if he's saying goodbye.

'I'll need your keys,' Noah says, coming back in.

'Oh yes. Right. They must be in my room.' It's days since I've seen them, many days since I attempted to move my car, when the snow was deep and frozen.

I'm rummaging around in my room, in my handbag, in my bedside drawer when Kong barks, long and loud.

'Shush, boy,' Noah says, his voice calm and authoritative, but Kong barks again, several times. Then he starts to growl.

There's a frenzied knock on the door, probably the cleaners, good job we're just leaving.

I find my keys, kicked just under the bed, I grab them. I'm about to march into the living room when I hear Noah speak, but it's not to me.

'Vic. What the hell are you doing here?'

Seventeen

I creep towards the door and spy through the gap. I can see her quite clearly, her back and side profile. If she turns she'll see me, but for now she's entirely focused on Noah.

'You could be more gracious. It's taking me hours and hours to get here. A train, then a taxi. Have you any idea how far from civilisation this place is? Even the taxi driver didn't know where it was. I had to Google it for him.' She lets out a long breath and so do I.

'Right,' Noah says, glancing over at me. He looks uncomfortable, miserable. As well he might. Cornered. Trapped.

In the corner of the room, where he's retreated to, Kong growls; it's long, low and deep.

'I see you brought him with you.'

'Of course I did, why wouldn't I?'

'Oh yes,' she says, tossing her hair, as though she's suddenly remembered that with Noah comes Kong. Kong growls again.

Vic's more beautiful in the flesh. I knew she would be. Her hair is long and silky, a pale blonde, it swishes from side to side when she talks. She's wearing a cream ski pants and jacket ensemble – she is definitely a woman who wears ensembles, not clothes – no home knitted jumpers for her.

'How did you even know where I was?'

'Yolanda. Though it took me a lot of texts and phone calls to get her to tell me. In the end, my charm worked.' She smiles and perfect white teeth almost split her face in half; that's a wide smile. 'Now I'm here, aren't you going to say hello properly?' She steps into his arms, wraps her own around his waist and pushes her head, her lips, up towards his. He pre-empts her and kisses the top of her head, gives her a quick hug then steps away.

Is it all for my benefit, because he sees me watching?

'How's Liam?'

'Old news.' Vic waves away the questions as though swatting a fly.

'What about his leg? I heard it's bad.'

'No. No. Sprained. Badly. He can't ski. He wanted to come home. I had to come too, someone had to help him. Honestly, what a baby. I told him Noah would have just got on with it. Waited it out. But not Liam. You know what he's like. Sulked until he got his own way.'

'Poor Liam.'

'Yes. Well. We're over. Done. I've realised what a fool I've been. I don't know how I could have left you the way I did. You're twice the man he is.' She pauses, a nervous smile on her face, before continuing, 'In every department.'

I feel a little sick. I feel humiliated even though I know it's not Noah's fault, it's not even perfect Vic's fault, she wasn't to know I was here.

'I'm dying for a drink, can you put the kettle on? Where's the bathroom? But even as she's asking, she's striding towards my door and I step softly back.

'No, it's here. This door.'

'Oh, ta.' I hear her turn on her high heel boots and stomp away.

Noah comes towards the door, towards me, whispers, 'I'm sorry. I had no idea.'

I force a little smile. 'No problem. We were fun, but that's all we were. You make it up with Vic.'

He smiles back at me, nods slowly then moves away.

'What a lovely bathroom, that bath, well, wow. Is that kettle boiled yet?' Vic asks as she bursts out of the bathroom, *my* bathroom.

'No. No. There's nothing to make anything with. I've had to clear everything up. I was just leaving. I'd just finished packing the car when you arrived. I have to leave, right now.'

I'm back spying around the door again as I watch her stomp over to the sofa and flop down. She's sitting in *my* spot on *my* sofa. Good job I picked up my knitting bag just before she came and stuffed it in my case.

'Oh,' she says with a sigh. 'I've had nothing since breakfast. And I'm exhausted. This place is so remote. How have you stood it on your own? Can't you go and at least bring some tea and milk in?'

'Not really. I need to leave.'

'But surely they won't mind if you just stay another half hour, they won't even know, will they?'

'I'm already here much later than I should be.' I can hear the urgency, the nervousness in his voice.

It's starting to get cold in the cottage. We let the fire die down last night, the heating has gone off and even though it's not as cold outside as it was, it's getting cold in here. I shiver and pull on my coat, grab my handbag and sling it over my shoulder.

I yank open my bedroom door and stride out.

I see Vic flinch at the noise then watch the shock register on her face at seeing me. The colour drains from Noah's cheeks. He looks from me to Vic and back again.

'Oh, I didn't realise you had company, Mr Steele. I thought you were here alone.'

'Um, yes. I was here alone. This is Vic and this is…'

'Mrs Sutton,' I jump in. Neither Vic nor I move to shake hands, we barely smile at each other, Vic certainly doesn't get off the sofa.

'Everything seems to be in order. I'll authorise a full refund on your deposit.'

Kong leaps up and gallops towards me, nuzzles his big head into the side of my leg. Without thinking, I pat him and stroke his ears. Vic's eyes widen.

'Such a friendly dog,' I say.

'Is he? Why did you have to pay a deposit?' she asks Noah who glances at me in alarm. 'It's just a holiday rental, isn't it? There's not usually a deposit.'

'We take a deposit for pets,' I tell her, my voice soft and sweet. 'Sadly, we've learnt the hard way.'

'Oh. Right. Well he…' She points at Kong who responds with a quick bark. '…is very well behaved. Aren't you?'

Kong's reply to that is to nudge me again to pat him.

'He's certainly very friendly.'

Vic grimaces, and for a moment it spoils her beautiful face.

'Anyway,' I continue. 'The weather is being kind for you today. Do you have far to go?'

'Yes. Miles. And I've only just got here. I'm dying for a cup of tea. Could we just do that before we go?'

Noah looks at me, there's a tiny little headshake; he just wants to get away, leave, take Vic with him and end this uncomfortable charade.

'I'm sorry,' I say, with a smile. 'The cleaning team will be here soon and they're paid by the hour.'

'Hey, come on, Vic. Once we're on the M5 we'll pull into the services, you can have whatever you like. My treat.'

'Aren't I the lucky one.' Vic rises up from the sofa and stomps over to the front door. She pulls it open. 'Come on then, the sooner we get going the sooner I can have a cup of tea. Maybe we could find somewhere a bit nicer before we hit the motorway. What do you think, Noah?'

He glances back at me and smiles while Vic actually taps her foot as she waits for him. Soon they're out of the door, Kong jumping into his place in the back and Vic climbing into the passenger seat, where I usually sit, while I watch from the window.

They drive off.

Noah and Kong are no longer in my life.

And he didn't even get a chance to bring my car up for me.

Or say goodbye.

I go into my room and slump down on the bed. I feel sad. Unreasonably, irrationally sad. I had imagined a long, fond farewell. Something to remember each other by, even if it was only a few quick words and a long sweet kiss. I feel cheated. Now the only image I have is of Vic's hair flicking and swishing as she walked away, Noah in tow.

I gather up my things and drag them into the sitting room. I drop them on the floor. It makes sense to get my car first rather than drag my case through the slush.

I pull my car up outside the door and head back into the cottage.

I gasp.

Noah is waiting. He's alone.

'I'm sorry about all that. I had no idea…'

'I know you didn't. Where is she now?'

'Just up the lane. I told her I had to give you the key, that she'd made me forget.'

'Ah. I have to return mine to Mrs Lane, via my friend.'

'Yes, similar.' He shakes his head. 'I didn't come to talk about the key. I came to say goodbye.'

'I know.'

'I just want you to know that I had the best Christmas I've had in a long time. You were just what I needed.'

'Me too.' I haven't fully realised just how true this is until now.

'I know we said no strings and all that, and I'm good with that, but I've loved every minute I've spent with you.' He steps forward. So do I.

'Me too.'

The kiss goes on and on and if Vic wasn't up the lane, sitting in Noah's car, I think we'd be jumping back into bed now.

He grips me in his arms, wrapping them around me so tightly that it feels as though he'll never let go. I rest my head on his chest, hear his heart beating out a fast rhythm, know that mine is doing the same.

'Bye, Ruby Sutton.' He pulls himself away.

'Bye, Noah Steele.' I watch him leave, he doesn't look back, he just keeps on walking, so I turn away and focus on collecting up my luggage.

Once I've packed my car, I take one last look around to check we've left nothing behind. And, other than our snow sculptures, which have already collapsed into distorted heaps, we haven't. Soon they will be gone and it will be as though we were never here.

When I finally drive up the lane myself, the only signs of Noah are his tyre tracks in the slush, and they will soon be gone because the sun is shining and it's definitely warming up.

❄❄❄

The journey home doesn't take as long as the journey down. It's daylight, it's not snowing. I don't have the radio on; I don't want to be distracted from my thoughts, my memories. Even Kong's pervert action with the towel makes me smile. I'm filing and sorting my fond memories away in my mind, the first kiss, the second kiss, the way he made me feel, the way we fitted together, the food we cooked together, for each other, the blue cupcakes, our snow sculptures. I can take these memories out and look at them whenever I like. If I like.

Each mile that passes between Christmas Cottage and home, pushes the last two weeks with Noah further into the past. Into another life.

❄❄❄

Back home the house feels cold and empty, unwelcoming. I override the computer timer and whack the heating on, then drag my bags in from the car.

There's some post on the doormat, mostly junk. I fling it on the giant kitchen island. I check my phone and go through my emails; there are several from Mum, with photos. They're on the beach again, hot, sunny smiles staring back at me. What a contrast to my own Christmas, so white with snow, so cold. There are several messages from Zara telling me that she still hasn't had the baby yet. I message back and ask her what she's playing at. Her response is several rolling eye emojis.

I put the kettle on for a cup of tea, or maybe I'll have hot chocolate, and wonder if perfect Vic has had her cup of tea yet? Are they still on the motorway because of their stop?

I settle back down with my hot chocolate, start to thumb through the photo gallery on my phone smiling at Mum's photos. Then it dawns on me, I have not taken one photo while I've been away. None of the cottage, none of the surroundings, none of Noah. I can't quite believe I never took a selfie of us together. Was that some kind of Freudian thing? All I have are the photos he took of us the day we built the snow sculptures. I study them carefully, expanding our faces, especially his. We're laughing. If I delete these photos, I will have no evidence of our rebound fling other than my memories. It has to be done. If this holiday has taught me anything, it's not to look back, only forward. I select them and press delete.

And we never exchanged phone numbers either.

I suppose if I really needed to get in touch I could via his dad's business card.

If I can find it.

But, really, why would I need to contact Noah? He's with Vic now.

Eighteen

I'm back at work. It feels as though I've never been away. It's the fifth of January and for a lot of people, like me, it is the first day back. We shut down over Christmas and a lot of people save their holidays to extend their break.

The trouble with such a long break is that there are literally hundreds of emails to go through. We all sit for the first hour or so diligently scrolling through, discarding the rubbish, answering the urgent ones, filing the others. It's so tedious. Then someone gets up and mentions a coffee break and there's a mass exodus for our break-out room.

Everyone is talking about their Christmases. I listen politely, smile genuinely and don't tell anyone about Noah. I haven't even told Zara about Noah, well not the important bits, and we had a long conversation on the phone last night, though it was mostly dominated by Zara's inability to give birth yet. I'm popping round after work to drop off the key to Christmas Cottage.

By the end of the day Christmas seems even more remote than it did last night. If I was fanciful, which of course I'm not, I could almost believe that I imagined the whole thing: him, his humongous dog. After all, I have no evidence, no proof, not now I've deleted those photos.

Unless you count my memories, how I felt when I was with him.

'Penny for them?' Zara says.

'What's that?'

'You were miles away. Did something happen down in Christmas Cliché Cottage?'

'Why are you calling it that?' Have I said something? Have I inadvertently let slip how I caught him watching me sleep, how he caught me doing the same? My telling him he was a creepy cliché, him laughingly agreeing.

'Well, all you've said is that you were snowed in, no phone signal and you built a snowman. Oh, and you just smiled then too. One of those special smiles.' She nudges me with her elbow.

'Snow sculpture,' I correct, a bit too quickly.

'Snowman, just because it was a man, woman and dog combo doesn't make it anything special.'

'No. Well, it's melted now, so it's certainly not special.' I laugh, kiss her goodbye and leave, so she can get on with feeding her hungry brood, and hopefully, give birth soon. I've played down my interactions with Noah, implying that he left as soon as he could.

Back home it's just me. Alone again. At least the heating has come on. I make myself a cheese toasty and sit up to the island to eat it. Once done, I flick through the post I flung there when I came home yesterday. I open all the bills, line them up, check the amounts – does the heating really cost that much? At least I don't need to take any further action because they're all direct debits. Maybe I should close off some of the rooms and switch their radiators off. But it's probably this barn of a kitchen where most of the heating goes, it's so big, and the ceiling so high that it takes a lot of heating, and that means a lot of fuel and that means a lot of cost.

I drop the envelopes in the recycling and come back to the island to clear away my plate. That's when I notice the white envelope with black spider scrawl on it, almost invisible against the white marble worktop.

I recognise the writing.

My heart sinks.

Susannah. What the hell can she want?

I make myself a cup of tea before I read it.

There are three pages stapled together, but her scrawl is large so there aren't actually that many words.

Dear Ruby

I hope this letter finds you well and Christmas wasn't too sad and upsetting for you.

'Fuck you,' I yell before continuing.

I know I found it terribly difficult, especially when it came to giving the boys their presents.

'Fuck you, you bitch,' I scream. How I wish she was here. Maybe I'll ring her up and give her a mouthful.

I can hardly believe that this is the second Christmas without our darling Clifford.

I wonder if her soon to be new husband knows that's how she refers to her long-time ex? I stop reading. Why don't I just throw her letter in the bin, or better still burn it? If I can find some matches, I can burn it in the sink and never know what other daggers she's going to stick in me. I start hunting around in drawers for a box of matches or a lighter or anything to set fire to the bitch's letter. Nothing. The hob is electric, maybe if I switch it on I could drop the letter on it and leave it until it catches fire. I flick the switch and watch the hob light up bright red. I grab the letter, drop it on the hob and wait.

At first nothing, then finally it catches, tiny flames lick at the corners and the top sheet lifts up.

£10,000 flashes before my eyes.

I snatch the letter off the hob, dash to the sink and run the tap, dabbing the corners of the letter under the water. The smell of singed paper fills the kitchen.

Although wet, and with her scrawl blurred, I can still read on.

Although you can live it in until you die Clifford left the house to the boys. I can't believe that you really want to stay there on your own. It's such a big place, far too big for one person and, as per the terms of Clifford's will, you can never take another partner and live there, so you'll always be alone. Obviously the boys are far too young to need the house yet and until they are, the house is under my management.

'It's under mine, actually,' I tell the kitchen. 'And you, Susannah Bitchface, have no authority over it while I live here.'

I can't imagine how lonely you must feel rattling around in that place. So, I wondered if you might be interested in my proposition? I am willing to pay you £10,000 to move out. This would be a full and final settlement and would mean that you can move on with your life.

Let me know as soon as possible as this is a time limited offer.

Kind regards

Susannah Sutton

I sit looking at the letter for longer than I want to, I reread it several times. I wish Mum and Dad were here but they're not due back for another few days and this isn't a conversation to have over the phone.

How do I respond?

Time limited offer! Who the hell does she think she is? Worse still, who the hell does she think I am? Some poor little waif who would be grateful for her pay out? I won't be accepting her offer. I will not be beholden to her.

What intrigues me just as much is why? Why does she want me out and why now? In the last two years she's never once hinted that she wants me gone, quite the contrary, she even told me she was glad that I was caretaking her sons' property for them.

She's really stuck the knife in, digging the wound deep and rubbing salt in it. I sting all over, inside and out.

I want to ring her; I want to scream and shout and swear and be abusive. I won't. I know that I will just look and feel a fool while she waits quietly until I've finished, I'll almost be able to hear the smug little smile on her bitchface.

Okay. Calm down.

What's the best thing to do here? I *will* be leaving this house, just not yet. I'm saving as fast as I can until I can get a deposit. I have a job of my own so I should be okay for a mortgage. I feel bitter because I put my everything into this house and while it wasn't much compared to the actual cost, it was everything I had. All the equity from my flat. And it was considerably more than £10,000. She's a cheeky bitch.

I'm not replying. Why the hell should I?

I don't sleep well, how can I?

As soon as I get up I race down to the kitchen and check her letter. There is no date, but the postmark on the envelope is over a week old. Good, I suspect that's already annoyed her. She doesn't know I've been away and is probably already assuming I'm ignoring her. I've decided to wait until Mum and Dad are back and discuss it with them before I tell her where to go.

Sod Susannah. She can wait.

I wish I had Noah's phone number, he heard enough about my situation and was suitably sympathetic that I think he might be a good sounding board.

Oh well.

***

Mum and Dad flew back today from Australia. I'm so pleased. Although I won't be able to see them until tomorrow evening because they're jet lagged, tired and just need to go to sleep. Mum rang me from the airport while they were waiting for a taxi to take them home. I'd offered to get them but they know I need to go to work, so refused.

I'm spending this evening sorting out my knitting. Quite a feat. I was so distracted by Noah that I've neglected my Fair Isle. Just the thought of his name makes my stomach flip – I have to stop thinking about him like this, he's no doubt happily making up for lost time with Vic. And why shouldn't he? Good luck to him.

I'm going through each line on the knitting pattern and ticking it off. It's taking me a long time but I'm finally making headway and manage to knit a line. I had thought I'd finish this while I was away, maybe even wear it. If it hadn't been for Noah...

I get to the end of the line and finish, not much to show for a whole evening but at least I know where I am. As I'm folding it away and tidying up my knitting bag I find the card Noah gave me, his dad's business card. I'll keep that safe because I might need to use it, it's possible I might be in need of a mortgage sooner than I anticipated.

❄❄❄

I'm having a lovely evening with my parents; they've shown me all their photos and we've had a good old catch up. My niece and nephew have grown so big and loved the presents I sent with Mum and Dad.

'I can't believe how much they've grown,' I say again, scrutinising the photos on my mum's phone again.

'I know. They're growing so fast. Next year you must come with us.'

'I will. Yes, I will.' I mean it too. My little holiday with Noah, my little unexpected romance, has made me feel as though I've turned a corner, as though there is a point to life.

'I must say,' Mum begins, 'I was concerned about you, miles from anywhere and on your own. And when I saw how badly Devon was hit by all that snow, I was really worried. But you look perkier now than you did before Christmas, so perhaps it's done you some good.'

I smile. 'It was fine, Mum. Great, in fact. You don't need to worry about me.' I'd love to tell them about Noah, about Kong, but they might get the wrong impression and think that I might be starting a new relationship, not just having a fling. I think Mum and Dad don't really hold with flings, not that they've ever said that, not in so many words. Just as they never said they didn't approve of Cliff, but I know they were very worried about the age difference, even though it really wasn't that much, only seventeen years and four months if anyone was counting. Not that it matters now.

Mum rolls her eyes, tuts at my comment about her not having to worry about me and puts the kettle on again for a cup of tea. This will be our third since I arrived.

'How's work?' Dad asks.

'Yeah, okay, you know. Fine.' There's nothing much to say about work, it's not especially exciting but it's not taxing either. It passes the time and pays the bills and frankly, that's all I want from work right now.

Dad nods sagely. That's his main topic of conversation dealt with. Now would be a good time to show them the letter, it's been burning a hole in my handbag all evening.

'There's been a development…' I start.

Dad frowns. 'At work?'

'No, no, nothing to do with work. No, I've had a letter… from Susannah.'

Mum flinches at the mention of Susannah. 'Oh?'

I pull the letter out and hand it over.

'Terrible writing,' Mum says as she and Dad huddle together to read it.

'Well,' Dad says, shaking his head. 'What's brought that on?'

'She wants to live in it,' Mum spits.

'Nooo,' Dad and I chorus.

'Bet she does,' Mum says, nodding her head. 'Mark my words. What's her place like?'

'I've never actually been in it. Been outside. It looks quite grand. Though Cliff did once mention that it's not as big as our place.'

'She wants to live in it,' Mum says again, absolutely convinced she is right.

'No. Although maybe they're feeling a bit cramped now that Adam has moved into her house and the boys are getting bigger. And I have a pool of course and Cliff did say that Susannah was envious of it.' Not that I can afford to heat it, so it sits full of cold water and is never used. 'Either that or someone has offered to buy it at a very high price.' I pause. 'No, it wouldn't be that, nothing is as good an investment long-term as property.' Cliff told me that often enough.

'She wants to live in it,' Mum says, her voice stronger now.

'Or maybe she's found a tenant who's willing to pay her a lot of money to live there. Now that's an investment. Increasing capital and rental income.' That's what Cliff had said to me about my flat, the best reasons for keeping it. Shame I didn't take his advice.

'In either case,' says Dad with a little grin. 'She can pay you fairly to push off.'

'D-a-a-d,' I admonish. 'I'm not taking her money.'

'Then you're a fool.' Mum looks at me with steel in her eyes. 'A real fool.'

Nineteen

After a very long discussion with Mum and Dad, we make a plan.

They've persuaded me that I should take the money.

'Sod dignity,' Mum said. 'There's no dignity in being poor.'

I'm not poor, but I'm not rich either. I never married Cliff for his money, despite what Susannah thinks and I don't want to prove her right by accepting her offer. But, as Mum pointed out I saved long and hard for the deposit on my flat, and *they* contributed so it's only fair I get that back. It feels wrong, it feels mercenary.

'Mercenary!' Mum shouts. 'Are you joking. She's the one being mercenary.'

So now, I have a plan.

I'm not going to reply to Susannah, I'm going to wait it out and see what happens. I'm not going to ask her for more money because that would just make me look either greedy or desperate, or both. I'm neither. Dad advised me to let the ball be in her court – he does like his sporting metaphors does Dad.

He then follows this by saying I have nothing to lose. I point out I could lose the £10,000 that they've just persuaded me to accept because she might just rescind her offer. It is, as she pointed out in her letter, time limited.

'She won't rescind it,' Mum says, her voice confident and sage-like.

Now we've made the *waiting* plan, I'm nervous. That money would boost my deposit savings considerably, I could just accept it now. Then it's over and done with.

'Do you think it makes me look grabby and greedy?'

'No,' Mum and Dad chorus before Mum adds,' It makes *her* look grabby and greedy.'

So there's the plan: Wait it out.

❄❄❄

As it turns out I don't have to wait very long; the second missive from Susannah arrives less than a week later. As I pick up her scrawled envelope from the doormat, I notice my hand shaking.

'Stop it,' I bark at myself, then hear my voice echo around the marble-floored hallway. So grand. So empty.

I take the letter through to the kitchen, make myself a cup of tea and sit up to the island. I flick the letter over, desperate, yet afraid to open it. I could leave it. I could take it to Mum and Dad's and get them to open it. It's Saturday and they usually spend the morning reading the papers and taking a long, leisurely breakfast, so I'm pretty sure they'll be in.

No. Open it.

I open it. This time she doesn't bother with any niceties or any bitchy comments or pretend empathy over the loss of my husband, this time the letter is just a few words:

Would £20,000 do it?

There's no greeting, no signature. Mum's right, Susannah is the desperate one.

I ring my parents and we agree that £20,000 is a very generous offer and I should accept it. That way I'm not out of pocket too much as this is almost as much as the equity from the sale of my flat that I put into our home. Mine and Cliff's.

I can't bear to ring her, just hearing her voice will be horrendous, and even texting her is too close, too personal. I'll write her a letter later, that's how she's communicating, so that's how it is.

It'll be strange not living here. Even though I haven't been happy here alone since Cliff died. It's definitely time to move on, to make my own life, to put the past behind me. I'll never forget Cliff, never forget how lovely he was, how kind, how we loved each other, the plans we made for the future, but that's in the past. And I will be taking some of the furniture from here, though not all. I need to make it clear to Susannah that the furniture I don't want will be her problem, as I don't think I'll be able to afford anywhere that can accommodate a sixteen-seater table and a giant-size four poster bed. Both of these were Cliff's idea, he insisted we'd need to entertain on a large scale, maybe we would have done if he'd still been alive, but we hardly did before he died. And the bed was a just a sheer indulgence. I hate it and haven't slept in it since that Christmas Day. When I could sleep I slept on the sofa and then I moved into one of the guest rooms. I might take some of the furniture from the guest rooms, it's far more normal.

There's one room I never go in, never. It's the one that would have been the nursery; thank God we never bought any furniture for it, never decorated it. It looks out over the rear garden and it's a really sweet room just off the master bedroom. I imagine Susannah using it as her dressing room, assuming she is moving in.

Maybe I'll get a dog when I move. Not a giant one like Kong. Kong. Now I'm thinking about Noah and feeling guilty about it for all sorts of reasons, not least because I'm standing here in Cliff's house and also because Noah is back with the perfect Vic, which is what he always wanted.

I hope they're happy.

I'll get a small dog, perhaps. Something that is happy to be left alone all day while I'm at work. Do such dogs exist? I'll see how it goes. If I have a dog I'll need a garden and I was imagining myself living in a flat, mainly because it won't have a garden. I'm not a big gardener, not a gardener at all in fact and living here has made that even more the case what with the team that keep the grounds here so well-tended.

Maybe no dog then.

❄❄❄

It's Monday morning and I wake up feeling awful. My throat is so sore that I can barely swallow. It's still dark outside and when I check the time it's 5am. I stagger all the way down to the kitchen where I shiver and shake and not just because the heating is off. I get myself a glass of water and some paracetamol and go back to bed, where I shiver and shake some more. I do finally fall asleep but when I awake, I feel worse.

I ring work. I'm sure they think I'm putting it on, I sound so husky, but I really do feel awful.

Whatever I've got, lasts a week.

And that is my excuse for not replying to Susannah straightaway as I had intended.

Which works to my advantage, which I feel guilty about, when she offers me £30,000 to go away. She's even put her phone number on the letter. She's hand delivered the letter too because I cannot see a postmark on the envelope, or even a stamp. She's also added that the offer expires by midnight tomorrow. Talk about dramatic. But I'm not going to risk it.

Even though this is the first day I've been out of bed for any length of time I decide to contact her. I hold my phone in my hand and tap in her number, then, just before I press call, I chicken out and end the call. Maybe I'll just text her. Later.

I make myself a meal of cereal and toast, although it's mid-afternoon. Mum has called the doctor's surgery for me, mainly because I need a sick certificate for work as I've been off sick for too long.

When the phone rings I jump, especially when I see it is from an unknown number. Could this be Susannah? Is she ringing me to hound me? If it is her, she *is* desperate. Of course not, my phone would recognise her number.

I answer it. It's the surgery, and there's no need for me to come in, a nasty bug is prevalent at the moment so they'll send a certificate in the post.

After my meal I haul myself back to bed and sleep deeply.

It's pitch black when my phone rings and I wake suddenly, jumping around and grabbing it. I expect it to be Mum, but it's not.

It's her. Susannah.

'Are you getting my letters?'

'Sorry?' I say, my voice groggy from sleep.

'I said, are you getting my letters?'

'Um.' I can't think straight.

'I know you got today's, I put it through the letterbox myself. You could have the decency to at least contact me, even if your answer is no.'

'It's not,' I manage.

'Not what?'

'It's not no.' Even though I am feeling a lot better my voice is still terribly husky and I unintentionally cough into the phone. 'Sorry,' I mumble. 'I'm ill.'

'Ah. So. Does that mean you accept my offer.'

'Um,' I'm not stalling, I'm just still half asleep.

'It's full and final, you've pushed me to my limit.' Her tone is condescending and snooty, typical Susannah.

'Why do you want me out?'

There's silence on the line and I suspect she's deciding whether to tell me the truth. Cliff always said that Susannah didn't like telling people too much because she liked to be the only one with the full picture, the full details. It meant she had control, power. He said she could be incredibly economical with the facts when it suited her, but I think the answer she gives is probably one of her more expansive and honest ones.

'The boys would like to live there. It's bigger than our house and now that Adam is living with us, we need extra space. And there's the pool...' Her voice trails off, almost as if she's said too much. So Mum was right, she'll be amused when I tell her.

'Okay. I accept. You do the paperwork or whatever. But I won't move out until I have somewhere to go.'

'Fine. Good. But you won't get the money until you move out.'

I end the call before she can.

❄ ❄ ❄

My first day back at work is long and tiring. It appears that half the office has been off sick while I have and the other half are brewing this illness. I blame the aircon for circulating it around and around.

I flop through the front door and almost trip over the post. It's not a bill or junk mail, but a letter from Susannah's solicitor. I have only to sign the forms and return them, they're suggesting that I leave the property by the end of February or suggest another date if this is not convenient. Considering that we're only half way through January I think the end of April is more realistic as I have nowhere to go yet. I could always move in with Mum and Dad but I really don't want to do that.

Definitely time to start looking for a new home.

'Sorry, Cliff,' I say to the vaulted kitchen ceiling. 'It's time for me to move on.'

After a cheese-toasty meal, followed by a low-fat yogurt, I pluck up the courage and ring Noah's father. It's no good looking for a new home if you don't know what kind of mortgage you can get. I will, of course, check with my bank to see what they can offer too, but it's always wise to know what your options are.

Noah's father is charming, and very helpful and I won't even need to go and see him as we can do everything on the phone and by email. He tells me what

I'll need beforehand and we agree a date and time when I will ring him so that we can go through all the forms. He gives me a rough estimate of what he thinks I can afford and I'm pleasantly surprised to discover it's more than I expected – and Susannah's generous contribution has helped that along.

Before the call ends, I pluck up the courage to ask after Noah.

'Oh,' he says, 'You know Noah?'

'Yes, it was Noah who gave me your card. We met…on holiday.'

There's a long silence. I'm now wishing I hadn't mentioned Noah and certainly hadn't said I'd met him on holiday.

'You're the Christmas girl?'

I'm silent for a moment or two. 'Yes, I suppose I am.'

'Ah, right. I see.' I can hear a smile in his voice. 'He's here at the moment, shall I fetch him, would you like to speak to him.'

I panic. Alarm makes me gulp.

'Oh,' I say. 'No thank you. That really won't be necessary. Goodbye.' I end the call.

I feel sick and stupid and I now wonder if I can even ring his father back at our agreed date and time. Why did I mention Noah?

Because you wanted to know about him, a silly voice in my head says.

'No, I don't,' I say aloud. 'I definitely don't and I certainly don't want to hear about the perfect Vic.'

Twenty

Once the decision is made, time flies.

I find a flat in a new-build block and make an impulse purchase off plan. It's Mum's fault, she's with me and urges me on. But I love it and I have no regrets. But it won't be ready until after Easter.

I ring Susannah's solicitors and inform them of my proposed moving date. I don't ring Susannah because I don't want to have a confrontation with her, even on the phone. That's the date I'm moving out of mine and Cliff's home and that's all there is to it.

My phone rings ten minutes after I've rung the solicitor. It's a landline and my phone doesn't recognise it. It's sure to be Susannah. I decline the call.

The letter arrives from the solicitor a few days later saying Susannah is disappointed that the date is so late but accepts it. Phew. I'm glad I never answered that call, she might have talked me out of it. Tried to lure me with more money even though I already feel guilty for accepting anything at all from her but Mum and Dad keep telling me she's only paid me what's fair.

I surprise myself by applying for a promotion at work. It remains to be seen if I get it, but at least I'm trying. I feel as though I've moved forward a lot since Christmas, since my adventures at the cottage, such as they were. We didn't do anything exciting. We didn't do much at all. Walk the dog, cook, eat, make love. Maybe that should be have sex. Make lust.

I think about Noah a lot, too much. In unguarded moments my mind strays to the colour of his hair, the touch of his fingers on my skin, the smirk. Even the smirk. I pull myself up when I realise I'm doing it. It's silly. Some days I find I'm thinking about Noah more often than I do Cliff. On those days I'm annoyed and disappointed with myself.

I'm not stupid, I do realise I've fantasised Noah into something he's not. I know this. I do.

I force myself to ring his father, make sure I make no reference to Noah whatsoever and we go through the forms. He gets me a better mortgage than my bank offers. So I'm going with him. Even though we have several phone calls he doesn't mention Noah either.

One evening when I'm visiting Zara, holding her six-week-old daughter in my arms, the subject of the cottage comes up.

'I thought you told me that mix-up man left the cottage soon after you arrived?' There's an accusatory tone to her voice that I don't like.

'Yeah, he left before me.' That is true, just.

'Well, Mrs Lane thinks he was there the whole time. How did that work out?'

'Oh, yeah. It was fine. Plenty of room, we hardly saw each other.' I focus my eyes on the children's books on the coffee, the top one, *Thunderpants* has slid over to reveal *Liar, Liar, Pants on Fire* below.

'It didn't sound like nothing. She said the cottage was double booked and it was her brother's fault.'

'There was plenty of room, it really wasn't a problem,' I say again. I don't want to have this conversation; I don't want to talk about Noah. He's my secret. And I know my fantasy Noah is probably more amazing than the real person, but he's *my* fantasy. 'This little one is growing fast, how much does she weigh now?' I pointedly change the subject, stroking her baby's downy hair.

'I don't really know,' she says, smiling down at her. 'She's number four so I don't have time for weighing and clinics and stuff. She looks healthy, she feeds and sleeps well, that's enough for me.'

Phew, I've distracted her.

'Anyway, back to Mrs Lane. She said, can you give her a call?'

'Why?' Did we break something at the cottage? If we did, why does she think it was me and not him? I rack my brain trying to remember if I broke anything. I don't think I did. I'm not aware of him breaking anything either. Maybe Kong did chew something he shouldn't.

'She didn't say.' Zara grins, so I suspect that Mrs Lane did say.

'Did I tell you I have an interview for that job I applied for?'

'No. That's wonderful. How are you preparing?'

'Oh, you know, swotting up on all the right answers and also working on my presentation.'

'Urgh, I hate those. How long?'

'Just five minutes. I suppose they're keeping it short because they have to listen to so many of them.' I don't know how I'm even going to fill five minutes. I also don't know how many other people they are interviewing or who my competition is. I'm just going to do my best.

Zara stops and looks at me, frowning as she does so. 'What?'

'You seem different. More… what's the word? Chilled. You've seemed different since Christmas. That break away on your own, well, nearly on your own…' She winks at me and I don't like it. 'Well, I think it's done you some good. What happened when you were away?'

'Nothing much.' Liar, liar, pants on fire. 'Anyway, back to my interview, do you have any tips?'

'Be yourself,' Zara says as she nudges the *Pants on Fire* book towards me. 'Whoever that is.' She grins and I choose to ignore her.

❄❄❄

I don't ring Mrs Lane, the reason for not ringing her is not even rational. My time in the cottage is there in my fantasy world and I'd like that fantasy to be kept intact, not sullied by broken things or whatever Mrs Lane wants. When my phone rings two days later and I don't know the number, a landline, I assume it's her, and I reject the call. Then I put my phone on silent so that I won't hear it if she rings again. Which she does, twice more.

My interview the following week goes well, so well in fact that it makes me feel overconfident. I kid myself that the job is mine.

Mrs Lane rings twice more that same week. Well, I think it's her, it could be scammers telling me my internet is about to be cut off or my car's been in an accident – it's why I try not to answer unknown numbers. There used to be a landline phone in the house but after Cliff died I received so many scammy calls, and some downright threatening ones that I took the plug out and put the phone in a drawer. I think Cliff knew some weird people, or maybe he didn't, maybe they just thought they knew him. Either way, it had to go and I haven't missed it. Even when it rang legitimately it was never for me anyway. Anyone who knows me knows my mobile number and my mobile recognises them. That makes me feel safe.

I'm celebrating getting through my presentation without freezing once, with a glass or two of white wine all alone in my kitchen, when I pluck up the courage to call Mrs Lane back. I find her mobile number in my contacts and press call. It rings and rings and I'm about to hang up when she answers.

'Mrs Lane, it's Ruby Sutton. You wanted me to call you. About the cottage?'

'Oh yes. How are you, Ruby? How's life treating you?' She's chatting to me as though she knows me which makes me think that Zara has been talking about me.

'I'm fine, thank you. Is everything all right with the cottage?'

'Oh yes. Yes. I just wanted to apologise to you over the mix up. I've been meaning to call you about it since Christmas. I do hope you'll forgive me.'

'Nothing to forgive. Anyway, we already discussed it at the time,' I say. 'It worked out fine.' Better than fine, much better and in my quieter moments I'm still enjoying it.

'Well, I've spoken to my brother and he's agreed that he was in the wrong.'

I don't know what to say to this, what's gone on between Mrs Lane and her brother is her business, not mine.

'So, we've agreed that you should have another week.' She pauses. 'For free.'

'Oh. Oh. That's very nice, but it really isn't necessary.'

'I insist. We insist. My brother feels as bad about the mix up as I do.' She pauses again before adding, 'Especially given the circumstances.' Zara has definitely been talking about me.

'Right.' It would be churlish not to accept. Very churlish. 'Thank you. Very much.'

'Excellent. Would Easter week suit you? We've just had a cancellation and, frankly, it's the only week available this year.'

'Okay. Thank you. I really appreciate that.' I wasn't planning on having another holiday but since it's the week before I move home, then why not. Never look a gift horse in the mouth I say. I doubt I'll have the time or money once I move. 'Thank you very much.'

We agree to sort out the details nearer the time and I mark the dates as vacation on my calendar. I've already booked a week off work to move and I can just add the week before. It shouldn't be a problem.

Something else to look forward to.

Yes, Ruby Sutton is definitely on the up.

'I still miss you though, Cliff,' I whisper into the air.

My phone starts to ring as soon as the words are out of my mouth. It's that same number again, the one I don't know. I reject the call then panic; it could have been Mrs Lane ringing from her landline. I think about ringing back but before I have finished the thought my phone rings again and I stare at it. Is it Mrs Lane? No, we just finished speaking. Has one of the Cliff's weirdos found my mobile number? I hesitate, letting the caller ring for a long time before I press answer.

'Hello?' I say. But the caller rings off. Ah, so it is one of Cliff's weirdos or worse still, a call centre.

I immediately block the number on my phone.

'Problem solved,' I say out loud. I really need to stop talking to myself. Or get a pet to chat to. Not a dog though, not in my lovely new flat. Totally unsuitable.

❄❄❄

A week later and I'm ecstatic. The first people I ring are Mum and Dad.

'I got it. I got the job. I can't believe it.'

'That's wonderful. Congratulations. Just putting the phone on speaker so Dad can hear.'

'Knew you'd do it,' Dad says. 'Never doubted it. When do you start?'

'When I go back to work after I've moved house.'

'Talk about new starts,' Mum says, sounding jubilant.

My parents are as pleased for me as I am and I sometimes forget that they've lived through my misery with me. Mum still feels guilty for being in Australia when Cliff died, even though I've repeatedly told her that it wouldn't have changed anything. My parents, but especially Mum, worry about me. They weren't that keen on Cliff, they felt he was too old for me. There are more than five years between Mum and Dad, so I thought they would have understood. I think it was also because of his ex-wife, his children, all the baggage. They never said anything against him, were always pleasant to him, as he was to them, but there was no real connection. They didn't say much to him or about him, not the way they had gushed over Kylie, my brother's wife – and still do.

Mum chats about how my life is finally getting back on track and Dad asks practical questions about my move, have I booked a removal company? Is the date for me to move in absolutely final? As they chatter away, I find my mind wandering and I wonder if they would approve of Noah. His age. His personality. His kindness. His humour. His body…

'When do you get the money from Susannah?' Mum cuts across my thoughts.

'What? Oh, when I complete on the flat. It's sitting between the solicitors now. Susannah's no fool, but I'm not complaining.' I don't add that I feel guilty for taking the money, but Dad hears it in my tone.

'No need to feel bad about it,' he says. 'It's only fair.'

'Yeah. I suppose.' I'm not actually any richer than I was when I married Cliff, but I'm not any poorer either.

'That house has increased in value since you moved there. She's getting a good deal, so don't feel guilty.'

Easier said than done.

'Oh well,' I say, changing my internal tone. 'Onwards and upwards.'

Twenty-one

The cottage looks different in sunlight. The walls are less a stark white and more a mottled cream, the slate roof which had seemed so dark in winter now shimmers a light grey. There's greenery in the front garden, a contrast to the bright snow that I remember. It seems strange, almost not the same place at all.

My drive down hasn't taken too long, no mishaps, no stops, no lashing rain or howling wind. The trees in the lane are lush with new leaves, fresh and green, the air smells of new growth and promise. Or maybe I'm just feeling it that way.

I park my car, get my case from the boot, trundle along to the front door, push the key in the lock. I dump my case in the smaller bedroom behind the kitchen, the one that overlooks the sea, but I don't linger at the window, I go back to my car. There are bags of shopping that cannot sit out in the spring sunshine, so I haul them in, and unpack my goods into the fridge. Then I stop and draw breath.

Inside looks just the same, the log burner almost smiles at me. I wonder if I will need to light it; it can be very cool in the evenings, but then there's always the central heating. Through the French doors and rear windows, the view of the garden is stunning. Someone has cut the grass recently. Its first cut of the year? I suspect so, because the gardeners in mine and Cliff's house only finished the first cut yesterday.

The infinity lawn slips away to the sea, a turquoise shimmer against a blue sky. How at odds this place seems to my winter memory, there is, of course, no sign of our snow sculptures, in their place a solid wooden picnic table and benches, painted blue.

I unpack my case, make myself a coffee and go out to the table in the garden. This is bliss. I can hear the sea, smell it almost. Sea birds fly overhead calling to their mates. Maybe I'll take a stroll down to the beach, the path must be less treacherous now than at Christmas. If the tide's right maybe I'll find that little cove, but I'll have to watch that I don't get trapped. The thought makes me smile to myself, remembering Noah saying how easy it would be to get caught out by a changing tide.

It's around noon when I pull on my walking boots because I'm not taking any chances with that path, push my phone, the cottage key and some cash into my jeans pocket and head off down to the beach. It's breezy and warm and I soon pull off the light jacket I'm wearing and tie it around my waist. Elegant, but who cares? Who is here to see me? No one. Or at least, no one I know. I can please myself. This is the kind of solitude I imagined back in December, except of course the weather wasn't like this, never could be. Perhaps I should think about coming here every year, every Easter, when the weather is kinder, the light brighter, the days longer.

Down on the beach there is just me, and a few seagulls strutting their stuff along the waterline, looking for fishy treats. They turn and look at me with their black-bead eyes, see it is me then turn away uninterested. I inhale the sea air, I feel exhilarated, free, alive.

I venture round to the cove; it's exposed as the tide is low. A large rock shaped just like a sofa, the perfect resting place, beckons me and I do not fight the urge to sit. I never noticed this at Christmas, but it was probably covered in snow and almost invisible. If I close my eyes, lean back, let the sun warm my skin, I could almost fall asleep. Yes, it would be so easy to get trapped here. Not that I will let that happen.

After a while my stomach rumbles and my thoughts turn to food. I wonder if the pub is open for lunch today. It will be, this is the start of the holiday season, it definitely will be.

I jump down from my rock sofa and, with a splash, land in an inch or two of seawater. The tide has, indeed, turned. So sly. As I walk back up the beach, I smile to myself, it would be so lovely to tell Noah how I could have been marooned in the cove. Oh course, I'll never tell him.

I don't know whether it's the sea air, the warmth, the effort of hiking back up from the beach, but I feel alive, more alive than I have in months, no years. I feel optimistic about the future, my new job, my new home, my new life.

And I only feel a little guilty about taking Susannah's money.

I've tried to imagine her living in our house with her fiancé and her sons, Cliff's sons. I cannot imagine it. I wonder what Cliff would think of it. Not that any of it matters because she moves in the week after I move out – she's having the house deep cleaned first. She hasn't told me this, the company she's employed made a mistake and sent someone round to assess the work needed. The woman, an area manager, stood on my doorstep and was mortified when she realised her mistake. I assured her that I wouldn't be telling anyone, least of all Susannah.

I don't mind, I'm moving on.

I reach the pub and I'm puffing and panting from the effort of climbing the beach path. My lungs are bursting with fresh sea air. Picnic tables line up against the pub's walls, on the end one sits a woman patting the head of a big dog.

I stop in my tracks. It could be Kong. It can't be. The woman and the dog are looking out to sea and are far enough away from me to not even notice I am here. The woman wears a sun hat but I can see wisps of silver blonde hair beneath it.

Reminds me of Vic. Reminds me of Noah.

No, I'm not going to think about Noah. He's as much in the past as the rest of my life is. It's onwards and upwards, or maybe that should be forwards, for me.

While I refuse to live in the past I do have my memories, happy times I've shared with Cliff. And Noah.

I don't need to ask if they're serving lunch in the pub because the delicious smell of food hits my nostrils as soon as I push on the door. It makes me feel even hungrier.

The pub is packed, far busier than it was at Christmas.

'Bit of a wait for a table,' the barman tells me as he pours me a large white wine spritzer. Take a pew over there and I'll let you know. Might be a while.' He grimaces and so do I. But patience is a virtue and I must be virtuous.

At least I have time to study the specials board and I instantly know what I'm going to choose.

'Ruby, Ruby,' voices call.

I don't even look up because they can't mean me, no one here knows me, more's the pity.

'Ruby, Ruby,' a male voice calls again, much louder this time.

I glance up; I'm curious to see who this other Ruby is.

Two old, smiling faces greet me, and I do recognise them. We sat with them at Christmas when the band arrived and we had to move from our table. Me and Noah.

If only I could remember their names.

I wave and smile back at them.

'Are you eating?' the man calls.

'Hope so,' I say, sounding a bit pathetic. Am I really *that* hungry?

'Join us, join us. We're just about to order.'

'Come on,' the woman calls. 'There's room.'

It would be rude not to.

I glance around me just in case there's another Ruby in the pub and that's who they are really talking to, then stand up and walk slowly towards them – just in case. The waitress is already taking their order but they stop and wait for me to sit down. We're snug on our table of three.

'Do you need a menu?' the waitress asks.

'No, I know what I'm having.' And I give her my order for fish pie.

She smiles her thanks at me, grateful that I'm not going to delay her any longer.

'Well, isn't this a nice surprise.'

'Um, yes,' I say. What the hell are their names?

'On your own today?'

'Yes. Oh yes. Just me.' I giggle. Really? I giggle. How old am I?

'Where's your nice young man today?' The woman asks.

Oh shit. 'Um, he's busy.' I smile and grab my drink. I think I'll be having another one of these soon. Was it a good idea to sit with these people who, that night over Christmas, thought Noah and I were honeymooners?

'Ahh, maybe you'll catch up with him later,' the woman says.

'Yeah,' I say, humouring her. I down my drink and stand up. I'm stuck here now, there are no other tables and my order's been placed. 'Would you like another drink while I'm at the bar?'

'Not for me,' the woman says. 'What about you, Arthur?'

Arthur, that's it!

'I'll have a pint of Doom Bar if you're going.' He starts rummaging in his pocket.

'No, my treat,' I say, moving past him.

'Doom Bar,' mutters the woman. 'I don't know why they stock that Cornish ale here.' She shakes her head.

'Joan, everyone likes it, that's why.'

Joan, Joan. Arthur and Joan.

'Plenty of good Devon brews to be had.' She shakes her head and I leave them to bicker about beer.

As I wait at the bar I idly look out of the window, out to the glistening sea. The Kong-like dog bounds past, probably following his owner, the Vic-like woman.

Maybe it was a mistake to come to this pub, there are too many reminders of Noah, more than at the cottage. Strangely.

I take our drinks back and sit back down.

'Are you sure you wouldn't like one, Joan?' I ask, seeing that her drink is now empty.

'Oh, no,' she says, sounding not at all convincing. 'You've just sat down. Arthur can go, can't you?'

Arthur frowns then takes a large gulp of his Doom Bar. I jump up.

'I'll go. What would you like?' At least it will stop them asking about my *young man*.

'I don't know. Surprise me,' she says with childlike glee. 'As long as it's not Cornish.'

So I get her a white wine spritzer too.

I take Joan's drink back and sit down, glancing around me, willing the waitress to bring our food and not only because I'm starving.

'We were just talking about you last night,' Joan says, with a grin. 'Talking to your young man.'

She's getting me confused with someone else, or maybe getting Noah confused with someone else. My thoughts must show on my face because she turns to Arthur for corroboration.

'Weren't we, Arthur? Talking to Noah, last night?'

'Oh yes,' he says, nodding but fortunately showing more interest in his pint than Joan.

Definitely mistaking me or Noah for someone else.

At that moment our food arrives and I am so grateful that Arthur and Joan now concentrate on eating.

I finish before them which says more about my greed that their slow eating.

'I'll just check the specials board for puddings.' I jump up.

By the time I come back they've finished and the table has been cleared. I recite the pudding list on the specials board and, as luck would have it, the waitress reappears and takes our order.

'I think they're keen to get us fed and out of here,' Joan says with a smile. 'Haven't seen it this busy in months. Not even at Christmas when we had live music. I suppose it's the proper start of the tourist season. Always makes it nice and lively then.'

'Yes. I imagine it does.' Please don't remind me of Noah and the band and that evening or the subsequent ones.

'Are you down for long?'

'Just a week.'

'Oh, yes, that's right, that's what Noah said. Shame you couldn't get the cottage again, isn't it?' Joan says.

'Oh, but I have. I mean, that is where I'm staying.'

'Well, that's odd. I'm sure Noah said he was staying here, in the pub. I must have got that wrong.' Joan frowns.

'No,' Arthur pipes up. 'He did say that. Said he was pleased that they allow dogs here. So few places do. Especially a big dog like his.'

I pick up a coaster and start to fan myself with it. Surely they have this wrong. Surely they're confusing Noah with someone else. Someone who looks like him and even has the same name? And a big dog? Just like the one I saw outside?

'Oh, there he is.' Joan nods towards the door. 'We can ask him.'

I freeze. I feel panic rising. Then I calm myself. It cannot be him. I turn slowly towards the door expecting to see a perfect stranger.

Instead I see someone who *is* perfect but definitely not a stranger.

'Ruby?'

Twenty-two

'Ruby, is that you?' He's as shocked as I am.

I sit there staring at him, blinking like an idiot, my mouth dropped open, wondering what to say, what to do. Then I remember who he's with, who I saw outside with Kong.

I stand up, pull some notes from my jeans pocket and press them into Arthur's hands.

'What's going on?' he asks, frowning.

'That should more than cover my food, and all the drinks. Can you sort it out for me please? I have to dash.' I don't wait for his reply, just yank my jacket tighter around my waist and march as fast as I can to the door.

'Hey,' Noah says. He's smiling. How dare he?

'Hi.' I dodge around him and hurl myself through the door.

Outside Vic is sitting at a table with Kong by her side, she has her back to me but the hat is off and displaying her hair in a sexy messy bun. Nooo.

Kong sees me and his tail starts to wag. He lets off a friendly bark or two.

I need to walk past them to get back to the cottage. But I can't. I won't. The last thing I want to see is the perfect Vic with the perfect dog waiting for the perfect man.

No, he's not.

Yes, he is, my defiant little heart tells me.

I double back around the pub and through the car park. Then I scrabble up a scrubby bank and hope that it will bring me up onto the lane so I can find my way home.

The bank is steeper than I anticipate and earth softer and wetter. I grab at roots and clumps of bushes until I finally manage to pull myself up six feet above the car park. Just as I reach the top, when the hard part is done, I slip and land on my arse, pulling my left leg in the process.

'Fuuuck,' I yell.

'Woohoo, yay,' a chorus greets me, followed by a round of applause.

A group of lads, late teens perhaps, are laughing and clapping me. Little bastards.

I stand up with as much dignity as my wet, muddy backside can manage and limp off. Whether this is the right way or not there is no going back. None.

Fortunately, I am on the right track. I can even see the cottage wall through the trees in the distance.

By the time I reach the cottage I am limping badly. I'm also seething with anger. How dare he turn up and make me do all that to escape him and his perfect life? How dare he spoil my holiday?

Again.

I tumble in through the door, kick off my boots, untie my jacket which is as muddy as my jeans and hurl it across the room where it lands on the back of the sofa. Then I unzip my jeans and yank them down. I get them half way down my legs to my knees and because they're wet, they're peeling my knickers down with them.

I'm crying now. Crying with anger, crying from humiliation, all sorts of humiliation, the pub, *him*, the bank, the lads in the car park laughing at me, the falling over on my arse. The wet muddy mess I'm in. All of it. And I'm crying in pain. The top of my leg really hurts. This must be how footballers feel when they have a groin strain injury.

I was having such a nice day and now it's all gone to shit.

And it's all his fault. Noah Bloody Steele has done it again.

I hate him.

And why did he have to bring *her* here, the perfect Vic, to our place? Why? Why? Why? It's ruined now. I'll be going home as soon as I can.

I'm standing in the middle of the room engulfed in self-pity, my jeans and knickers at my knees, snot dribbling out of my nose, pathetic tears dripping off my chin when, behind me, the door flies open. Kong bounds in and barks a greeting.

Where Kong goes his master follows. And no doubt he's trailing *her* along with him.

I scrabble desperately to pull by clothes back up, but the pain in my leg is almost unbearable.

'Fuck off,' I shriek as I turn to see Noah Steele in the doorway. 'Fuck off and leave me alone.' And all the while I'm trying to at least get my knickers back where they should be. But it's all too much. Much too much. And Kong is so excited to see me that he takes a running leap and knocks me to the ground.

'Just fuck the fuck off.' What a foul mouth I have.

'Are you okay?'

'Just go. Go.'

Noah grabs my jacket from the sofa and lays it across me, covering the bits that matter while I lie there wincing and seething.

'What can I do to help?'

'Go away, that's what you can do and take your bloody pervy dog with you. Fuck off. And if you've brought *her* with you, I swear I'm going to kill you both. Fuck off.'

Noah whistles. 'Kong.'

They leave quickly and quietly, but not before Kong lets out a little whimper and a sorrowful glance at me. Noah closes the door behind them.

I lie on the floor for ages. I don't even know if I can get up because every time I try, the pain is excruciating. Eventually I cross my arms and lay my head on them to form a makeshift pillow, then I fall asleep.

I don't know how long I sleep but when I wake up, I feel horrible. I'm angry and upset and in pain. Although the pain doesn't feel quite so bad as it did so I try moving. I manage to roll over onto my back then scoot my way to the sofa where, after three attempts, I pull myself upright using the back of the sofa as a support.

My jeans and knickers are still around my knees and my discarded jacket is now on the floor.

I try a few steps and it's not so bad. I slow walk to the front door and deadlock it. Should have done that in the first place then I could have spared myself the ultimate humiliation. I close the inner porch door then attempt to get the jeans off. It takes some doing as they keep sticking, but finally they're down and soon followed by the knickers.

It takes me a few minutes more get the rest of my clothes off, the socks proving especially difficult.

Finally, I'm standing in the middle of the cottage naked. Which, given how he and his dog are wont to creep up unannounced, is not a good idea. I scoot into my bedroom, grab my dressing gown and clean towels and my washbag.

In the bathroom while the bath is filling, I take a couple of painkillers using my hands to scoop up water from the tap to wash them down. A good soak in the bath is going to really help this, I tell myself, as I climb in and flop down. I don't quite flood the bathroom.

❅❅❅

The cold water wakes me and for a moment or two I don't know where I am. Then it all comes thundering back. Oh the humiliations.

I may not have paid anything for this holiday but the cost is high. Very high. My dignity, my modesty and almost my sanity. There is, as I should know, no such thing as a free holiday.

I pull the plug out using the toes of my good leg and wait for the water to go before I attempt to get out of the bath. There's no need to add the weight of water to my effort.

And it is a little bit of a struggle. It takes me four attempts, all accompanied by profuse cold sweats and panics about getting stuck there, before I'm finally on my feet in the bath. I grab a towel and wrap it around myself; at least the cleaners won't find me dead in the bath, or just waiting there, drinking from the bath tap and crying. I assume they will come at the end of my week.

Imagine that. No doubt it would make it onto someone's Facebook feed.

But it's okay. I'm upright. I struggle out of the bath and although I'm in pain it has definitely eased. The combination of painkillers and hot water has done the trick.

It's all his fault. Him and his pervy dog.

I cannot get over the bloody cheek of him, turning up here like that. In what universe does he think that is acceptable?

Okay, he didn't know I had the cottage this week, just as I didn't know he was staying at the pub. I'll give him that; it's just a horrible coincidence. But once he saw me you'd think he would have had a bit of decency and kept his distance. He didn't even move aside to let me leave the pub easily, I had to dance around him. Then he greets me with a jolly 'hey'.

I can't believe him. I really cannot.

Why did he have to follow me? Just to rub it in? Just to say, hey, here I am back in my happy life with my shit hot, gorgeous girlfriend. And he must know that I'm moving out of mine and Cliff's house and that my life is downgrading as his upgrades. I can't believe he hasn't asked his father.

I just want to go home, leave this place and never come back again and never think about it again.

Move forwards. Move forwards.

At this rate the entirety of my life before this moment will be a place I do not visit or refer to. It's all getting too ridiculous.

I stumble out of the bathroom, get myself a drink of water and head for my bedroom.

Funny how I've not chosen to sleep in the main bedroom, the one with the biggest bed. *His* bedroom.

'It's because of the view,' I tell the walls, because there's no one else to hear me.

Even though I've been asleep for I don't know how long, I might just have another little nap. I rip off the towel, climb into bed, pull the covers over my head and shut my eyes.

I'll go home tomorrow.

❄❄❄

It's morning when I awake, the sun is shining and the sky is blue. I can see both quite clearly because I didn't draw the curtains last night. I've slept well, deep and dreamless. I move my leg a little to test the pain, it's a lot, lot better. Good, I'm going to need that leg to drive home.

I lean against the window sill and gaze out to the sea, it's glorious, a beautiful blue that reflects the sky.

I pull on some clean clothes and venture out to the living room. I make myself breakfast, sit down on the sofa and switch on the TV. The local weather man is forecasting wonderful weather for Devon. They move onto the national weather and the forecast isn't so good for where I live.

Typical.

The prospect of sitting in the car in this sunshine doesn't appeal to me either. It's such a waste. I put my breakfast dishes in the dishwasher then pick up my dirty clothes from last night. The mud has dried hard. A plan starts to form in my mind. What if I stayed for the rest of the day and headed home early evening? That would make far more sense. In the meantime, I could put my muddy clothes through the washing machine here and lay them out to dry on the picnic table.

Just one flaw with that plan, I don't have any washing tablets. Should I just wash them without? At least it would get the worst of the mud off. Yes. I load the machine, then, just before I switch it on, I have a brainwave, I'll drop a bit of washing up liquid in there, not too much, obviously. But it will definitely remove a lot, if not all, of that mud, after all, it cuts through grease on pans.

The machine will take an hour so I make myself a nice cup of coffee and head out to the garden.

When the washing is finished I'm going to wander down to the beach. I think about the muddy boots in the porch and decide against wearing them, it's too warm for boots. I'm going to wear trainers. I didn't really need the boots yesterday except for climbing up that bank behind the pub and I certainly won't be doing *that* again.

I won't be going near the pub. I just hope him and her and Kong don't go near the beach.

Well, a little voice in my head says, they most definitely will. Kong enjoyed the beach in the winter, he'll love it even more now.

Damn it.

No, I won't be prevented from enjoying myself, I *will* go to the beach.

The hour is up and I wander back into Christmas Cottage and on the way I spot a washing line in the corner, complete with pegs. Perfect.

The washing has finished.

My clever trick with the washing up liquid wasn't so clever. I've overdosed the machine and there are suds all over the floor, spreading in a whirl from the kitchen to the sofa and beyond; it's like a foam party.

It's only soapy water. Just get a mop and clean it up. I paddle over and pull out my jeans and jacket. They look lovely and clean. I decide to hang them out first before mopping up.

When I come back the suds are still there and still spreading. I hunt around for a mop, but can't find one. There must be one, there must be. Unless the cleaners bring one with them when they come at the end of the week.

I'll have to use towels to mop up instead, then I'll have to wash the towels because they're the only ones I have, I didn't bring my own. But I can't use washing up liquid to wash them, can I? Wait, I won't need to because they'll be soaking with it anyway.

Yep, it's the towels.

I wade across the room to the bathroom and just as I get there, there's a loud knock on the door.

I freeze. Like a criminal caught in the act. Which I suppose I am in a way if you count flooding with suds as a crime. I'm going to ignore it, it'll be him. Who else could it be?

Knock, knock, knock.

He's so bloody persistent.

Knock, knock, knock.

It's even louder this time.

I grab the towels and head back to the flood.

Knock, knock, knock.

Right. That's it. Why can't he just leave me alone? I'm seething now.

I still have the towels bundled up in my arms when I yank open the front door.

'What the fuck do you want? Oh...'

Twenty-three

'I'm so, so sorry for that,' I say as a puzzled looking Arthur and Joan stare at me. 'I thought you were someone else. I don't normally swear like that.' Actually, I do lately.

'We brought your change,' Arthur says, his voice quiet. He holds out his hand with a few coins in it. 'Four-pounds-twenty-three.'

'Um. Right. Thank you. No need.' I shuffle the towels about in my arms trying to find my hand to take the money. 'Please, why don't you keep it.'

'Oh no,' Arthur says. 'We couldn't do that.'

'Oh, um…'

'Is everything all right?' Joan asks, evidently far more perceptive than her husband. 'Are you having problems?'

'You could say that. I've flooded the cottage. That's what the towels are for, to mop it up.'

Joan pushes past Arthur and steps into the porch. She reaches past me and opens a cupboard next to the coat hooks, a cupboard I've never even noticed before. Has it always been there? Then she pulls out a bucket and mop.

'This will be better than soaking those towels.'

'Yes, yes. I couldn't find it.' I feel doubly stupid now as Joan marches into the cottage and starts mopping and wringing out the mop in the bucket. She's very efficient, very quick.

I trot off and dump the towels back in the bathroom and when I come back Joan has mopped more than half the room. Arthur has ventured inside and is standing with the money still in his hands. I am not taking it, now. Definitely not.

'Please, let me take over.'

Joan relinquishes the mop and smiles at me. 'I'll empty it down the loo,' she says, picking up the bucket. 'Back in a minute.'

Once the bucket is back I carry on and it really doesn't take very long, especially when Joan opens the windows to let the floor dry off.

'Thank you so much. So, so much. I had no idea the mop was there. How did you know?'

It's Arthur who answers, 'Ahh, well. Our Belinda used to clean here, that's our granddaughter, and more than once she didn't make it, did she Joan? But it had to be done.' He rolls his eyes and Joan shrugs her shoulders.

'Yes, that's how I know.' She laughs. 'Judging from how dirty the water was I think it's probably been a while since it was mopped properly anyway, so you've done the floor a favour.'

Talk about positive spin.

'Your change,' Arthur says, offering the coins again.

'No. Please, please, keep them. Buy Joan a great big glass of wine from me.'

Arthur looks at me, then at Joan, then pockets the coins. 'Thank you.'

'We were a bit concerned about you anyway,' Joan says. 'After you ran out of the pub like that, last night. And Noah came back later with a face like thunder. Not like him at all, he's always so smiley, isn't he?'

Why did she have to mention him?

'Oh, I'm fine. Just remembered something I had to do, that's all.' Like get the hell away from Noah Bloody Steel. 'Have you seen him today?' What do I care? Maybe he's pushed off home.

'No. No. But we haven't been in the pub today. We don't spend all our time in there, you know.' Joan laughs. 'Even if some of us would like to.' She nods at Arthur whose response is to keep his face impassive.

'I really can't thank you enough for helping me with the floor.' I really can't. Now it's mopped up and dry it feels as though it never happened.

'My pleasure.'

'We'd better get off then, Joan, if we're going to Exeter.'

'Oh yes.' Joan turns to me. 'Would you like to come?'

I pretend to consider her offer, then decline.

'Well, maybe we'll see you in the pub later in the week,' Arthur ventures, putting a hand on his wife's back and steering her towards the door.

Joan's response is to roll her eyes at me and smirk.

From the doorstep I watch them as they wander down to the parking space, get in their car and drive away. It dawns on me that I don't know anything about them as any conversation between us has been centred on me and *him*. If I do see them again, which is unlikely given I'm leaving tonight, I'll be asking about their love story. Definitely.

❄❄❄

There's no one on the beach, not one single person. It's just me and the seagulls again, and they show not the slightest bit of interest in me. Maybe if I had a bag of chips or an ice cream they might be more interested, but happily I don't.

I wend my way round to the cove and settle down on the sofa rock. The sun has warmed the rock and it's so comfortable it's hard to believe it is actually not a soft sofa. I pull my phone out and take a few photos of the gulls as they waddle along the shoreline. Then I take a few longshots of the cove then the wider beach. This is a little slice of heaven and it's all mine. For now.

Such a shame I have to leave. But, looking on the positive side, it does mean that I can get an early start on my house packing ready for my move. I'm leaving behind the giant table, no use to me, I've not used it since Cliff died, never likely to either and it won't fit in my new place anyway. The same goes for the four-poster bed that Cliff loved so much. I'm taking very little furniture really, two beds and assorted bedroom furniture from spare bedrooms, the sofas which I love, and all my personal bits and pieces obviously. I'm also taking the entire contents of the kitchen, even though some of it has never been used and won't fit in my new place. I'd rather sell it than leave it for Susannah to sneer at, especially since some of it came from my old flat. Cliff had even sneered at some of my kitchen paraphernalia, saying we should get high end replacements if I really needed a lemon squeezer (mine is yellow plastic and came from IKEA), and a spaghetti spoon (also plastic but from Asda). Neither have been used since I moved in with Cliff, or since his death. Maybe I need to make more of an effort in the kitchen in future.

The sound of voices jerks me from my musings and I look over to see a pair of lanky teenage boys paddling and splashing each other on the main beach. They're tall with mops of dark hair and the wind carries their half-broken boy/man voices towards me.

I hope they weren't among the lads who witnessed my arse fall yesterday. Weren't they a bit older? I slink into the sofa rock and hope they don't notice me.

'Don't get your clothes wet, we're going for lunch soon,' a female voice calls, carried on the wind in my direction.

Two groans come from the teenagers. I think *that* wet ship might have already sailed judging by the water dripping off their clothes.

'Look at you both,' the female voice says. 'You're absolutely soaked. Well, you can sit outside with Kong.'

Kong? Kong?

Oh no. Has he brought his whole family with him? Go away. Go to lunch now.

I spin around and see the perfect Vic, her back to me, hair in its messy bun again, standing with her hands on her hips. She's dressed in another colour co-ordinated ensemble, pale blue this time. She has a soft blue padded bodywarmer on too, very elegant – my mum would certainly wear it. Am I being bitchy? Maybe. I look down at my own clothes, hastily pulled on jeggings and a t-shirt, I have a fleece tied around my waist. My hair is hanging loose although I have clipped the front back. Vic looks put together; I look thrown together. Designed versus dishevelled.

What do I care?

There's another groan from the teenagers and a matching one from me too. I need to get off this beach and fast. But I can't escape without walking past them, and no doubt *him*. I scan the beach for Kong who will be easy to spot but there's no sign of him. Thank God for that. Maybe they'll just head off the beach if I sit here quietly.

I slink back down onto my makeshift sofa, close my eyes and wait.

The bark that greets me makes my heart leap, swiftly followed by my body. It's the friendliest of barks and the cold nose that nudges against my hand is all too familiar. Trust Kong to find me.

'You,' I say. 'Haven't you caused enough trouble?' I ruffle his ears and stroke him under the chin. At least he appears to be alone, there's no sign of *him* here in the cove. Hopefully he's way up the beach and will call his dog back without venturing closer. I slide back down again trying to make myself invisible.

'Go, Kong, go. Find your master,' I whisper.

But Kong isn't going anywhere. Instead he jumps up and puts his paws on my knees. His tail is wagging and he's so pleased to see me.

'Kong,' a voice calls, but it's Vic's, not Noah's. Maybe Noah isn't on the beach at all. And Vic won't know who I am, if she remembers me at all it'll be as some inspector for the cottage rental.

'Go, Kong, you're being called,' I say as Vic calls for Kong again but naughty Kong doesn't go, and it's obvious he has no intentions of responding to Vic's calls. Didn't Noah say they didn't really like each other, Kong and Vic?

Kong paws at my leg again and barks, it's not a loud bark but I'm going to be caught soon enough if he doesn't go away.

'Off you go, Kong. Go on, go.'

But Kong doesn't go, instead he starts to whine. Really? Does this dog love me that much? I feel a little tinge of superiority over the perfect Vic. Kong likes me better than her.

'I know you've got good taste, Kong, but really, you need to go.'

Kong whines again and pads my knees with his giant paws, again. I wish he wouldn't do that.

'Kong,' Vic calls again, this time her voice very stern.

Kong gives me one more whine and then goes, bounding off and leaving me to my peace. I stay where I am until their voices are distant and I'm sure they've completely left the beach. I sit up and scan the horizon to check. Yep, it's just me and the seagulls and the softly crashing waves.

Disaster averted, peace at last.

A little bit of sea spray hits my face, I can taste the salt.

Sea spray? How close is that sea?

I sit up and am horrified to see that the tide is coming in and the rock is now an island.

Oh. My. God. I'm marooned in the cove.

Can I sit here until the tide turns or will this rock be completely submerged? I feel sick with panic.

That's what Kong was trying to tell me. That's why he was whining. It wasn't because he loved me so much, it was because the tide had turned.

Calm down. Calm down.

I look into the water. It really doesn't look that deep. Yet.

I take off my trainers and stuff my socks inside them. Then I tie them together and loop them around my neck. I roll my jeggings up to my knees, they're so tight around my legs that they're almost cutting the circulation off. That might be a good thing given how cold I know the water will be.

I lower myself down and do actually squeal. The water is deep and bloody cold, even more so than I expected. I start to wade through it towards the sand of the main beach.

It's deep, already lapping at the bottom of my jeggings. They'll soon dry in the sunshine, I tell myself.

Gingerly I edge forward, watching where I put my feet because I have no way of knowing if there are dips or crevasses under the water.

A big bark shocks me.

Kong.

He's on the sand, wagging his tail and egging me on.

'I'm fine,' I call, in my best calm voice because the last thing I want Kong to do in run in to rescue me and knock me over in the process. 'Good boy, you stay there.'

I return my attention back to my feet, it's not far now.

Weirdly the water seems to be getting deeper as I get nearer to the dry sand. I thought it would just slope up but it doesn't. In fact I'm starting to struggle now, I'm going to have to go on all fours and pull myself up. I'm going to be very wet. It's so annoying when I'm mere feet from safety.

I yank off the shoes around my neck and hurl them onto the dry sand, quickly followed by my fleece. I'm just about to perform my crab act when a voice breaks through my concentration.

'Give me your hands.'

Noah Bloody Steel.

He sees the hesitation on my face.

'Don't be silly, come on. Would you rather drown?' He's holding out both his hands.

He's right. I am being silly. I take his hands and he hauls me out of the water. At least only the bottoms of my jeggings are wet.

'Thanks,' I say as I pull my hands from his and march away. I grab my fleece from the sand, then my shoes.

'Are you okay? I'm sorry I didn't get here earlier. When I heard that you were trapped here…'

'What?' I turn and sneer at him.

'Apparently there's a sort of a riptide, an undercurrent around the rock. I was so worried, I got here as fast as I could.'

'I'm fine. I was doing fine. I don't need you or the perfect Vic to save me.' With that I stomp up the beach as fast as my wet and now sandy legs can carry me as Kong bounds along beside me, tail wagging furiously.

'Fucking bastard,' I mutter under my breath.

Twenty-four

I slow down as I approach the beach entrance. There are two reasons for this. One: I'm puffed out, two: I'm trying to maintain my dignity in front of all the people sitting outside the pub having their lunch in the sunshine, Vic and her sexy, messy bun included.

I want to put my shoes back on but my feet are so encrusted in sand and I don't have a towel so I don't think I will even try. I scrabble up from the beach and start to march down the lane towards the cottage.

'Ruby,' Noah calls as he gains on me. 'Ruby, stop.'

I march on. I don't want to look at him, he's wearing those soft blue jeans and a dark t-shirt today and I don't want to see how perfect he looks. Just the sight of him pulls my stomach into a tight knot. Perfect Noah. Perfect Vic.

'Ruby, wait.'

I don't. I know he can gain on me, he's bigger and stronger, but I don't care.

And, of course he does gain on me and overtakes me and stands in front of me, blocking my way. Kong, I notice, stands beside me. Noah and I are having a face off and Kong has chosen me, my side.

'Ruby. Are you all right after that?'

'I'm fine. I told you I was fine. Now step aside please.'

He steps aside and I attempt to stride on. But the lane is less forgiving than the sand, it's stony and hurts my feet and it's hard to stride on. I hobble on past the pub then spy a small bench and flop down.

Noah sits down next to me, far too close for comfort.

I use my socks to start cleaning the sand from my feet. Once I get my shoes on I'll be much better equipped to escape him and his pity.

'Ruby?'

'What do you want?' I hiss, my face screwed up in annoyance, not a good look. I bet the perfect Vic never does that.

'Just want to talk to you.'

I take my time brushing the sand out from between my toes, I'm not going to get chafe burns because of *him*.

'I don't think we've got anything to talk about, have we? You have your life and I have mine, thank you very much.'

'Right. Okay.' He stands up, flicks his fingers at Kong who comes straight to his side. 'You're staying up at the cottage then?'

'You know full well I am, you sent your pervy dog in to molest me yesterday. Remember?'

He lets out a little snort that could be a laugh, but it's not his trademark smile, or its best friend, his smirk.

'I'm staying at the pub,' he says.

'I know.'

'Yes, I would have stayed at the cottage but it was booked.'

'Yes. By me. Not that that stopped you last time, did it?' I want to bite my tongue after the words are out because he might think it's an invitation and it most certainly is not. I've got my socks and shoes on now and I stand up and grab my fleece off the bench.

'No. Right.'

'Well, why don't you trot off to your perfect life now, eh, because I've got things to do.' I stomp off in the direction of the cottage and I don't look back until I'm about to round a bend. He's still there, standing, watching me, with Kong by his side.

I think the sooner I get out of here the better.

But all that wading through water, stomping and being nasty has made me hungry and thirsty. As I approach the cottage I decide that I won't be forced away earlier than I'd planned. I'm going to have lunch – I've got enough supplies in the fridge for a week – then I'm going to spend the afternoon in the garden before I drive home this evening.

To Hell with *him*.

✿ ✿ ✿

Two hours later, my jeggings are drying on the line, I've changed into a little cotton skirt, I've had my lunch and a nice sunbathe in the garden. I'm back in the cottage loading the dishwasher when there's a knock at the front door.

It had better not be him.

If I ignore him, he'll go away.

Another knock, and the door disproves that. I'd better answer just in case it's Arthur and Joan again. I don't want a repeat of earlier.

I open the door carefully, slowly, just in case it is the elderly couple, but fully prepared to tell Noah Bloody Steele where to go. Then I'm stunned into silence.

A woman in her late forties, stands before me. She smiles.

'Hello, you must be Ruby.'

I'm so confused. Is this Mrs Lane? No, it can't be, why would she be here? Anyway, I imagined her older than this woman. Yet there's something very familiar about her.

'That's me,' I say, with caution.

'Great. Noah sent me. He wanted me…'

'No.' I hold up my hand. 'I don't want to hear anything he has to say. Goodbye.' I go to close the door but the woman puts both her hands against it and pushes back.

'Hey,' I say in my best stern voice, then I realise why she looks familiar. 'And why are you wearing Vic's clothes?'

'I'm not. That's why Noah sent me. I'm Yolanda, his stepmother. He thought you might have mistaken me for Vic, from a distance. Still quite flattering though.'

'Oh. Right. I see.'

'Anyway, I've done as he's asked. Job done, box ticked, and all that. Bye.'

'No, wait. Does that mean that Vic isn't here?'

'I'm not answering any questions, I just had to tell you who I was. If you need more information, you'll need to ask him. I didn't want to get involved in this at all.' With that she turns and leaves while I step out after her and watch her retreating form. She definitely does look like Vic from the back, same build, same hair colour. So I'm not completely stupid.

Right, what now? What do I do? What do I want to do? Do I want to go hunting for Noah and ask about Vic?

I don't know what to do? I don't want to go chasing around after him. Just because she's not here – assuming she isn't – doesn't mean they're not still together.

I really don't know what to do for the best.

Go find him, my heart tells me.

No way.

✿✿✿

When in doubt, do nowt.

I don't know who first said that, but I do know it's been around for a long time. Dad sometimes says it and claims his granny, who came from Yorkshire, invented it. I doubt that. However, it's what I'm going to do, nothing, because I don't know what else to do.

I have poured myself a large, cold drink – non-alcoholic of course because I'm going to be driving this evening – and I'm back in the garden enjoying the sunshine and the view. The sea is definitely at its best today, the sun glinting off it. Gulls are soaring across the sky and squawking to each other and there's a sweet, warm breeze playing with my hair and stroking my skin. It is quite idyllic here.

If only it wasn't for Noah Bloody Steele.

I could just ignore him. Pretend he isn't here, either down on that beach or in that pub. I could do that, it would be easy, wouldn't it?

Yes, that's what I'll do.

Inside my head, in the far depths of my brain, a chorus of laughter echoes.

Who the hell am I kidding?

I want to see him. I want to know if he's still with Vic.

Then what?

Do I want him?

Is that even an option? Does he want me?

In an effort to be pragmatic I consider the evidence. He chased after me when I made my escape from the beach, didn't he?

Yes, but he only wanted to make sure that you were okay after your near drowning incident. Any decent person would do that.

I wasn't nearly drowning; I just got my leggings wet.

He seemed keen to speak to you in the pub when you were with Arthur and Joan.

He was just being polite.

He came up to the cottage after that.

Yes, so he could set Kong, the pervy dog, on me and enjoy my humiliation.

He covered you over with your jacket to protect your modesty.

He could have just left immediately and shut the door behind him, that would have been far better than coming inside. He enjoyed seeing me humiliated.

I sigh and take a long gulp of my drink.

The evidence really isn't evidence at all and even if it was, it's all very subjective.

I'm stumped.

So I'm going to do nothing.

And in a few hours I'll be loading up the car and leaving.

Ah, my inner voice says, then you've decided; you're not going to pursue him.

'I was never going to pursue him,' I say out loud, annoyed with myself.

'Pursue who?' a voice asks from behind me.

Noah Bloody Steele.

'Oh YOU. Don't you ever stop?'

'No.' He looks me in the eye.

I look away. There's not a hint of a smile or a smirk on his face. In fact, I cannot tell what he's thinking.

'What do you want? I ask, evidently not doing nowt, because I could be opening a big can of worms just by asking that question. He could be about to tell me he has a horrible sexually transmitted infection and I need to get tested because he might have infected me.

Now, you didn't think of that, my nasty brain tells me.

'I want to talk to you.'

Yep, definitely an STI. That would explain his insistence on speaking to me.

I wave at the bench opposite me on the picnic table, inviting him to sit. Should I offer him a drink? It's hot and he looks as though he's caught the sun. No, if he's delivering bad news I want him to say it and leave immediately.

As Noah sits down, Kong appears from nowhere, bounds over to me, rubs his giant head against my leg, and pants.

'It's hot, he's thirsty,' Noah says.

Right on cue Kong rests a paw on my lap and looks up at me with soulful eyes, even raising his eyebrows. He whimpers. This dog is well-trained.

But I already knew that.

'I'll get him a bowl of water.' I stand up. 'I suppose you want a drink too?'

'Yes. Please. If it's no trouble.'

'Okay.' I slope off back to the cottage, aware that he is watching me, that they both are.

I return with a bowl of water for Kong and a glass of the same lemon squash that I am drinking for *him*.

I clamber back down onto my bench and wait for the bad news, but he's more interested in gulping back his drink than talking to me.

'Thank you. I needed that.'

'You're welcome. So what did you want?'

He gives me that same unfathomable look he did before he sat down.

'I've tried to ring you several times.'

'Have you? You don't have my number.' Get out of that lie.

'Ah, well, yes, I do. Or at least I thought I did.' He smiles the faintest of smiles.

'You got it from your dad? I didn't think financial advisors were allowed to pass on clients' details, that's…'

'Whoa,' Noah cuts in. 'He didn't give it to me. I snooped and found it, on his phone. He doesn't know and he certainly wouldn't give it to me even though he knew I needed it. Anyway, you never answered did you, not if I rang from my mobile or landline, so maybe I have the wrong number.'

I shrug. I can't deny I didn't answer him because I think I'd remember if I'd spoken to him.

'I don't answer numbers I don't know.'

'Oh. Right. Why? It could be important. It could be me.'

'Because I don't like unsolicited calls. Had a lot after Cliff died. A lot of weirdos…'

'Oh, I see. That must have been unnerving.'

'Yep, so if I don't know your number, I block you.' I smile now, or maybe I smirk. 'Anyway, what did you want?'

'I wanted to talk to you.'

'Fire away.' Hit me with the bad news, tell me about the STI, let me get it sorted before I move house and start my new job.

'How are you?'

'Fine.' I wonder what symptoms I should be displaying?

'Yes, I can see that.' He pauses and studies me. I don't like it, even though I feel compelled to study him back, our eyes meeting before I look away fast. 'Why are you so angry with me?'

'I'm not.'

'You are. You definitely are.'

I shrug again.

'I sent Yolanda up to explain about Vic. Yolanda was quite flattered to be mistaken for her.' The way he speaks, his very tone, suggests that everything between us should be wonderful now.

'Yeah, she came.'

'So why are you still angry with me?'

'I'm not anything with you.'

'You clearly are. What have I done?'

'Nothing.' Except you got into my life by stealth, then you got into my heart. Then you buggered off with the perfect Vic.

'I'm not with her.'

'You went home with her.'

'I took her home, to her home, a rented flat she was sharing with Liam, she collected her stuff then she decamped to her mother's.'

'Not yours?' I imagine they were going to take it easy for a while, not rush back into how they were before.

'No. Not mine. Not ever mine. We're over. We were over last February. And, okay, yes, it took me a while to get over Vic, but then I met you.' He looks into my eyes again, and I look into his and I find that this time I cannot look away.

There's a grin starting to form on his face, playing around his lips, if it turns into a smirk, I swear I will scream. But it doesn't. I can feel the start of a smile tugging at the sides of my own mouth.

'And…?'

'I couldn't get you out of my mind, couldn't stop thinking about you. So I stole your number from my dad and tried to ring you to see how you were, to tell you I wanted to see you again, away from this place…' He nods towards the cottage, then moves his hands across the table, takes mine. 'Away from the romance of this place and the surreal atmosphere it created. I wanted to see if there was any chance of us connecting in the real world.'

It's a lot to take in. He likes me, I like him. I'm not jumping straight into bed again with him though. No. So I say the first thing that pops into my head.

'You haven't got an STI then?'

Twenty-five

To be fair he takes it in good humour.

He laughs. Really loudly. Even Kong joins in, barking along with his master. Then his face turns serious and he lets go of my hands.

'No, I don't. Do you?'

It is so tempting to say yes.

'No. Of course not. And if I did I would have caught it from you.'

'Ditto,' he says.

'No, you might have got it from Vic, or Liam, well via Vic… You know what I mean.'

'No, because I hadn't been with Vic for over a year so I could only have caught it from you.'

'Well, I'm fine.' This joke, if that is what I meant it to be, is backfiring horribly. 'So we're both fine.' Let that be an end of it now, please.

'So neither of us has an STI then?'

'Well I don't.'

'Me neither. So why did you ask?'

I have to stop this now. 'No more talk of STIs, it was a joke. It's finished now.' It hadn't started as a joke, just my paranoia.

He smirks. 'I know it was a joke.'

I don't answer, I'm not going to say another thing about it.

'So, tell me what's been going on in your life?' He watches and waits while I consider where to start. Once I do start, there's no stopping me and he sits patiently while I unload the last few months of my life.

'Wow, you have been busy. And when do you start your new job?'

'A few weeks, after I've moved house.' I sit back feeling happy and pleased with myself.

'I'm glad it's worked out so well. Go you.'

'Yeah, go me. What have you been up to?'

'Well, after I explained to Vic that we were well and truly over and that I'd met someone else, I've been mostly trying to get in touch with *you*.' He gives me a smile, a smile that seems more like a challenge.

I give a little shrug. 'You know where I live.'

'I know the village you live in, yes. But there are a lot of grandiose houses down that gated street. Anyway, you weren't answering the phone to me so I doubted you'd be very happy if I just turned up on your doorstep, assuming I could get through the gate without knowing the exact house number.'

'It would have been creepy, but we both know you are creepy.'

'And a cliché,' he adds.

'Hold on a minute, did you say that you'd been in my street?'

'No, I didn't say that…' he pauses and smirks. 'But I did drive past it once or twice, on the same day, it wasn't like I was stalking you, or anything.'

'I'm flattered, I think.'

'Can we stop playing cat and mouse and be honest here?' he asks as I squint into the sun. It's getting lower and it's shining in my eyes as I look at him. Then I notice there are beads of sweat on his forehead, I imagine the sun is hot on his back, unless he's nervous.

'Let's go inside where it's cooler.' I stand up then wonder if he thinks that's an invitation into my bed. It most certainly is not.

Once inside Kong finds his favourite corner, flops down and goes straight to sleep. I put the kettle on and make us both a coffee. Noah sits on *his* end of the sofa. I feel his gaze on me as I shuffle around the kitchen.

'No double booking this time,' Noah muses.

I smile to myself. I feel smug. I take our mugs over to the coffee table before I speak.

'No booking at all, Mrs Lane offered this place to me for free to make up for Christmas.' I grin at him. A nasty part of me wants him to be annoyed, but he grins back.

'And has it…?'

'What?'

'Made up for Christmas?' He's still grinning.

'Don't know. I was planning on going home this evening.' That wipes the grin from his face.

'No. Why?'

'Why do you think?'

He shakes his head. 'Not… Vic? You thought I was still with Vic?'

'Maybe.'

'Right. Well, going back to being honest again, I'm going to tell you how I feel about you and you can do the same.'

'Can I?'

'Well, if you want to. I'm still going to tell you. You can please yourself.'

'Yes, I can. I do.'

'I know.' He rolls his eyes. Noah Bloody Steele.

'I think I'm in love with you,' he starts, watching my face, gauging my reaction. I struggle to keep my face impassive. Am I teasing him? Maybe. 'After I left you here that Sunday, and sat next to Vic all the way home, I knew I wanted to see you again. I kicked myself for not telling you when I came back to say goodbye. But you didn't seem to want that... us... to continue. I don't know if you do now. But I do, so I'm being straight with you here and now.'

'You think you're in love with me?'

'Mmm.'

'Maybe it's lust.' I am definitely teasing him.

'Yep.' He's sulking now. He's laid his heart out for me to see and I'm being mean. I know it. So does he. But I feel I'm owed for my humiliation. Is that sick of me? I can't carry on doing it.

'Well, maybe I feel the same.'

'You do?'

'Put it like this, I'd like to get to know you better.' There. I may not be declaring my love, because it's too soon for that yet, but I'm encouraging him, aren't I?'

He smiles. Smiley, smiley Noah, the one that Vic finds so boring.

Right then, right when we could have sealed our attraction with a kiss his phone buzzes loudly, and vibrates so violently in his pocket that I can feel it reverberate up through the sofa and into my backside.

'Woah,' I cry, laughing. 'Do you get a signal here now?'

'No, no, it's the alarm. Yolanda set it. She gets annoyed with me if I'm late. We have a table booked for dinner. I have to go.' He stands up and I feel so deflated. Is Yolanda his master, like he is Kong's? Or would that be mistress? No, that's just too creepy, a step too far. Stop thinking.

'Why don't you come with us?'

'No, I couldn't…'

'Why not? We have a table booked in town, some swanky place that Yolanda found. That's why I have to go now because I have to change. Apparently, my normal attire isn't good enough. I can't take Kong either.' At the mention of his name Kong leaps up.

'You could leave him here?' Is that a good idea? Maybe I shouldn't have said that.

'No, you're coming with me.' He holds his hand out to me and I take it. He pulls me up and hugs me, then we kiss. Oh, how we kiss. 'You're definitely coming with me. Now I've found you again I'm not letting you go. Anyway, the pub staff are happy to entertain Kong, it's all arranged.' He steps away from me, whistles for his dog and heads for the door. 'I'll pick you up. It'll be good for you to meet my family. They've heard so much about you…' He grins and leaves, calling out the time I have to be ready by.

I have less than an hour so I dash into the bathroom, have a shower, then run into my room to see what I can wear, rummaging through my hastily repacked suitcase. I have brought nothing dressy. Nothing at all. In the end I opt for a sundress which is new and rather pretty and team it with my jacket, the one that has had a trip through the washing machine, so at least it's clean. I'm going for funky, smart casual, I think I'm just about pulling it off. I slap on some makeup, play around with my hair until it looks presentable, grab my bag and sit on the sofa waiting for my lift.

He arrives on time, a knock on the door and I jump to my feet. I feel nervous, I don't know why, I've already met Yolanda.

'Hi,' I say as I open the door. He looks me up and down. 'Will I do?' I feel irked by his action. He's wearing a dark shirt and dark trousers.

'Oh yes, more than,' he says, holding out his hand to me.

He leads me to the passenger seat in his car, that great big, black four-wheel drive thing. It's only as I get in that I notice Yolanda is sitting behind me, and next to her a man who I assume is Noah's dad. He leans forward and introduces himself, it's pleasant to finally meet the man who's arranged my mortgage and helped me move forward with my life; James, Noah's father.

'And you've already met my wife, Yolanda,' he says.

'Oh yes. Hello again.'

'Hello again, too,' Yolanda says, with a broad smile. 'I'm glad to see you and Noah have sorted yourselves out. These two moody brutes are our sons, Kit and Matt. Say hello, boys,' she calls to the back of the car, where a pair of sullen teenagers lurk. I recognise them from the beach.

'Hello, boys,' the pair say in unison. Oh, teenage humour.

'Hello, boys,' I call back.

'I'm the designated driver, as per, so these two can drink,' Noah says, rolling his eyes as he drives up the lane.

We make polite conversation during the drive and, while it's pleasant to be in the heart of Noah's family, a bit part of me wishes we were on our own. I glance over at his strong profile, his jaw, his lashes, his freshly shaven face — has Yolanda issued a clean-shaven instruction? I could kiss the face off him, right here, right now.

I have to admit to myself that he's drop-dead bloody gorgeous. Physically he's even better than my fantasy Noah. Let's hope the rest of him lives up to my expectations.

Let's hope I live up to his.

My heart sinks. How can I possibly compare with the perfect Vic? How can anyone?

Noah parks the car and we clamber out; Yolanda grabs my arm and links hers through it.

'You're all we've heard about since he came back after Christmas,' she whispers, nudging me. 'Ruby this, Ruby that.'

'Really?' I'm not sure I like the sound of this. Wasn't he obsessed with Vic too?

'Don't exaggerate, Yolanda; I mentioned her twice to you.'

'And how many times to your father?' She looks behind for her husband to confirm. 'James, how many times did he mention Ruby to you?'

James looks between our faces, deciding on what best to say. Shakes his head and shrugs then speaks to his younger sons. 'Before you ask, boys, no, you cannot drink beer.'

The boys roll their eyes in unison and grunt something that could be anything.

Noah laughs and grabs my hand, holding it tightly in his, but Yolanda doesn't let go of my arm. It feels a bit weird. I'm in the middle of a threesome.

In the restaurant I end up sitting at the end of a table for six, flanked by Yolanda and James. Noah is at the other end, flanked by his half-brothers.

'Oh,' I say. I don't even attempt to hide the disappointment from my voice.

'Don't worry, you and Noah already know each other and will have plenty of time alone,' Yolanda says, smiling and picking up a menu. 'It's our turn to get to know you this evening. And vice-versa of course.'

I look across at Noah and he raises his eyebrows and mouths, 'Okay?'

I tell myself to grow up and nod and smile back at him. I suppose I feel that we've wasted so much time without each other since Christmas that I don't want to waste any more.

James and Yolanda are lovely, they do ask a lot of questions but it's in conversation and they tell me as much about themselves as they ask about me. I don't feel too interrogated. We also have all the wine at our end of the table and manage to down two bottles between the three of us. There's just coke and water at Noah's end.

'Okay,' Noah says, as we leave. He's back next to me and holding my hand.

'Yeah, good.'

'They're not so bad. They were all desperate to meet you.'

'Even the boys?'

'Yes. Well, yes, sort of.'

We both laugh. The boys are pleasant and polite but I can't imagine that an evening meeting their brother's potential new girlfriend is particularly interesting to them. I hardly compare with Vic for glamour.

We pile into Noah's car and head for home. Me to the cottage, them to the hotel. I sit next to him and wonder where he will go, does he expect to stay with me tonight? Do I want that?

Hell, yes.

'Do you want me to drop you back at the cottage first?' Noah asks.

I smile over at him, but he has his eyes on the road, not on me.

'No. Why don't you drop everyone else off first?'

He chances a glance at me and grins.

From her seat behind me, Yolanda leans forward and speaks. 'I much prefer you to Madam Victoria,' she says, with a sardonic tone to her voice. 'You're much more genuine and real.'

''Right. Thanks, I think.'

'My pleasure.'

'Okay. I didn't realise it was a straight compare and contrast. So pleased I passed the test.' Obviously, I'm not pleased, and I hope my tone conveys that.

Yolanda doesn't answer and no one else speaks, but I do notice Noah steel another glance at me. I don't look back. There's an atmosphere in the car now. When I look back into the rear of the car, I can see that even the boys are alert to it.

'Hey,' I say. 'I'm tired. It's been a long day. Why don't you drop me home first.'

'Are you sure?'

'Absolutely.'

'Should I pop...'

'No,' I cut in.

I cannot wait to get out of this car and be alone.

Being interviewed to be Noah's girlfriend is not my idea of fun, especially when I'm so blatantly compared to his perfect ex.

Twenty-six

It's six am and I've been awake for ages. I've hardly slept at all. I drag myself to the kitchen and fill the kettle.

I'm irritated and annoyed and I don't even think it's Noah's fault, but he did sort of go along with it and that irks me. How would he feel if I paraded him in front of my family and waited for them to pronounce their approval?

There's a sudden noise from the front door, not a knock, more a flap. I look out of the window but see no one. I approach the porch door and open it with caution, if there is someone at the front door, I don't want them to see me. It's far too early for people, even Noah, to call round.

On the doormat is a letter – the post arrives early here I think to myself and laugh out loud. I pick it up. Hand delivered, of course.

I wonder where he is? Hovering along the lane, waiting, poo bag in hand, while Kong does his business?

I pick up the letter, turn it over and over. I assume it's from Noah, who else would it be from? I'm not familiar with his handwriting, but this is small and neat and written in purple ink. Surely he's borrowed the pen from Yolanda?

I tear it open, noticing how my hands are shaking a little.

Dear Ruby

So sorry about last night. Yolanda was mortified at her clumsy attempt to make you feel welcome. She's usually so good at saying the right thing, let's face it, it's her job to. The sentiment was genuine though, they all really like you and I hope you feel the same about them.

I hope you forgive us all.

If you do, please meet me later.

12 noon on the sofa rock in the (almost) secret cove.

I'll bring a picnic, you just bring your lovely self.

Please come…

Love

Noah xx

PS, I expect to meet your parents as soon as possible, for their approval. ☐

PPS, the pen and paper are Yolanda's, in case you were wondering.

I survey the letter, reading it over several times. I wonder if he would have sent a text if the mobile reception was better? Instead I have a letter.

A love letter?

I make myself a coffee and sit down on the sofa with it, turn on the TV and flick through the breakfast shows. The main topic of news is the wonderful weather spreading right across the UK and expected to last for the whole of Easter.

How different from Christmas.

I'm wearing my little summer skirt again, with trainers. I cannot trust that coast path with flip flops, convenient as they are on the sand. I've given myself ten minutes to reach the rock: five minutes along the path, five minutes across the beach. I'm taking nothing with me except my keys, stuffed into my skirt pocket. He did say to just bring my lovely self.

When I reach the beach I pull off my trainers and stuff the socks inside them. It's nice to feel the soft sand between my toes, especially as my feet are dry and there's no rubbing this time. There are more people on the beach today than there were before. I suppose all the holidaymakers are arriving now with it being so close to Easter. I wonder how secluded our almost secret cove will be – weird how I've come to consider it *our* cove. I feel as though we were the first to discover it back in the depths of winter, so I've staked a claim – silly, I know.

It seems to be taking me ages to trog across the main beach, longer than I anticipated. I don't want to be late because he'll think I'm not coming and I wouldn't want that.

I've had a good talk to myself, told me to grow up and not be so tetchy. I think, on reflection, I behaved a bit like a teenager last night, throwing a strop over a few missaid words. I'm bigger than that, better than that. And, while I don't like being compared to Vic, if I'm honest I know my family will compare Noah to Cliff, even if it's not their intention. I must ensure they don't say anything in front of him.

I've compared Noah to Cliff, just not out loud.

I'm finally across the main beach and just around the curve is our cove. I'm hot from rushing, and even though I don't know the time, I know I'm late. I stop, take a deep breath, smooth down my skirt and hair and head for Noah.

He's on the rock, the sofa rock, sitting on a large, tartan rug. He's staring at me; he smiles and waves and I return his smile and wave. I'm here, finally, just twenty-feet from him.

Oh shit.

'How long have you been there?' I call over.

He gives me a sheepish grin. 'About half an hour. I didn't want you turning up early and wondering where I was.'

'Right. Umm…'

'Come on then, join me. I have our picnic.' He points to the blue cool box beside him on the rock.

I shake my head. 'I think you'd better come back over here,' I say.

'Why?'

''Cos you didn't notice the tide coming in.' A part of me feels smug, a part of me wants to say, see, that's how it happened to me. But I don't because I'm actually worried. The water is deeper than it was when I waded through it, and yes, he's taller and stronger than me but even so.

'Quick,' I yell. 'Look at it.'

He looks at the swirling, churning water and alarm finally registers on his face.

'Bloody hell, that was fast.'

He rolls up his trouser legs then lowers himself into the water. It's not much past his ankles there, which is good, but I know how steeply the cove shelves, how deep that water will be when he takes just a few steps towards me. He turns back to the rock, rolls up the rug, grabs his shoes and wades towards me, even he notices that the water is deeper almost instantly, than it was immediately by the rock.

'Mind out,' he calls from half way across as he flings his shoes and the rug in my direction. They land on the sand as he turns back for the cool box.

'Leave it,' I shout. I can feel my heart beating in my chest. I remember the feeling of being dragged down and him having to pull me out. Yes, he's bigger and stronger than me, but I don't have the power to pull him out and the water is definitely deeper today.

'No way,' he shouts back, grabbing the cool box and wading back. He can't throw that onto the dry sand, it's far too heavy. He wades towards me, and the water is so much deeper.

I can feel panic rising in my chest. Get a grip, I tell myself, he's hardly going to drown here, just get his trousers wet like I did.

'Here, can you grab this?' He leans over offering the cool box and I lean over to grab it. But I can't.

'No.'

'Hang on.' He takes another step forward and I can see him sinking. This is where I struggled, the sand beneath the waves is like quicksand. 'Grab it now?'

I struggle but I do get it, it's heavy and I almost drop it but finally I haul it onto the dry sand.

He takes another step forward and I can see it's an effort, even for him. Another step and he sinks deeper and even though his trouser legs are rolled up to his knees, the bottoms are now wet.

'Come on,' I urge, holding out my hands for him to grab.

He looks as though he would laugh if he could. Another step, another struggle. I keep my hands out but I don't say anything to distract him as I can see he's putting all his concentration into getting out of that swirling sea.

Finally, just two more steps and he'll be safe, providing he can claw his way out. He will probably have to do what I planned before he rescued me, go on all fours. But would that help? Would his hands just sink like his feet are?

I hold out my hands for him to grab.

'Move back, Ruby,' he says, instead of grabbing my hands.

I step back and he lunges for the sand, his hands landing on dry land and pulls himself out. He makes it look easy as he jumps upright.

I rush towards him and wrap my arms around him.

'I was so worried. I thought you were going to get sucked under.' I can feel my heart beating in my chest, beating against his chest.

He laughs. Laughs!

'What's so funny?' I step back and wait. How dare he.

'I could have just waded down and into the sea and along the beach. I was never in any real danger. I just didn't want to get my clothes wet.'

'Oh. Yeah.'

He steps forward and grabs me, wrapping his arms around me in a big, bear hug. 'I'm so touched you care so much, though,' he says, holding my face in his hands. Then he kisses me and I let him. 'I have to admit, though,' he says, when we come up for air, 'That sand is like bloody quicksand. A child, or a small person could get sucked down there.'

'I'm not a small person,' I say, narrowing my eyes at him.

'Oh, Ruby, there's no pleasing you.' He laughs, puts his arm around my shoulder and we wander away from the edge of the cove. He grabs the cool box, rug and his shoes with his free hand. I'm rather impressed by that. 'Let's have our picnic.'

We find a more secluded spot against the rocks and settle down on the tartan rug. He opens the cool box and produces plates, china plates.

'Well, wow,' I say, with a laugh.

'Nothing but the best for you.'

'Right.'

Then he produces a box of sandwiches.

'Ham for you on the left, ham and mustard for me on the right.'

I take one and bite into it.

'Nice bread, nice ham,' I say between mouthfuls. 'How did you manage this?'

'Pub kitchen. They were very helpful when I explained what I needed.' He throws me a small bag of vegetable crisps and I tuck into those. Afterwards there are strawberries and clotted cream.

In the distance I see an old couple, hand in hand, walking along the water's edge. They're barefoot.

'It's Arthur and Joan.'

'Where?'

'Over there. Look, he's carrying her shoes. How sweet. I keep meaning to ask them about their lives. Whenever I've seen them it all seems to be about me. I wonder how they met, how long they've been together.'

'Met when they were five and six or something,' Noah says, dipping a strawberry in the cream before cramming it into his mouth.

'How do you know?'

'Told me about it a few nights ago. They were both orphaned during the war, bombed out in London, met in the orphanage, then they were adopted separately. They both ended up down this end of the country but obviously, being little kids, they didn't know where the other was and even if they had...' Noah shrugs. 'But they bumped into each other fifteen or so years later at some wedding, it seemed they had mutual friends. Been together ever since. Said it was fate. They're big believers in fate.'

'How sweet. I thought they were a sweet couple.'

'They have four children and ten grandchildren.'

'Wow. It's a good story, isn't it? The fate bit too.'

'Yeah, it is.'

'Do you think we were fated to meet? It was quite weird, wasn't it? The mix up, the double booking.'

He doesn't answer. Doesn't even look at me. Have I said something silly?

'And finally...' he says, taking my plate from me and giving me a champagne flute. 'Cava, sorry it's not champagne.' He grins at me.

'What happened to nothing but the best for me?'

'The cheapest champagne was forty-five pounds a bottle and I don't even know if you'd like it. I think you're probably used to the very expensive stuff.' He gives me a little mock grimace.

I take a sip of the cava. It's sweet, which I like and the bubbles instantly go up my nose. It's also ice cold. 'It's lovely. I love it. Thank you.'

If this had been Cliff it would have been the most expensive champagne in the place; he was fond of grand gestures, was Cliff. He would probably have paid the pub chef to come down on the beach and cook us a steak on an impromptu barbeque. But this is much better, so much more intimate.

'I'm sorry about last night.'

'Yes, you said in your letter.'

'I didn't know Yolanda was going to say something like that.'

'I overreacted.'

'Even so, as I said, she was mortified. She's blaming the wine.'

'For my reaction?'

'No, no.' He laughs. 'For her blabbermouth.'

'Let's forget it. This is turning into the STI conversation again.'

'Yes, about that…' He smirks and I lean over and playfully nudge him with my elbow.

'Don't start that again.'

'*I* didn't start it.'

'You must have been up early this morning.' I change the subject.

'Hardly slept.' He looks at me, his eyes soulful.

'Me neither.'

'Spent half the night and a lot of paper writing that letter to you, over and over.'

'Nice colour ink.' I giggle.

'I know.' He shakes his head. 'So we're okay now?'

'I'm sitting here eating and drinking with you.'

'Yes but, Ruby, even when we hated each other we ate and drank together.' He arches his eyebrows at me.

'I didn't know *you* hated *me*.'

One of his trademark smirks plays across his face. 'I resented you being there, a little bit, once I'd got over the delight of seeing you squirming naked on the floor.'

'Pervert.' I look around, up and down the beach. 'Actually, that reminds me, where is Kong?'

'The family have taken him; I have to get him back later.'

'Right, is that so you could seduce me without a pervy rival.' My hand goes up to my mouth. 'That didn't sound the way I meant it.'

But Noah is laughing, really laughing. He leans over and kisses me and I kiss him back and then we decide that we had better go somewhere private. Immediately.

And Christmas Cottage seems like the perfect place.

✿ ✿ ✿

It's getting dark when we wake up in *his* bed, in *his* room, in *my* rental cottage.

'How long are you booked into the pub for?'

'Tonight is our last night. The pub was fully booked for Easter."

'Oh. Oh.' I feel genuinely bereft. The thought of him going home now that I have found him properly upsets me more than I imagined it would.

'It's okay.' He wraps an arm around me.

'Did you drive everyone down? Do you *have* to go back?'

'No and no.'

'Well, as you know Sunday is the turnaround day here and I have this place until then, even though it's Easter Sunday.' I smirk at him.

'I see.'

'So you could come and stay here, but we will have to vacate by ten this time.'

'Okay, Ruby Sutton,' he says. 'If you insist. But right now, I'm starving and I'm already late picking up Kong. Shall we go and grab a bite at the pub?'

'Okay.' We start to pull on our clothes. 'You know, I think our love is built entirely on eating and drinking, it's all we've done since we met,' I say.

He catches my eye and smiles the widest smile.

'Are you admitting that you love me now?'

I stand and stare at him for the longest time, watching his face, so earnest and serious.

'Suppose so,' I say, shrugging and smirking and holding out my hand. 'Come on we have a meal to eat and a dog to collect.' We let ourselves out of the cottage and head for the pub.

'I never doubted you for a moment,' he whispers into my ear and I feel a shiver of excitement run down my spine. 'And the answer to your earlier question about fate bringing us together – I think so. Even if it kept us apart for months so that you could come to your senses and realise that you felt the same way about me as I do you.'

'Don't push it, Noah Steele.'

'As if,' he whispers just before we kiss again.

'By the way,' he says. 'I'm still off Facebook.'

'Good for you. And…?'

'Haven't missed it at all. That said, if you were on it, I might have sneaked on and checked up on you.'

'You know that's creepy and stalkerish, don't you?'

'Yeah. I wouldn't do it.' He shakes his head. 'I did watch *Pride and Prejudice* though.'

'Really? Which version?'

He looks at me blankly. 'Um. It was a film?'

'Who was in it?'

'That guy who used to be in Spooks, I think. I was a teenager when it was on, my dad used to watch it.'

'Matthew MacFadyen. Yeah that's a good film but the BBC series is so much better. We'll have to watch it together.' I grin and so does he.

'Okay.'

'And did you learn anything from watching it?'

'Yeah, I think so.'

'And what was that?'

'Um...' He grins before speaking. 'That we can't always trust our first impressions. Although I knew how hot you were when I first saw you lying na...'

'Enough,' I cut in. 'No more talk like that, we're nearly at the pub.'

We stop outside the pub and he turns to face me. We're holding hands, we have been all the way here.

'I love you, Ruby Sutton.'

'I know.' I grin. His face is mock-sad. 'And I love you too, Noah Bloody Steele.'

'That's okay then.'

We kiss and it's a very long time since I've felt this happy and I'm definitely looking forward now, not back.

The End.

Other books by this author:

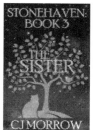

Printed in Great Britain
by Amazon